WE EARNED OUR STRIPES

A TIGER'S TALE

BJ TENCH

WORKBOOK PRESS
RECOMMENDED
LITERARY BOOK COMPETITION 2021

WORKBOOK PRESS LLC
187 E Warm Springs Rd,
Suite B285, Las Vegas, NV 89119, USA

Website:https://workbookpress.com/
Hotline:1-888-818-4856
Email:admin@workbookpress.com

Ordering Information:
Quantity sales. Special discounts are available on quantity purchases by corporations, associations, and others.
For details, contact the publisher at the address above.

Library of Congress Control Number:
ISBN-13:978-1-956876-20-8 (Paperback Version)
978-1-956876-21-5 (Digital Version)

REV. DATE:09/11/2021

We Earned these stripes: A Tiger's Tale

BY

Bernard "BJ" Tench

When I was a child, I talked like a child, I thought like a child, I reasoned like a child. When I became a man, I put the ways of childhood behind me.

The Holy Bible

The book of 1st Corinthians

Chapter 13

Verse 11

The stories in this book are based off young men and women's real-life experiences in Beaver Falls (PA). Some of the characters are fictional but the stories are real. The purpose of this book is to get you (the reader) to compare, contrast and later assist some one that maybe going through similar trials and tribulations. We all can assist in raising a child or destroying a child.

Dedication

I dedicate this book to my family and friends. To the
teachers who truly helped our experiences at BFHS,
you know who you are. To all the coaches, role models,
mentors, and boosters. Youth leagues, Jr High and Varsity
Athletics, you know who you are.

Acknowledgement

My deepest appreciation and warmest friendship extended to all those important and wonderful people who have helped me to create this book. You helped by simply being a part of my journey. I especially thank those listed below who took the baton of excellence and continued to run with "our" (Beaver Falls 2003) tradition and apply it to their everyday life. Some of you are fathers, husbands, boyfriends, coaches, trainers, teachers, leaders…etc. The Lord brought us all together in that small town to make a large impact in the world.

Kenny Johnson, DeJon Alford, Rory Berry, Douglas Beauford, PJ Ceriani, Blaire Cockfield, Allen Karczewski, Nate Lewis, Tony Pharr, Daniel Tomaino, Tianna Van Kirk, and Seth Job: thank you for always displaying brotherhood. We fought and argued at times, and it was not always pretty. I never had a brother growing up; now I have too many.

Regis Bolden: thank you for being the "standard" both in the classroom and on the field. You always showed boys how to be men by accepting challenges.

Aaron "Shakes" Shakespeare, Rodney Slappy, and Nathaniel

Lewis.: thank you for being the balance we needed as a group. During turbulent times we needed people talk to. Thank you for showing us a different way of beating the odds.

DeWarren Ford and Ascheley Brown: Thank you for being the prayer warriors and joyous devotees when everyone doubted us. You men weathered storms that were both boisterous and silent at times. No one noticed but I did. Loyalty and honesty seem to be your formula for success.

To the Beaver Falls Class of 2001 (Gerris Wilcox, Jacob Pacella, Vince Moye, Nate Jones): I recognize you all as trendsetters and "peaceful renegades." You lit the spark that turned into a long-lasting conflagration. Other classes such as 2002(Tyrone Goosby, Leo Clements, Rory Thomas, Brian "Bullet" Pitts), 2004(Brandon Tymous, Jordan Potter), 2005(Cameron Mobley, Shane Curry, Kaylin Slappy, Carliss Jeter) and 2006(Cassandra Washington, Lance Jeter, Dom Henderson, Timmy Rose and "Jordie Beauford"): I thank you for providing stories and opinions that would help me to write this book.

To the Slappy, Jeter and Washington Family: you put up with me and my brothers by coaching us, teaching us, and ensuring our needs were met.

The list is too long. Charge it to my head and not my heart, please... you know who you are, thank you.

To the Aliquippa, Pennsylvania community, this book is only to highlight the rivalry, NOT to diminish reputations, household names, and history within the Beaver County borders. I appreciate you and I want to thank you all for allowing us to compete with you on the fields, courts, and classrooms. Let us continue to push each other towards excellence. Let us also continue the blue-collar, Western PA, small town tradition.

And to all the others who took time to talk to us and love us: I love you and appreciate you. Be wise and blessed. All praises to the Most High.

Table of Contents

Introduction

Many moons ago I had the opportunity to meet a "tribe" of great men; big families with big expectations-- in the classroom and in athletics. With some skepticism they allow me to mingle with their sons and some allowed me to date their daughters. What I found in this small town in Western Pennsylvania. were driven, hungry, and dedicated children. These children turned into curious adolescents and damn good people.

This story begins in the late 90's. The "Bling, Bling" era. Boy bands were still in style and Southern Rap had begun to peak due to the deaths of West Coast rapper 2pac Shakur and East Coast rapper Biggie Smalls. Michael "Air" Jordan was on his way out of the NBA. Kobe Bryant, Allen Iverson, Randy Moss, and Vince Carter were a part of every middle school boy's hallway and lunch table conversations... especially in the so called "hood."

What hood or neighborhood am I talking about? Compton California, Philly, Washington D.C., or Baltimore Maryland? None of those! This story began in the Steel City, Northside of

Pittsburgh and moves further west to Beaver Falls, PA. Beaver Falls is about 30 minutes from the Ohio border and 38 miles from Pittsburgh. It is the home of Joe Namath who played quarterback for Alabama University (1962-1964) and New York Jets (1965-1976).

In this story, you will find out that Joe left no *Broadway Path* for these Tigers (no shade thrown at Joe). It is just a different time and different story about... different men.

You will find in this book how children from small towns go up against the same "big" deals: peer pressure, violence, politics, anger management, self- awareness, and temptations of all sorts. You will see these young folks were given life's test with little to no studying. They were able to pass their test through trial and error. They overcame only because they had gone through their individual journeys.

Enjoy!

Precocious Naivetes

The year was 1997 and it was the first day of school. Football signs were everywhere. The signs were for the Little Tiger's youth football team or the varsity teams. The tiger was the mascot for Beaver Falls. You would think the Beaver Falls Tigers would be the Beavers, right? Wrong! The weird thing was that Beaver, PA is another small town about 20 minutes up the road... and their team is the Bobcats. To make things more confusing, there is a South Beaver, Beaver, and Western Beaver all in Beaver *County,* PA

"Tyrell Goosby-- report to the office. Again... Tyrell Goosby report to the office." The intercom boomed with the announcement.

"Tyrell Goosby report to the office. DeJon Alford, Tyrell Goosby report to the office."

These announcements occurred what seemed like every half an hour.

Mr. Otter, the school principal, had a strong presence. He was an *African American* Principal who had children of his own, and at times he made the children at his school   feel like these were also his own biological children. His office was as soon as you came in the front door of the school. You could not miss him because he greeted most of his students with a firm handshake or a fist bump.

"Damn Tye, it's the first day!" said Carlos Clemons.

"I know… can't really say what he wants from me," Tyrell responded.

"BJ Timmons!" Tyrell yelled when BJ "BJ" Timmons left the library where they were all sitting. BJ was BJ's nick name. "Rev" was another nickname that his friends and teammates liked to call him because of his father. BJ was a "P.K.": A preacher's kid.

BJ Timmons was the son of Pastor Timmons of the 2nd Baptist Church in Beaver Falls. BJ's father was a strong man from the Manchester neighborhood in Pittsburgh's Northside. Both he and BJ's mother were from the Northside of Pittsburgh and decided to move because of his parent's calling and because Pastor Timmons had seen too much violence in his neighborhood. BJ admired his father because although he was loving, he was no chump! To some children he reminded them of Malcom X or Mufasa from Disney's The Lion King.

It was only second period and both Tyrell and DeJon had been in the office for 20 minutes.

"What did Mr. Otter want?" BJ asked when they came back.

Tyrell looked at BJ and said, "To let me know he was the H.N.I. C."

H.N.I. C?

"What's that?" BJ asked in front of both DeJon and Carlos.

"The head Negro in charge." Tye said with a big laugh following.

The four boys knew Mr. Otter meant well and could speak their language.

Tyrell Goosby went by several nicknames but was well known as "The Goose" or "Gizzard." He was six foot two, 185 pounds and had zero percent body fat. The young man had been dunking a basketball since the 6th grade., but he would tell you the 5th. When I say dunking, I do not mean on a Nerf 5ft hoop--I mean regulation 10ft! He was in the eighth grade. He and his compadre, Carlos "Los" Clemons, were the monsters of the school that year. Of course, there were other big eighth graders like Brian "Bullet" Pitts, "Big" Steve and "Big" Rob Tomlin. They were all 6ft or taller, but Tye and Carlos were ahead of their time.

Tyrell was fun loving, project, kid who could manage his emotions very well. Beaver Falls has six housing projects. Tyrell never displayed the stereotypical project behavior other than wearing the du-rag in school and he had his way with the ladies. They adored him for his balance of childlike behavior and dominance on the school grounds. He also had a twin; a beautiful girl named Tara. She too was popular and had many boys that were interested in her. Since the junior high school only went up to eighth grade, the eighth graders were the seniors in a sense. Tyrell was big man on campus, all the high school athletes knew he was coming.

BJ on the other hand was a seventh grader. He played sports because it was the thing to do to stay away from juvenile detention centers and drugs. He was not so popular and not yet a star in any of the three major sports. At BF (Beaver Falls), the main three sports were baseball, basketball, and football. BJ had some "baby fat" that started to shed around this time. In the seventh grade the core athletes were Tremon Barksdale, Dominique Taylor (who would move a year later), and Regis Bolden a.k.a. "Man Man," but the star of stars was Calvin "Hollywood" Jackson.

Calvin Hollywood Jackson was known by some as C.J. and by others as a jerk and a jackass. Calvin had been battling Tyrell for the future number one spot since they were in elementary school. Calvin was fast, strong and always two steps ahead of his opponents. He, Tremon, and Regis had always played up against kids one or two grades ahead of them. So, all these guys had been competing for years. Tyrell knew Calvin and all his teammates. The scary thing was there were great athletes in the grades seventh, eighth, and ninth. Ninth grade had some great football players like Gerris Wilcox, Vince Moses, Jacob Pacella, and Jake Jones. That means that Beaver Falls had a promising future, right? Maybe.

Calvin, like Tyrell, started off playing ball in the same housing projects as Tyrell. Calvin was the oldest boy of eighteen children on his father's side. His mother loved Calvin deeply, but the streets sometimes would get in the way. She would often find her way into jail for fighting some other lost soul. She was Calvin's biggest supporter, and she had no problem letting the world know. Just ask him. At games she would be so loud that he would have to turn around and tell her to "Shut it, ma!" It was not the most respectful approach, but Calvin had a rep, and she was jeopardizing it. When you are twelve years old, image is everything.

Calvin had his way with the ladies also. He was sexually active and would let the gals know from the start. Calvin had to grow up fast. He had the gift of gab and fast hands to get him in trouble. He and BJ grew up on different sides of the tracks. So, at times, they would clash about certain topics.

As the first day of school started to wind down the boys began to get into their simple childish debates. Favorite topics of that year were: "*Who's better. Kobe Bryant or Allen Iverson? Terrell Owens or Randy Moss? Wu-Tang or Ruff Ryders?*" The simple arguments of 7th graders.

That afternoon Calvin ran into Bernard in the hallway.

"What's up, Timmons?" Calvin hollered from the opposite end of the hallway.

"What's your *cowgirls* looking like this year?"

"Cowgirls" are what Dallas Cowboy haters would call their fans.

"I don't know," BJ responded, "better than them Bronk-Hoes!" He was referring to Calvin's favorite team, the Denver Broncos.

In those days, no one rooted for the home team, the Pittsburgh Steelers. A couple of guys liked the Steelers but the fanbase was split down the middle. DeJon liked Indianapolis, BJ liked Dallas, and Calvin liked Denver. There were even guys like Blaire Ameen and DeWarren Ford, who liked the San Francisco 49ers and Los Angeles Raiders! The arguments about who was the best were legendary.

As the day went along, the seventh-grade conversations fluctuated. From 7:45 am to roughly 3:15 pm, you would hear every argument from who is the best rapper to who stole whose extra pizza slice. In every school, junior high is full of hormones. Beaver Falls Junior high at times disengaged itself from being any different.

"Aye Timmons, who you got your eye on this year?" Calvin asked. "I think Angela likes you, man."

"Nah I don't think so," BJ replied. "She likes my cousin Darren, I think. She's been eyeing up that cat all summer I heard."

Darren Shakespeare was a cool laid-back fellow, no smack talk or funny hand gestures. He was a God-fearing Christian who the ladies loved, and he was BJ's cousin through marriage. Darren was the kind of young man parents wanted their children to look up to. He was athletic and could sing like a member of the R &B group New Edition... but he just wouldn't let you know it.

BJ smiled, "I don't know if I'm her type. But she's mine!"

BJ was excited that Angela might like him. She was a cheerleader on the Little Tiger football team she was bi-racial, and full of sassiness. BJ thought about it and thought about it some more. It was the first day of school. Did she tell Calvin she liked him?

"Besides, it's the first day of school man." BJ said. "We got practice before y'all." The Junior high practiced right after school. The other youth league teams practiced at 6pm.

BJ made up his mind. "I'll write her a letter tonight."

Back then you expressed your feelings with smooth literature through note writing. You would begin with a *"What's up?"* Then, you'd tell her how pretty she was and how you noticed her. At the end of the note, you put two boxes for the girl to mark if she was interested: *Yes, or No will you go with me?* You would fold the note, draw two eyes the best you could and title it: "For your eyes only."

The next day BJ passed Angela the letter.

He was surprised at her answer.

"She actually checked yes!" BJ thought to himself.

"Yo! You go with Angela!" DeJon said the next morning.

The relationship only lasted for 4 days but hey… it was genesis for BJ's love life.

BJ and Regis played Junior high football because they were too big for midget football where the weight limit was 130 pounds. Calvin barely made weight and he was small compared to Regis and BJ. The midget football team was for 12-13-year-old boys. Calvin, DeJon, and Tremon all played midgets. Those three along with Douglas "Dougie" Benson and Blaire Ameen would lead the troops to a 2nd place trophy. All the football teams had a diverse group of children. Where BJ was originally from was all "black". The only so called "White family" was "White Mike's." Mike blended in with the rest of the neighborhood. In Beaver Falls there were about 40 "White Mikes" …or White kids that stuck out like a sore thumb. When BJ first moved to Beaver Falls, he thought some of the other kids in the area were Spanish or Middle Eastern. He was wrong; a lot of the children were bi-racial, and their parents were mostly men of color who had children with women of European descent.

At the Junior high practices, Tyrell, Carlos Clemons and Regis all displayed their gifts which included hard hits and dashing moves. BJ observed most of this because he was getting used to a new body and he was not yet strong enough to compete with the bigger lineman. He was also not fast enough to keep up with the faster athletes. Because of this, he was considered a tweener. He and Regis were the only seventh graders on a seventh, eighth, and ninth grade team. Regis would eventually start as a 7th grader. He was impressive, but nothing was too much for "Man Man." BJ and Regis would wash up and head down to the youth league practices watching their friends.

Calvin, Tremon, Dominique, and Dougie too, would dominate practices on the 12 through 13-year-old team. DeJon, like, BJ had been coming into his own but not quite a standout. This young team would end up being runner up in the championship. DeJon and Calvin would both sub in and out during the playoffs with older players. Tremon played backup quarterback but starting flanker. On a talent level, Calvin was the best wide receiver on the team. The following year he would become the MVP of the team. DeJon would grow some and his speed would turn heads.

The high school coaches and Junior varsity coaches would come observe the Little Tigers and ask: "Who's number 22? Who's number 3? Who's number 42 and number 10?"

These groups of young men had won or come in second

place their whole lives. or at least since they were six. Winning had become a culture. High schoolers had been told the 2002 and 2003 classes would be the best to come through in a long time because they were precocious and arrogant. Some of the community wanted to put these cubs in their place. These two classes had watched closely how losing had become the norm. Finishing in the bottom half of the section, they become the butt of the jokes in the county.

Guys like Tremon, Calvin and Tyrell would let it be known that they thought these high school athletes were losers. Sure, those kids tried their hardest. They went to practiced and did all the right things to be successful. However, they didn't have the one or two special players that could take them over the top. This caused dissention within the community. Parents took note and some school officials could feel the arrogance that these classes pushed out; sometimes unintentional, other times blatant, depending on who you asked.

At the Junior High-level Tyrell would play second fiddle to Vince Moses and Gerris Wilcox. The next year he too should have been the MVP but fell short due to school sports politics. Sometimes, if you did not have the right last name, you would be held back. During his freshman year, Tyrell stayed down and played freshman football even though he should have played Junior varsity. He dominated even more. His story is testament that sometimes God puts barriers in front of you to push harder so you become stronger.

That winter (97-98), basketball season would be intense. Calvin would be kicked off the team because of his smart mouth. Tremon and Regis would lead the team in his absence. Practices against the eighth graders would be legendary and consist of curse words, fights, and other disputes. BJ would be in a few.

BJ's favorite sport at the time was basketball. He was Regis's back up. He had started to get taller, and Regis helped his confidence. Regis and BJ spent numerous hours practicing all kinds of sports.

Regis would always say, "Keep working hard. Your time's going to come."

Regis Tremon and Calvin all had been hand selected by the high school basketball coach to lead the team to the promised land one day. The crazy thing was if you took those three off the seventh-grade team, they would still come close to winning a championship. Dougie Benson, Allen Fife, Darren Shakespeare, DeJon, and Timmons all could play. It is just that those three were so dominant that they would start on any freshman team let alone the seventh grade. They were all very precocious.

A Change in Roles
(1998-99)

Now that the 2002 class was gone, the 2003 senior class were the new upperclassmen of the junior high. There were plenty new and hot couples dating. Calvin Jackson and Dougie Benson made the 2003 class more popular in the high school than they did in junior high. They had started to date high school girls on the regular. A few high school girls liked DeJon and Barksdale too. Dougie and Calvin made sure that their names were spoken at a few schools' lunch tables. Calvin had been dating a girl from New Brighton who was in ninth grade, a few seventh graders in the BF junior high, and had befriended Tyrell's girlfriend Tara Bonds. Tara grew up with both Calvin and Tyrell. She had good grades and did not do drugs. Even if Calvin pursued her, she wouldn't bother with him because she knew he had messed around with her sister and a few other girls.

Calvin's reputation was misunderstood by girls, but she was one of the few that understood "Hollywood Jackson." Tara knew that his relationship with his mother was fractured.

Because of this fracture Calvin would look to his grandmother for that matriarchal advice. DeJon was also partially raised by his grandmother, so he too was misunderstood by the lady folk at times. He also dated a girlfriend that was two grades ahead of him. Calvin only loved ball or competing over ball, basketball, baseball, football, dodgeball, volleyball. The absence of a mother can make a man cold towards women; especially one that is just learning how to be a man.

"Calvin you're nasty." Calvin you're a hoe!" He heard this all the time. He got used to it.

"Man, you know Tara Bonds?" Calvin asked BJ and DeJon.

"Yeah, don't think about it." BJ said back to Calvin.

"If Tye mess up, I'm on." Calvin said.

"This dude!" Said Tremon and Regis shaking their heads.

"You say that about every girl." Tremon Barksdale chimed in.

"Why can't you just be with one girl?" Lindsey Sales, a classmate of Calvin's asked. "Is it that hard?"

"Is it hard for you to leave bad boys alone?" Calvin retorted.

Lindsey was a preacher's kid, and she dated a gang banger. Calvin had feelings for this girl, but she continued to lead him on and choose based off her own appetite.

"Won't leave them knuckleheads alone huh?" He said. "You and Tianna never learn." Calvin said shaking his head rapidly.

That afternoon, Tara Bonds and Tyrell both walked by the

middle school who had been dismissed.

"Tyrell, you still got detentions that you need to serve from 5th grade."

"Yeah, well since you're the H.N.I.C. how about you serve them?" Tyrell replied with smirk. He paused and added, "I need to rap with you later." You been trying to get at my lady man?"

. "Nah, I just like what I see." Calvin replied.

Tyrell knew that Calvin's ego would never let him admit that Tyrell had something he wanted. The roles had changed. Tyrell had the same success growing up in athletics except for the fact that he added more excitement. He was a tad bit bigger, stronger, and jumped higher. He noticed Calvin's height changing, his strength was growing, and he too started to add some ferocity towards his dunks at the playgrounds all around the neighborhood.

Now, Calvin was not only the best basketball player in the middle school... he believed he was the best player in all the area schools. There were rumors that Calvin beat a couple seniors from the 1999 class one on one. All Calvin needed was a few thoroughbreds like Tremon and Regis to back him up and he could win. He had some utility players like DeJon, Doug and BJ. With this combination, Calvin, Tremon, and the gang would beat the varsity basketball team in scrimmages. Calvin and Tremon were the backcourt of the future.

No one was a high- flyer like Tyrell though. However, even he was not the all-around player Calvin was. Tyrell was the combination of elusiveness and strength and really was geared more towards football. Calvin was speed, athleticism, mentality and had some follow through. He had the Randy Moss ability on the field and the Allen Iverson ability on the court. Calvin also knew that Tremon was a rivalry in his class and Tyrell was the Shaq to his Kobe. The two never realized how they could have pushed each other to be the best of the best. Tyrell dunked on grown men and Calvin embarrassed grown men. Tyrell would also eventually start as a freshman on the varsity basketball team. Coach Demona, who was the head basketball coach of the high school team knew that Calvin, Tremon, Regis, Clemons and Goosby all would have a chance to change the way "b-ball looked in the town." Coach Demona knew two things: he wanted Tyrell to be his starting forward as a Freshman and Calvin to be the starting point guard the following year. Tyrell had all the physical gifts to be a starter. He lacked in some areas, but his strengths outweighed his weaknesses. Calvin had all the makings to be the next great one yet, he lacked in structure and leadership.

The Tigers had a coach, Tim Jackson who was Calvin's cousin. He had coached this team since they were in the 5th grade. He introduced Calvin, BJ, Regis, Tremon, and the rest of the eighth-grade team to set short term goals. These short-term goals turned into long winning streaks. Winning became contagious. From youth to Junior high the Tigers always finished top 3.

Despite everyone growing in height the eighth grade, the young men were lacking in awareness. Calvin had become hard to deal with and his new role of best athlete went to his head. He was only a few pegs above Barksdale and Bolden. But once he started dunking basketballs his mouth became just as toxic. He would get into arguments with his classmates and teammates. Most fights were about girls' sports and… girls! BJ and Calvin fought over dodgeball. Calvin fought "Fast" Larry Walker over different girls. Barksdale wanted a piece of him a couple times when he hogged the ball or manipulated the practices. DeJon and Calvin fought over another dispute. Basketball was Calvin's time to shine so initially he acted out. It seemed like everyone wanted a piece of Calvin at that time, even guys that were not as physically imposing like little Nate Lewis, Tyler Marx, and Ascheley Brown. These were fun loving guys who occasionally played ball. They were belittled and tormented at times. What Calvin didn't expect, was that he would have to grow up mentally. He also had to learn everyone else grew in other ways. New roles were handed out the following Spring.

Points to Prove

From the high school campus to the middle school hallways, Tyrell and Tara's names were written everywhere on lockers, benches, and walls. The Janitors had to be ticked! With all that talent and everyone telling Tyrell that "*You're the man,*" it was a crash course headed to nowhere. Not to mention a 13-year-old girlfriend who thought he could do no wrong.

"Do you love me?" Tara asked.

"Come now. Of course, I do," Tyrell said taking off his Michael Jordan Jersey so Tara could put it on.

"After I go to Pitt, I'll go pro and buy my mother a house." He said.

"What about me?" Tara replied. "Just your Ma, huh?"

"Come on now. You know I'm playing." He said with devilish grin.

Tyrell had that charisma with the girls. He could tell jokes and leave them laughing. Tara knew Tye loved her, but she forgot Tye was lacking in his schoolwork. He had to do summer school so he would not repeat the eighth grade. He had been to a few workouts for football and not really concentrating on hoops either. Why would he? He had been levels above the competition for years. No one prepped him for high school athletics. If you train a child up to think a level above, he normally is ahead of the children his or her own age. Their character is more developed when adults prepare well.

Tye should have been working out with juniors and seniors. That way, by his junior year he would be an "All- American." He was not preparing well. Tyrell went along with the seasons. When it was football season, he was all about football. When it was hoops season, he loved hoops. Who knew he would excel at track? When it came to sports, freshman year for Tye was a breeze.

One late school morning, the principal called over the intercom: "Would the following students please report to the principal's office: DeJon Alford, Calvin Jackson, Douglas Benson, Allen Fife, and Bobby John."

Mr. Otter repeated the same sequence over the intercom. As all the boys entered the principal's office Mr. Otter smiled and slammed door holding the office phone.

"Who did it?" He asked.

"Did what, yo?" DeJon said with a surprise look.

"Come on......tell me." Mr. Otter replied. "I got the Beaver Falls Police on their way over here for some predator."

"Wait.... what?" Calvin asked. "Why are you calling the cops?"

"I'll tell you why, someone assaulted Amanda Foley." Mr.

Otter said. "She is in the vice principal's office right now telling my V.P. that someone put their hands where it wasn't supposed to be in the pool."

The boys started all yelling at once.

"Now calm down, not everyone at once," Mr. Otter said to the screaming adolescents. "Calvin Jackson, you sir, are already in hot water. You and Dougie cut school twice this month. Police Chief Jones said he had some men that chased you boys a few blocks. Didn't think I heard huh?" Mr. Otter said with his hand on Douglas's shoulders. "Now cut the bull and tell me who did it?"

He demanded the boys to come clean. Tears were rolling down the young men's faces. "She is trippin', yo." DeJon said.

"I don't remember no one touching her in the pool." Bobby chimed in.

"Yeah…. I mean yeah… I mean yes sir."

Allen Fife followed up. "Listen do what you gotta do Mr. Otter."

Calvin said with his arms folded. "I ain't saying jack."

"Oh, I plan on it, Fife!" Mr. Otter responded.

Then, Bobby John pointed up at the door. It was Amanda. When Amanda, the Vice Principal and Mr. Otter all went into the conference room to talk and BJ peeked in. He could see that his friends were trying to be strong. He knew that this could end Calvin, DeJon, or Dougie's whole reputation. It seemed like the meeting with Amanda took 40 hours. No one knew exactly what happened except those young men and her. Calvin appeared to be main culprit. He had been zeroed in on since beginning of the school year.

"Jackson, one day I won't be there to save you." Mr. Otter had once told him.

He knew that Calvin had a rough upbringing. He knew he was an at -risk youth. Chances were he, DeJon, and Dougie would all be criminals in someone's jail cell. He loved them boys but had a job to do. The boys had a lot of growing to do; when you are young, you think you are going to stay young.

As time progressed with the 2003 class. The boys would end up all graduating from Junior high. Was it no child left behind? The No Child Left Behind Act was a law that created to help kids who were struggling in math and reading more support. It was most talked about when kids just needed to get passed through because they were problematic. Who knows? There would be several points that needed to be made as this group went from one test to another. Who would lead this group? Who would push Calvin to look in the mirror? Would this group take Beaver Falls to the Promised Land like the elders predicted?

The summer of '99, BJ would end up becoming the 9th grade captain on the Freshman team. He, Douglas, DeJon and Regis would all be handpicked by the coaches. Regis and BJ were both asked by the varsity coaches to move up with Tremon Barksdale. Tremon's father was one of the coaches for the varsity and the head coach for the Freshman team. Regis and BJ stayed down to develop with DeJon and Dougie. Barksdale ended up starting at Free Safety, as Tremon moved up and two more studs moved into town: Rory Lamar Santiago, and Austin Macklin.

Rory Santiago had moved to Beaver Falls at the end of 8th grade. He had been quiet but greatly confident leading up to football season. All Spring and Summer he would ride his bike 20 miles from his house to football practice. He would not say much but he would let it be known he could not wait to do some tackling drills.

"Who's the Santiago kid?" The coaches asked BJ.

"He just moved here from the Valley, but I think he's from Pittsburgh."

The "Valley" was Seneca Valley which was a prestigious high school that was three times the size of Beaver Falls. Rory was originally from the West Side of Pittsburgh. He played youth sports with BJ's cousin. BJ had heard he could play, but he had not really seen Rory in pads. Streetball and organized ball are different, but you can tell what a kid brings mentally by watching him play in the street. Rory, on the other hand, had hands and heart; two things that can make a player. Rory would make it clear to the Beaver Falls program that he was taking someone's spot on the varsity team one day but remember... he was not a household name. He would have to prove a point in hitting/tackling drills so, he proved it on well-known athlete: Regis Bolden, a big, strong, young man that would easily run through a guy like Rory. Rory at the time was about 5'10" and 135 lbs.

After stretching the first day of full pad practice the coaches made it known they wanted to see who the biggest hitters on the team were. Douglas caught Calvin and BJ with some vicious hits.

"Regis... Rory... next." Coach Barksdale said.

There was a growling sound that came from inside Rory's helmet.

"*Beep...Beep*", went the coaches whistle. *Crack...Crack ...* and then *THUMP*. That was beginning of Rory's impact to the program and Beaver Falls lost a great Linebacker for a year: Regis had to get surgery. Rory ended up playing linebacker that year.

Macklin or "Mack" ended up moving to Beaver Falls following the football season of Timmons 9th grade year. He would show his allegiance while he was attending another Junior high school. He and his family had moved into a house downtown by BJ, but he went to Blackhawk Middle School. Blackhawk was another rival to Beaver Falls, however, there was a class dynamic and racial dynamic. Blackhawk had the same zip code as Beaver Falls but made it clear that they were *not* Beaver Falls. Blackhawk had made their own school district based off *"cultural"* differences in the 1980's. Barriers were mentioned often, and the kids were told to stay away from each other.

"That is Western PA for you," Rev Timmons would say to BJ.

A lot of schools were split down the middle like that. Others were Montour and Sto-Rox, Beaver and Midland, Aliquippa and Hopewell, and Moon and Cornell. These were all school districts that could easily combine, but there was nothing new here.

Macklin had proved himself to be not only allegiant to Beaver Falls, but also to his teammates. BJ had gotten into a fight with four or five players from the Moon Area High School football team. He had been clipped, which is a penalty, then kicked.

"Coach take me out the game" BJ said to his coaches.

They thought he was bluffing but, BJ ended up fighting the football team. He tried to fight some parents and coaches as well. DeJon had got into a similar situation like this. He, Calvin, Tye and Tremon fought Blackhawk's basketball team with their parents watching. Some parents had also hopped into that fight. It did not go so well for the parents. That was a summer league game but the Moon fight was during a regular season game so there would be some backlash for BJ's clashing with the Moon Tiger football team. DeJon and his father were the only two people that attempted to defend BJ. Maybe some of the other players were shocked.

After the suspensions were handed out, BJ and Macklin talked.

"Number 76, right?" Macklin asked BJ at the tennis courts that evening.

"Yeah man, dude clipped me and called me out my name," BJ said. "Then he kicked me.".

"Aye we play them next week." Macklin said. "I'm gonna get him."

He did. He ended up blasting that number 76 from Moon. He ended up getting a personal foul also.

Austin Macklin had a sister. Her name was Stacey. She too

dated Calvin on and off and a lot of boys wanted to fight Calvin over her. Sometimes Macklin also wanted to.

"I like you Calvin... just not for my sister." He would tell him.

"So, I'm not good enough but them thugs are?" Calvin would go back and forth with Macklin all the time.

Macklin knew he could not control the situation. Stacey was his older sister. She was very athletic and loved the BF culture. Macklin's parents had raised him right and he seem to be on the right track. His mother was a God- fearing woman and his father was a war vet. Fairly good combo, right? It also did not hurt that Macklin was 6'2" and 200 lbs. with moves. This White boy had jets, hands, and was good tackler.

The Freshman football team finished 500 but should have won more than half their games. Dominique Taylor, who would have been the starting tailback by junior year, moved to Steubenville, Ohio. Regis injured his knee and did not recover. BJ was suspended one game and severely ill the other. When you missed school the day before a game, you could not play, but the biggest blow to the team was Calvin "Hollywood" Jackson.

Calvin had been late for Practice. The team was playing Center Township that Thursday. The coaches asked Calvin to stay behind as the other players went to stretch and Calvin never returned. Following practice that evening, Timmons, Alford, and Benson all saw Calvin walking on the main avenue downtown.

"I'm done, yo." Calvin said to his boys.

"What you mean you're done?" BJ asked Calvin.

"I'm done, he kicked me off the team." Calvin replied. "They cursed me out and told me I am done."

Calvin started to say some things under his breath. "Who the hell do they think they are?!"

In disbelief, DeJon questioned Calvin quickly "Which coach kicked you off the team, yo? there?"

"Look nigga, I'm done." Calvin shouted back. "Forget him too. If they don't want me on the squad, then so be it." He said before turning his back to the huddle of 9th graders.

Everyone knew Calvin's mouth and primadona antics had gotten him into trouble before. He could be a coach's dream and a coach's nightmare with that mouth. As Calvin went into his plans for 9th grade basketball. BJ started to see the frustration in Calvin's eyes. BJ knew how important Calvin was to the team. All these guys were competitive and talented. Tremon, Calvin, Regis, Dougie, and Dominique all had been interchangeable with the number one athlete in the school, depending on the sport and who you asked. Calvin had been the star a year before and he would tell you this even now. The point is, the Tigers could have used him. Tremon would score touchdowns in the J.V. games and make impact plays Friday nights. Calvin would watch and sometimes smirk. Calvin knew that this incident would carry a lot of weight. Pants sagging and all.

"I'll see you niggas hoop season." Calvin said.

Everyone went home that night in disarray.

BJ went home upset that night.

"It ain't right pop." He said to his father at the dinner table. "Why is it always something with our team?"

"BJ before you say anything, get all the facts." Rev said. "You never know what was said to Calvin, and you don't know what he said to them coaches."

"Dad I'm telling you; we need him." BJ said back to his father. "Something ain't right."

BJ went to bed upset and confused that night.

Rev. Timmons knocked on the door "Maybe coach was trying to teach that boy something."

Ms. Timmons entered the room and followed up. "Try not to let it get to you."

"Calvin will never be the *"programs"* favorite." BJ told his parents. BJ knew if Calvin put his mind to it, he, Douglas, Macklin, Calvin, Blaire, and Rory all could have dressed Varsity. Tremon was special, but his whole class was special.

BJ started to feel like his days of being a Tiger were numbered. He had dreams of moving back to Pittsburgh to play with his cousins at Perry Traditional Academy. Situations like what happened to Calvin gave him more reason to be pessimistic about politics. BJ's mother was a special education teacher, so she offered to take him to school sometimes when he was running late because the day after Calvin was kicked off the team, BJ was 2 hours late.

By the end of Freshman year in 2000, there was a rumor

going around the whole school that Calvin was afraid to play Varsity basketball. He turned it down because he wanted to stay with his boys. In all reality, Calvin should have moved up. Tremon tried out and made the JV, but the coaches wanted him to stay down with Freshman.

"Is Hollywood scared?" Tyrell asked Calvin.

"I ain't trying to play with you bums." Calvin replied. "Y'all be losing every other game."

"If we had you maybe it would be different superstar," Tyrell said walking by the locker room.

If Calvin would have had that push from another male role model, he would have played. If Beaver Falls cared about Calvin's overall character development, he would have forced Calvin to move up. It was true; Calvin lacked in work ethic and leadership. Why wouldn't you try to get that ball rolling on these two major flaws as a freshman? The two flaws caused Beaver Falls yet another championship. Calvin quit on the team in the Shaler Tournament that year. He had let his emotions get the best of him.

"I could have killed that guy." Regis said the next day in school after the debacle. "Sometimes he holds us back." Darren Shakespeare said.

"Luckily, DeJon started balling." Tremon said.

The day before, or the put the timeframe here Calvin exploded in front of scouts and varsity coaches.

"That guy needs to grow up." Dougie said.

Coach Demona would ride Calvin home that night and tell him about himself. "We need you next year to grow up and stop the bull shit. You are our point guard. You got to prove yourself to your teammates."

Calvin looked at his coach before getting out of the car. "So, I guess I need to prove a point *again*?"

If Calvin only knew, in life you always must prove yourself.

"She Is into You"

Like most High Schools, BFHS was a high intense playing field for picking up the opposite sex. Most teenagers by the end of their freshman year become curious, bolder and some hungry for passion. Calvin had been a master chef at cooking up the souffle for late night get- togethers. He had been after a few older women in the school and would continue to be on the hunt much later when he was out of school. Tyrell was locked up which meant in full committed relationship now. Most of the fellas had a running mate or someone that they were pursuing. BJ, however, had a few young temptresses that were pursuing him.

The group had met up at the weight room outside of the middle school. There was a sign posted for varsity/JV basketball on the door that listed the names of Goosby, Hollywood Jackson, Tremon Barksdale, and Clemons. These were all shoe ins to make the team. There were some seniors who had been put on the team for merit. The only sure senior that should have made the team was "Black" Jake Jones. He was called that because of his complexion and his addiction to "blacks", which is something like a cigar. He also blazed a lot of blunts. He got the team into a couple nail biting games due to his smoking and his mental and physical conditioning were both in question. Overall, he was a great defender and a slasher that the Tigers needed that year.

"Alford, yes I'm in there baby!" DeJon read out loud. He continued: "A.B., Dougie, Fife."

DeJon may have been doing this to set a tone for the season. The Tigers were under a different mindset now.

"The losing year after year, that's over."

BJ read down and noticed his name was there also under both JV and Varsity. Keep in mind all these boys were sophomores. Shakespeare, Nate, BJ, Fife, Dougie, DeJon, Regis, Tremon, Calvin, Paul, and Ascheley Brown. Rory tried out freshman year, made the team and said, *"Nah to hell with it this year."* He was funny like that at times. Rory was extremely aggressive on defense and could leap. He did not mind playing at the playground, but not for Demona.

"Letter from Avalon: Sharon, Brittany and the lovely Denise from Houston Texas. Damn Rev, I see you!" DeJon said to his buddy BJ.

"My fault yo, you weren't supposed to see that." BJ replied as the overflowing composition paper fell out of his Boss Jeans pocket (Boss Jeans were a popular brand of jeans back then). DeJon and BJ were the last two to come up from the locker room that day for basketball practice.

BJ smiled, "Me and Brittany go back some. I used to like her back in middle school. She big but she cute."

"I dig it." DeJon said.

"BJ Mac." Regis chimed in as the two entered the gymnasium.

After competing at practice that day, BJ had a busy phone line.

"Aye boy, some girl called here with a southern accent." BJ's father said.

"Yeah, what you tell 'em?" BJ asked quickly.

"I told 'em, you had been at practice, and you would call them back when you came home...or whatever." Pastor Timmons sounded incredulous.

"What you mean whatever?" BJ inquired with a worrisome tone.

"Anyway, the dishes waiting for you." His father ended their dialogue just like that.

In the early 2000's, your parents were your secretaries or to a certain degree a human deliverer of your text messages... if they decided to write down the message. BJ had spent the next few weeks rushing home and tying up the phone line being a "Casanova." Every night, one of the cd's (*compact disc*, kids look it up!) alternated in his multidisc player: Michael Jackson's *BAD* album, Jagged Edge's *J. E. Heartbreak* or the "*mix.*" The mix consisted of several songs from LL Cool J, Usher, Ginuwine, or New Edition, and all the way back to the Isley Brothers. He listened to rap too, but not while the ladies were on the phone with him. He would let these songs play low as he interviewed these girls.

Some would spill the beans to him about how long they had liked him. Some would tell him their secrets, fears and dreams. But one gal, she not only told him everything. She told him everything about him. She had known about his family, his whereabouts, his past, and she wanted to be his future. She was very aware that there were girls who liked him, but she had enough personality for twenty girls!

As time went on that sophomore year, BJ had played a good bit of basketball and was a great practice player. He, A.B., Dougie, Nate, and Shakes, Regis, and Fife had been solid practice players and saw some varsity time. DeJon had been sidelined for being a rebel in school and arguing, cursing, and challenging everyone to a race.

"I'll smoke everybody in this school," he would let everyone know.

As DeJon was spectating from the bleachers Tremon, Calvin and Tyrell dominated the headlines of the paper. Thunderous dunks, sharp shooting, and flashy passing; these guys were tough, and the whole county knew it. BJ, right as he started to become a more vocal leader, sadly fractured his foot making an offensive move in the New Brighton Game. Denise, meanwhile, would target her future hunk and wait to make her move.

"You good cuz?" Darren asked BJ the next day as he limped to the school elevator.

BJ had a walking boot for his foot.

"Yeah, I'm cool, Shakes." BJ answered. "You see how Denise been looking at us lately?"

"Yeah, in Ms. Cooley's class she is always laughing at your jokes." Darren said. "I think she's into you!"

Calvin interrupted the cousins talking. "Yeah, she's feeling you, but I gotta rap with you later."

Later that evening, Calvin would meet up with BJ to talk in front of the McDonald's on 7th Avenue. This store had a lot of teenagers hanging out in and around it. 7th Avenue had a lot of restaurants, mom, and pop stores and… junkies. Crackheads, heroin addicts, pill poppers and even women were available if you were into that sort of thing. Not quite Skid Row but if you had an itch, you could get it scratched.

"Yo, let me tell you about your girl Denise." Calvin started that conversation. "When she was in Houston, she used to get down. Like… all the way down, bruh."

BJ nodded his head.

"I don't want you to get all deep, falling for the tail," Calvin continued.

BJ cut him off with conviction, "Alright, Alright, CJ I get your point. How you know all this?"

"She told me bruh." Calvin said.

"All I know is she dance and cook." BJ said.

"Yeah, she cooks aight. "Anyway, ain't she with Big Rob?"

Big Robert Tomlin was one of the starting tackles on the football team and hailed from the Class of 2002.

"Look man, I don't know, I don't care either." BJ replied.

"All I'm saying, I don't want you to get hurt, bro." Calvin said.

"What is this, the quiet storm?" BJ replied.

"She is wild man," Calvin continued to express his concern for Denise's interest in BJ. "This isn't your little summer fling with Sharon, Tianna, or Angela in middle school. She going to chew you up and spit you out."

"That's not so bad," BJ said with a smile on his face.

"You nasty dog, you!" Calvin said. The average beat cop or teacher would have thought the two were talking about bricks of cocaine the way their hand gestures and mannerisms were.

Calvin started to talk more with his hands as DeJon and Tremon entered the scene in front of McDonald's.

"What the hell is going on, y'all?" DeJon said with Tremon beside him.

"This fool warning me about Denise." BJ said.

"Yo, that's my people," DeJon said. "But she is giving you crazy rhythm."

"I think she's into you." Tremon said following DeJon's confirmation.

"Look I know about Rob, I heard about Jake Jones…" BJ said.

"But I'm telling you shorty's experienced!" Calvin yelled. "You must be a virgin."

Everyone would begin to laugh. Were they laughing because

they could relate to BJ or Calvin? As the crowd became bigger in front of McDonald's the teens would leave for BJ's sake and his reputation. Calvin knew BJ was not ready for action just yet. He had seen BJ as a rookie in the league of women. Denise was already in year 3… does that make sense?

"Sex? Who said anything about Sex? "I just want you to come over for dinner." Denise said that Saturday night. "I'm a Southern Bell; I love to cook. You ever had spicy Jambalaya?"

"Nah, but I'm interested." BJ replied.

Broken foot and all, BJ would make it to her house that evening.

Denise played basketball, ran track and later she would be cheerleader. She showed every muscle in her body that evening as she entered the room with a short jean skirt and tank top on.

"How's your foot?" She asked as she brought her guy friend a bowl of her famous Jambalaya.

"I should be back by the playoffs," BJ said. "Not like they be playing me like that anyway. "Coach hates me."

He paused, savoring the food before he asked, "Hey, before I forget what's up with you and Rob? Y'all like a couple still?"

"No, and we been done." she replied.

"Ok, because me and him cool but not that cool. He a Tiger, but not my mans." BJ said.

Back then like most big high schools there were teammates and there were cliques within the team. The BFHS Class of

2003, no matter the sport, was like a separatist movement at times, but even within that group there were cliques. It varied but at times, Regis Tremon and DeJon were a clique. There were times Rory, BJ and Blaire were a clique. Then there were other cliques such as A.B. (Ascheley Brown) Tyler Marx, P.J. and Nate. Then there were even smaller groups. You could also find Darren and BJ together a lot. Calvin hung with everybody, but his loyalty was to himself mostly, and to a certain degree, everyone understood why. He had been betrayed, lied on and manipulated in so many ways.

"Yeah, we're done BJ." Denise said. "I've been digging you for a minute. I used to see you talking to Avalon and Brittany. Burned me up!"

"Why?" Asked BJ.

"Because I always thought you could do better." She replied. "I knew I was going to get you even when I was with Rob."

"And Jake?" BJ asked.

She laughed, "Yeah done with that fool too."

Then her voice took a serious tone.

"I had some problems when I was younger. My mother was killed, and I've pretty much been on my own ever since."

Denise started to cry. "It's been rough, BJ."

BJ would listen to her story for a while forgetting everything that Calvin had told him… maybe because he was sad, maybe because he was fleshly heightened. Men become weak in certain moments. This was one of them.

After the two ate, they begin to watch some television.

"So why are you so afraid of me?" Denise began to come closer and closer. "Kiss me."

After the two kissed, she began to challenge him to make a stronger move.

"Don't be shy," She slyly coaxed him.

After a few minutes of getting to know each other a car door slammed.

"Denise! Denise!" Their make out session was interrupted by her grandmother's calls for immediate attention.

"Denise Wilson, come out here and get these groceries girl!" Her grandmother Ms. Emma said. "Oh, you got a friend here. I thought I told you no company."

BJ limped down the steps to help her grandmother with the grocery bags. "Hi, my name is..." "I know who you are, you're Pastor Timmons son." Ms. Emma interrupted his greeting. "Nice to meet you son but she is not permitted to have any company when I'm not here. And why do I smell food?"

As Denise rolled her eyes walking back up the porch full of groceries she said "Grandma!"

"Goodnight Timmons boy."

Ms. Emma dismissed BJ and he began his limping journey back home.

For months, Denise and BJ were a couple without being a

couple. She would escort him to the elevator and offer to carry his books to his classes. She would cut off the upper-class women from helping him in any way. The buzz was that D and BJ were a couple. Truth was, he was courting her. He had hung out with her and some, but he was more worried about his foot and having a great junior year. BJ started the second half of the year in football, though he was still a sophomore he had been thinking on the level of a collegiate athlete. Other girls would drop out the race because of the rumors of the two being official. Calvin and DeJon knew that eyes were watching but mouths were *running*. The closer he got with Denise the more Robert caught wind that he was replaced. Then the envy devil popped his nasty head out his hole.

It was a cold February afternoon. School had just let out and the student's conversations were overflowing with so called "Valentine's Day plans." BJ's foot had healed, and he was cleared to play basketball again. As everyone was talking on the walkway of the school, BJ had noticed that Denise and Robert were talking. The talking turned into play fighting, the playfighting turned into shoe throwing.

"Why in the hell are they throwing shit?" Rory Santiago said while he laid up against the wall with his girl. "Someone going to get hurt."

"I know if I get hit…" he warned.

Rory was with his girl Kristi-Ann at the time. He started talking to her around the same time BJ started talking to Denise.

"We got weightlifting so I'm about to wrap it up babe," he said. Tremon, Calvin and BJ all started to look closer at the playfighting scene that Robert and Denise starred in.

"You a** hole!" Denise said as she slapped his face.

"What you say?" Robert said.

Carlos Clemons and Brian Pitts tried to break the two teenagers up from playfighting.

"Aye Timmons... BJ Timmons... I had your girl already. Forget you and that slut!" Robert followed it up by calling BJ a bi**h. But what turned the moment into more drama was the size 14 shoe that hit Denise in her face. Robert laughed and went back into the school for a football work out.

Brittany Mosby and Denise attempted to walk BJ to practice. BJ with discernment, started to examine Denise Wilson a little harder. He was still naive to the fact that Denise was equally wrong, but his manhood was on the line. Robert was a big strong Division 1 football recruit. If BJ was going to remain in good standing with the lady folk, he would have to prove a point again. He had already gained some stripes in the so-called "hood" fighting the football players in Moon. Now a 6ft 4 inch, 300-pound mountain of man, was standing in his way this time.

"How could you let him talk to me like that?" Denise asked.

"D, let it go." Brittany stopped her in her rant. "Let him go to practice before he snaps."

BJ continued to shake his head and look at Denise at the same time after punching a random Wendy's customer's car door.

"Now I gotta see this dude."

"I gotta do something." He continued to convince himself. "I'm going back, yo."

BJ walked back in as Tremon and DeJon were talking in the waiting area of the high school with some cheerleaders.

"Yo Rev, what you doing?" DeJon asked BJ as the fumes came off his head.

"He fitting to snap." Tremon said.

BJ went to his locker and gathered every lock, exacta knife, and pencil he could find. He kept saying to himself: "I gotta do it."

DeJon and Tremon followed BJ to the high school basketball gym where the football players who did not play basketball were playing the administrators. A policeman who was a coach, a gym teacher and a few other coaches were present.

BJ entered the gym.

"Rob, can I talk to you?" BJ asked Robert. He repeated the questions twice as Robert ran up and back on the basketball court.

"Get out my face punk." Robert rejected BJ's question. "What do you want pu***?" Robert asked BJ with force.

Crack!! went BJ's book bag up against his face.

The first strike stunned Robert. He couldn't recover in time. *Boom...boom...boom!* BJ's fist pounded his face.

Tremon and DeJon observed everyone in the gym in case they planned on jumping in.

"BJ, you trippin'!" DeJon said while he and Tremon watched Robert's friends who thought about jumping in.

The gym teacher and policeman grabbed BJ and drug him to the girl's locker room to separate the two.

"Let's take it to the streets." Robert yelled.

"Son, I've been here 25 years. I've never seen anything like this before." Mr. Ace the gym teacher said to BJ as he punched the lockers. "You've got to control that anger."

"He had it coming, man." BJ said to Ace. "He's been poking the bear all damn year! Saying little slick shit with the quarterback Jason Sparrow. They can all get it!

Rory also had heard the commotion, and he ran to the gym to check what happened. "What happened to Timmons?" Rory asked DeJon.

"That mouth... BJ ain't with that shit." DeJon said.

BJ got suspended for 3 days.

This fight was not about Denise. She just happened to be the straw that broke the camel's back. Robert was an old-school bully. He along with Jason Sparrow and a couple other guys had always had their eyes on BJ, DeJon to a certain degree, and Tremon and Calvin. These four boys were always in someone's doghouse. BJ had believed because his father was a Pastor, and his mother was a teacher's aide he was on a leash... like a ferocious rottweiler. BJ had wanted to jump on a few boys.

"I'm going to tell your father. I am going to tell your mother." Those two sentences kept BJ in line, but every man or woman

has their limits.

Robert had threatened BJ a few times in Junior high, but nothing came of it. Probably because Tyrell, Regis, and guys like that kept the peace in between the grades. Those two were far from soft but likeable guys but at that point, BJ had to keep Robert in the back of his head for the remainder of the year.

"When your man BJ come back, I'm going to get his a**." Robert told Tremon and Regis.

Tremon and DeJon made sure they kept their boy informed so he could not get caught sleeping. Getting caught sleeping means getting caught off guard. Many men and women have got knocked out for being "sleep."

When BJ returned to school, he and Robert had not spoken again until the Madi Gras dance. Part II of their story was provoked because Robert's boys continued to fill his head with lies:

"BJ doing this and that."

"Timmon's thinks he this and that."

Robert had enough. He and Timmons would square off again outside of the school until Pastor Timmons and Denise's uncle came. This time BJ grabbed a Louisville Slugger. If Pastor Timmon's and a few other kids would not have held BJ back someone might have got killed, and Pastor Timmons was no stranger to violence. He wanted his son to be smart above everything. He also enjoyed watching his son change from being a passive chunky child to a courageous competitor. Robert had no clue the tide had turned.

In the end, BJ and Denise did NOT work out. Not because of Robert, but because of life. In life, people help you grow by causing you to move in different directions. That kind of growth is needed: it's called "growing pains". Denise gave BJ a few growing pains the next couple of weeks. She had even kissed Tyrell at a track meet. This was the deathblow to she and BJ's relationship, and it did not end well. BJ and Tye discussed the kiss for a few days. It hurt, but BJ was able to move on because the truth came out of it. Calvin was right... he did a good thing for warning BJ.

"I didn't want to see my boy go out like that." Calvin said.

As the spring turned into the summer the wounds of puppy love would heel. BJ's parents would see Denise and still talk like nothing happened because they understood Denise's situation. These two young attractive teenagers were moving fast and thank God someone prayed for a slowdown.

"That girl loves you, man." Pastor Timmons said. "I think it's for the best if you two split before someone gets hurt."

"Someone already did." BJ said sadly.

Calvin would also go through his own growing pains. He would get played by Stacey who happened to be Austin's sister. Calvin had his way with the women to a fault. He had given some girls pain and his time to hurt had come. Through that experience, he was taught a lesson about loyalty. He also got taught a science fact: *What goes around, comes around.* DeJon would get lied on also. People would tell his girlfriend who lived in another town about his flirtatious ways. Who told on DeJon? Was it a friend? No one knew. Rory would have his time too. Everyone needs that butt whipping to help them learn how to fight against adversity. These young men were battle tested by 15-16 years old. They had earned some more stripes.

Tye would later gain a brother from the moment that he and BJ reconcile. When you do your brother wrong, admit it and tell him your sorry, that way you can move on and learn from it. BJ learned a lot from both Denise and Robert also. He learned his temper would never leave but he would have to find an outlet. And find it fast.

"The Junior's Ambition"

"I won't deny it, I'm a straight ridah,

You don't want to f*ck with me."

That is what you heard in the locker room entering the 2001 football season. *My Ambitions as a Ridah* by the late 2pac Shakur. You heard this at least four times during a weightlifting or conditioning session. The Beaver Falls Tigers had one goal in mind this year. To win the championship and earn a state medal. They were ranked #2 in the state of PA. The papers and experts picked them to win because the number of seniors and juniors on the team.

"We been nice since midgets." Dougie said.

"It's on now!" Tremon Barksdale said.

"I can't wait to strap (put on equipment) em up this year." Macklin chimed in.

There were several Juniors inserted into both sides of the ball (offense and defense) this year. BJ Timmons now started at the tight end position and defensive End. The previous year he started four games at nose tackle. Austin Macklin was the middle backer with Regis right beside him. Macklin and Regis saw a lot of playing time as sophomores. Both he and Macklin played Fullback and Tight End also. Dougie was now the starting corner with Tye and Barksdale in the Defensive Backfield. Spencer Wallace, a senior, was a dynamite player. Blaire Ameen was now an importance piece to the defensive line. He had grown and was ready for war, but Jason Sparrow, who was also a senior, now had four unstoppable forces on offense. He would notice this when the team was still in shorts and shirts.

The football team had a big offensive line with Mike Nardone, Robert Tomlin, Brian Bullet Pitts, Mickie Cooper, and Randle Minkins. All the seniors and had known each other for more than ten years. The team possessed a trio full of tight ends: Austin Macklin who could run and block, BJ could block and had great hands...and Sparrow knew this because BJ played baseball the year before in the Spring.

Sparrow's dad had noticed BJ's glove on defense. BJ played pitcher, third base, and sometimes first. A lot of the boys grew up playing baseball. Sparrow's dad helped the coaching staff make the decision to put BJ as the tight end. BJ also grew an inch and lost 15 lbs. from basketball. Tyrell now went from running back to another back side Tight End/wide receiver. Tyrell Goosby could do anything he wanted on the football team, but for the greater good, D. Williams would be the starting tail back with Dougie backing up. The biggest increase on the team was the number of wide receivers, which would be the most noticeable force. The junior combination of Rory Santiago and Tremon Barksdale would put on clinics at the passing camp. Was this Rory's year? Coach Hilton noticed Rory's height and hands. He would leap above 95% of the defenders.

"Rory is the most improved athlete on the team." Pastor Timmons would tell his son BJ. "Jerry Rice." He would always call Rory "Jerry Rice" or "Cowboy Rory".

With a strong senior led offensive line, good tight-ends and dynamite wide receivers, this would be enough groceries for Jason Sparrow to start cooking, but would it be enough to bring home the gold? With a new coach who happened to be a man of color, all eyes were on the Tigers this year.

"Wait... where you going, DeJon?" BJ asked one evening at practice.

"Rev, I gotta go. They keep doing me dirty." DeJon said.

He had a monster finish as a sophomore wide out and defensive back. Because of his grades slipping and conduct in school, he needed a man in his life. His parents did not live together. It was time for his father to get his son full time. DeJon's mother had done everything she could along with his Grandad keeping him in church and around good family. She needed to sort out some things in her life and she did not want her son to be affected by it.

Where did DeJon go? Only to the Tiger's nemesis for the last 3 years: Aliquippa.

D, like Calvin felt, the effects from "coaching politics." DeJon's father watched his son sit for three quarters of a blowout. DeJon would make huge plays in the junior varsity games. Nothing would change. Calvin was still sore about the way the program had did him. With the coaching change, this would have been the best time for him to reassert himself. but he didn't. He stayed back and watched his boys lift and run in the hot summer. Calvin did something else: he got a job. He was going to need it for what he was about to come his way.

There were also other changes happening in the town. Since BJ and Tye Goosby were free agents due to the Denise stuff, they would interview other girls for being the other half of a power couple. The breakup with Denise caused BJ to look at girls like an employer looking for an employee and he had a list of criteria. First, she would have to pretty and all. He also wanted someone who had more balance in their life.

Tye who was a senior now and a future first round draft pick would also take his time interviewing girls.

"What about Maria and Sierra?" BJ asked Tyrell.

"Nah, they are crazy, and I know both their families. We all grew up in Morado Dwellings together." Tyrell replied. Morado Dwellings was a housing projects right before the expressway in Beaver Falls.

"I'm up there almost every night now." BJ said. "

Rev, I'm telling you they will come to you. Be patient, it's going to be a long year. Championship after Championship." Tye said laughing.

"They be on *me.*" BJ said with a smile on his face.

While those two were living the life, Rory and Barksdale were laying low in commitment. Barksdale had been with his girl for two years now. She went to another school and kept a low profile. "Tre" or Barksdale liked it like that because he was high maintenance, but he also liked his privacy. Rory was still with the Cameroonian princess Kristi-Ann. Rory and Tremon both got their driver's license so they both were at the top of the food chain when it came to the females.

Regarding football, both Rory and Tremon had the charisma of diva wide receivers. Rory had an old school beamer (Mercedes). The system could be heard from Australia. Three Six Mafia, Jay-Z, Afro-Man, Nas, Soulja Slim, and his favorite Ice Cube, were playing loud in his car.

"Here comes Bibby." Macklin would say.

Bibby was another nickname for Rory because he favored the Sacramento Kings point guard Mike Bibby. Light-skinned guys got compared to everyone back then. BJ was called LL Cool J, Nelly, or Allen Iverson. Rory and Little Nate Lewis were called a couple members from B2K. Ascheley Brown even was called "Tweety" (tweety bird) at times because he was (yellow) light skinned with a bald head. It's just like that.

With all the hype how did Rory keep a level head? He remembered all those nights riding home on his bike. He remembered waiting for parents to offer to take him home. 20 miles is a long ride, but he did it. In a sense it was like God was blessing him. Rory knew it and he would tell you that right now. *It was God Almighty.* If you ever tried to call him spoiled because of the car, he would let you know about the grind. He worked at Liner Ellies Furniture on the weekends. He even got a job at McDonald's to stay in good standing with his family.

Calvin who had been working for a few weeks at Eat-N-Park on 7th Avenue in Beaver Falls was still dealing with the breakup. He and Stacey were done, and he knew it.

"How could she play me?" Calvin asked BJ one night at the court.

"I mean bro, you did a lot of girls wrong." BJ said. "I mean think about it, there are a lot of girls who think you got what you deserved."

"I guess that what I get for messing with white girls, huh?" Calvin asked.

"Hahaha! Don't tell Macklin that man." BJ said. "That's what you get for dating your boy's sister fool."

Macklin had his moments where he wanted to fight Calvin… it's natural; your sister is your blood. Would you want your sister, your daughter, or your mama to date a man like Calvin Hollywood Jackson? If you say yes, then there are some changes you need to make. He was a certified player. He had a reputation for moving fast and hurting women emotionally.

"Girls come a dime a dozen men ain't that what you told me?" BJ asked Calvin.

"Yo…speaking of girls, what's up with you and Cassie?" Calvin asked his friend.

BJ smiled from ear to ear. "Yeah, yo…."

Cassie "Sassy" Washington a young "tenderoni." What is a

tenderoni?

"The truth about a Roni, she's a sweet old girl
About the sweetest little girl in the whole wide world
She'd make the toughest homeboy fall deep in love
So once you've had a Roni, you will never give her up
She's a special kind of girl that makes her daddy feel proud
You know, the kind of girl that stands out in crowds
Found a tenderoni and the Roni is so right
I think I'm gonna love her for the rest of my life."

Lyrics and music Performed by Bobby Brown...And sung by BJ Timmons to Ms. Cassie S. Washington.

"She is dope son." BJ Said.

"She young though, bro." Calvin said.

"You may be young but your ready…." BJ sung out loud.

"O.K. *Keith Sweat* but is you for real about to get on?" Calvin asked.

"Nah, it's going to take a while." BJ answered. "She ain't like that I gotta ask her some questions about some dumb rumor."

"Like Denise rumors?" Calvin asked.

"Not quite like that sir." BJ said.

Cassie had her eye on BJ for years now. She had been around Denise and her sister when they would talk about BJ. She also kept her secret crush to herself. It took an uncanny conversation for she and BJ to officially start talking. There

64

was a rumor about her being involved with a Senior in high school the previous year. BJ stepped to her one day at Sunday School. After BJ got clarification on the rumor, Cassie really took notice to him. She knew he cared.

Cassie had been a member of Pastor Timmons's church. She sat right behind BJ's grandparents. She was also a member of the book club, Meals on Wheels (cooking club), and the Audio-Visual staff for the newscast in the mornings for the school district. She was a shy, withdrawn, reserved girl. Small in stature but big in virtuousness. Baseball games, basketball tournaments, dances…. she was always there. BJ would always notice her and spark up a conversation. In the back of his head, he always wanted to ask her out. They were 2 ½ years apart.

The two began talking on AOL instant messenger. Messenger was not only a form of communication, but a visual voicemail, secretary, and matchmaker at times. For high schoolers, whose parents were too lazy to write down the messages, it worked like a charm! A real love shot!

Speaking of love shots, Cassie threw first blow. She had to be the aggressor because BJ knew he needed to ensure her safety. Safety from what? BJ was now an upper- classmen so he was a vet in the romance game… at least in his eyes. He had ducked and dodge a few girls all summer and he did not want Cassie to be a target. If the other girls even heard BJ was interested in this young girl, they would try their hardest to sabotage her chances. It wasn't personal, but some of the girls that year wanted the limelight.

Cassie had everything going for her. She came from a well-known family and had a God-fearing mother who was one of

BJ's biggest supporters. Ms. Lisa had a way of making you feel welcomed. One day, she offered BJ a ride home with Cassie in the car following a baseball game. He played horribly but she and Cassie made him feel like there would be a tomorrow. Little did he know, Cassie was crushing on him then. He was so mad that his braids came loose. BJ wanted to show Ms. Lisa as well as her daughter that she was worth the wait. No woman should feel rushed to grow up fast.

"If you're 13, be 13. You're only going to be 13 once." All Ms. Lisa asked was for BJ not to take advantage of her child. She wanted Cassie to have a healthy relationship.

While BJ was aligning the stars with Cassie, Rory "Bibby" Santiago had to get ready to battle some stars for headlines on his team. The coaches had no clue of the drive that Rory had. He had a crazy weight - lifting regimen. He also had an appetite for destruction. He loved hitting his opponents head on. All was going well, or was it?

"Rory go stand by Coach Gillard." Coach Hilton said. "Wallace and Clemons, you're in the starting lineup. Rory, just wait your turn, baby."

Shaking his head, Rory began to become frustrated. After practice, Rory left without talking to anyone. The rubber on his Mercedes is all the Tigers heard... with some Ice Cube music being played extremely loud.

"What's with Santiago?" Pastor Timmons asked BJ when he picked him after practice.

"I think he's ticked." BJ said.

BJ had watched his friend work hard at home and on the field all summer, coming to passing camps and weightlifting. Learning a new offense was tough. It is even tougher when you work across town at a burger joint four days a week. Not to mention Rory's home life wasn't the greatest. He moved around a little bit. Living with his grandmother off and on. His Pops wasn't present, and his mother displayed tough love at times. Rory needed some nurturing. By the time, a young man hits about eighth grade, if he hasn't been babied, don't baby him. It won't work.

BJ had seen a lot of his friends in single parent households become spoiled and neglected. Sometimes mothers overcompensate for their sons if the father is not present. They buy their sons all the Jordan's, video games and junk food. But not Rory. His grandmother taught him the do's and don'ts of the world. Rory was very guarded at times. If you crossed him, then you were as good as dead.

"Where is Bibby?" Goosby asked Barksdale before Thursday night's practice. The Freedom game was a day away.

"I think he had to work." Barksdale said.

"He better stop doing that, he going to miss his chances." Tye said.

"Honestly Tye, he catches everything, and he runs crisp routes." BJ said to Tye.

Tyrell continued to shake his head and he asked some more Juniors about Rory's where abouts. Tyrell was like that. He wanted to make sure everybody felt included. He knew Rory was a solid receiver, but he also knew he needed to focus on himself.

"He's a 3.2 student, a boyfriend and working part time." Austin Macklin chimed in.

"I'm going to rap to him later." Tye said.

Opening night for the 2001 football season was a beatdown by the Tigers. The Freedom Bulldogs had no chance. Intense hitting was done by Macklin and Nardone. The sold-out crowd was mostly full of Beaver Falls fans. BJ, Dougie, and Regis played solid defense while Barksdale and Goosby put on an offensive clinic. The final score was 27-0 Beaver Falls with the win.

Guess who had a touchdown? Rory Santiago.

"See you can't quit on us now." Tye Goosby said.

"There was scouts there tonight!" Tremon said.

"The University of Pittsburgh, Syracuse and I believe Toledo." BJ said.

"You think they're looking at me?" Rory asked the boys on the bus. "Bullshit."

"They saw you tonight bro." Austin said.

When the bus got back to the high school to drop the Tigers off, Rory was the first one out the locker room.

"I gotta be up at 7:30 am." Rory said.

"What about films? BJ asked.

"Forget them man." Rory said.

Rory was still upset that he got demoted for an unknown reason and he believed the quarter back Jason Sparrow had a lot to do with his demotion. Sparrow wanted to stick with his classmates. Rory was the better receiver. Truth be told, Rory might have been the 3rd best option in the passing attack. Tremon and Goosby would have led any team in the state that year. Rory wasn't no slouch though. He would have to earn some more stripes by practicing patience.

Game 2: Austin Macklin and BJ split time for tight end. The tight end position is an incredibly unique position in football. Normally the Tight End is faster than the line man but not as fast as the wide receivers. Austin Macklin and Tye were both faster than some receivers and running backs. BJ was the more traditional high school tight end. Austin was stronger than BJ and faster. They would push each other daily. There may have been some friendly competition, but it was hard to tell because the beatdowns were so thorough. Tigers would crush Shady Side Academy in week 2.

Week three was the first of many rivalry games that year, but the plan of attack was from another unexpected enemy.

"*Pst... Pst*! Timmons... what you put for number 3?" Robert Tomlin whispered to BJ during Psychology class.

"I put R.E.M. sleep cycle." BJ answered.

Big Rob Tomlin was nobody's fool. He was on his way to college for sure. Psychology was taught by great teacher. His teaching style was hard to follow, but he made everyone laugh. Mr. Byers was the most animated man you will ever meet. He was a huge sports fan so he would love to have small talk with his two football players.

"What you put for number 2?" BJ asked Tomlin.

BJ and Rob put the conflict from last year behind them. They both would need to depend on each other. Rob and Bullet made BJ's life good. The tackles are lined up right beside the tight end. Therefore, when a run play is called if the tackle blocks his man good then the tight end gets to beat up on the corner or safety. Sometimes the tackle and tight end double team line backers or defensive ends. For those who follow football, it is like watching a great music group's choreography.

That day, Mr. Byers kept walking in and out of class. BFHS had block scheduling. Block scheduling meant only 4 classes a day with a long lunch.

"Everyone: Stop writing." He said with a puzzled look on his face.

Pencils stopped moving.

"I just got word that a plane crashed into the World Trade Center." Mr. Byers said shaking his head.

Mr. Byers turned on the television in the classroom. Every news station had the first crash on. In between classes that day the students all had mixed emotions.

"Is it the end?" BJ asked Tremon Barksdale.

"This is crazy!" Barksdale said.

"The book prophesizes about these days." Ascheley Brown said to his friends.

"What book?" A freshman asked him.

"The Bible" A.B. answered quickly.

"These are definitely some signs." DeWarren Ford said.

"Where is Bush (U.S. President) at?" BJ asked.

September 11th was the topic of discussion in everyone's household including Cassie Washington's. BJ went to Cassie's that evening.

"What if the Lord came back tonight?" BJ asked her.

"Don't talk like that baby." She said. "You're scaring me."

"You ever been to the Tribulation House?" BJ asked.

"Yeah, but I don't remember everything. It was scary." Cassie answered.

The Tribulation House was a walk-through haunted house that was based off Biblical prophecy. The rapture, mark of the beast, plagues…etc. Calvin, Tremon, BJ, Rory, Blaire, Regis, A.B, "Shakes", DeJon, and Nate all had been there. Some more than once.

"If you pray about it and asked Jesus to come into your heart…" BJ said.

"Look everything is going to be alright." She stopped him. "We're going to get married, have babies…"

"Babies huh?" BJ said with a smile on his face. "We can't tell the Lord what to do. If it all goes down tonight, I'm ready to live in Paradise."

A lot of the boys grew up in church in Beaver Falls. They belonged to different denominations, but Sunday service was meant for church back then. In Beaver Falls, a good chunk of the youth went to some sort of church service. Not just for religious purposes but also social events. It was a way to keep the youth off the streets. Whether it was meaningful, that would depend on who you asked.

The New Brighton game was an emotional one. Due to the country being on notice and it being a rivalry, it was known as the "Little Brown Jug" game. The brown jug was full of nasty river water which smelled like crayfish and frog urine mixed with rain. There was a bridge that separated the two towns. Whoever lost the game, the captains had to return the jug to the school at the following pep rally. If the team that has the jug continued to win then there was no return, just bragging rights. The game got moved to the following Monday night which meant no NFL Monday night football in Western PA. This resulted in there was only being standing room at the game. The game was neck and neck until the final three minutes when Barksdale scored the final touchdown to make it a tie game. Austin Macklin scored the two-point conversion.

That night, while most of the team went their separate ways, Rory and BJ stayed back to talk.

"Look man, we all know you and Tre should both be the starting receivers." BJ said.

"I'm ready to say to hell with this shit." Rory said.

"Just wait, your time is gonna come."

Rory waived BJ off.

"For all that, I could be working." Rory said while staring

at the ground in the parking lot of the middle school. "I got college prep English classes, too."

BJ nodded his head knowing the importance of studying for this class.

"Plus, this girl won't stop tripping about time." Rory continued.

"Who?"

"You know who." Rory said. "I'm about to bounce now and head up there."

The next few weeks the Tigers would cruise through the conference, beating everyone convincingly. However, there was one small stumbling block: they lost to Center Township. Sadly, Macklin broke his fibula and would be out for weeks. The high- powered offense and ferocious defense drew a lot of colleges to come see what these boys were about. The whole state was on notice. DeJon who was a member of the Aliquippa Quips, also ranked, heard about how the Tigers were going to get destroyed again.

"Watch I'm going to break Barksdale. Goosby ain't all that."

DeJon would hear it all day every day.

Gerris Wilcox who moved to Aliquippa his Senior year also heard how the Quips were going to rock the Tigers. It had become ritual to beat the Tigers by 30 points. DeJon would read the papers and shake his head in disbelief. He had wanted to go back. He had a decision to make: move in with your dad to have a better life? Or stay to be with your boys? Calvin who had been working at the Eat-n-Park also took notice to the BF buzz.

Calvin who had become a spectator and a critic sat through all the games that year. He always remained confident still contemplating on playing the next year. He was anticipating his junior year for hoops and basketball was still a few weeks away. He had got used to his new schedule going to conditioning and working every other day to ignore his home life. He also kept money in his pockets from tips he made from running food out to guests and washing dishes.

"Did you catch that game last night, Calvin?" John the manager asked.

Shrugging his shoulders Calvin replied, "Yeah I caught it."

"Some of those guys got serious, serious talent." John said.

"They ok. They ain't play Quip yet or Washington or North Catholic." Calvin said. "I'll wait to crown them the champs."

As Calvin was stacking plates John went into a rant. "Look Calvin, I know about your mother's situation."

"Aye you don't know shit" Calvin cut him off.

"All those guys out there, you could be one of them Calvin!" John said with his hands folded.

"Of course, I could be but I'm not one of the good boys." Calvin said. "Offense, Defense, Special teams... I could contribute. I don't have a dad like Timmons, and I don't have a mother like Regis. Or Barksdale, he has the system. Tre has the system and the family to take him to the top."

"Calvin, let me stop you right there," John interrupted. "BJ

Timmons worked his ass off. Rory Santiago doesn't have a support system".

"Yeah, me and Bibby ain't close like that but they dogging him." Calvin said.

"Who the hell is Bibby?" John asked Calvin as he started to sweep the dining area.

"Rory, we call him Bibby." Calvin said. "Like Mike Bibby from the Kings."

After running the potato soup to table three, John continued he and Calvin's conversation. "Why do all you guys…"

"Whoa buddy… who is you guys?" Calvin asked with a mean mug on his face.

"Like why you guys always compare someone to an athlete or celebrity?" John asked.

"The reason is…. John……because most of us relate to athletes." Calvin said. "Most of us don't know any politicians, doctors or lawyers. And if we did, they normally ain't for us. Niggas live-in reality not a fantasy."

"Calvin you can't use that word around me." John interrupted Calvin with an index finger pointing up.

"NBA players, NFL…. Actors…" Calvin continued. "Hell, even the black doctors, teachers and coaches most of them sold us out."

He paused. "Let me ask you something John? What do Tiger Woods, Jay-Z, Kobe Bryant, Michael Jackson, and Calvin Jackson have in common.

"They're all black?" John asked.

"Nah there all niggas."

John shook his head, "Good night Calvin. But before you go, does Macklin know you talk like this?" John asked locking the back door of the restaurant.

Calvin untied his apron. "His sister dated me, and your daughter likes me. He's heard the word end in e r and not a." He laughed, "His family loves us, John."

John shook his head, "Why did I even ask?"

This topic was a sticky topic all around the country and still is to this day: "Why do you guys say that to each other?"

Young people of color get those questions every day. Here are the reasons: 1) Black is a color. So is brown, yellow, red and white. None of the boys in Beaver Falls were the color of a tire. What is so-called black culture? Is it chicken... dancing... slang... sagging... skinny jeans now? 2) When you get called a name so much, at first it hurts. Then you get mad, and then you get desensitized. Most men of color made the word stick every time they said the word nigger. Brotha would say it so much that other nationalities and races would cringe when they heard that word. Then they turned "er" to an "a". In the 1990's, 2pac Shakur made it an acronym: N.I. G.G. A. which meant *Never Ignorant Getting Goals Accomplished.*

Eazy-E taught young so called "blacks" to monetize the word through his group N.W.A. or Ni**as With Attitude. This group could be heard in every car, radio, or walk-man in the 1980's. Rory and BJ stayed with this music in their ears. It's a dirty game, but who made the rules? You can find this word repeated in most of the 90's "black" films. Above the Rim, Friday, Boyz N da Hood, Menace II Society, Life, The Program, Juice, House Party...pick one. All those movies were constantly being acted out in Beaver Falls and all around the world. In conclusion to this topic: It didn't matter what background they came from; all the guys had been called it before. The only thing "black" was these Tiger stripes. Think about it.

"HUMBLE PIES AND SALTY FRIES"

Every team has a nemesis, a rival, an antagonist. The Tigers had some rivals all through the county. But none as big as the Quips. The prestigious Aliquippa Quips. There football team was always a powerhouse and ranked nationally. The previous three years, the Tigers had been outscored 75-14 by the Aliquippa Quips. Mike Ditka, Tony Dorsett, Tye Law, Vashon Patrick, Josh Lay, the list goes on. That year they had a couple future pros. Mike Washington, Darrelle Revis and Thomas Campbell. Great tradition, tough town and committed fans. Perfect set up for the Tigers. That's what they were thinking that week. The head coach, Coach Hilton, was also from Aliquippa. He was fine athlete in his day. All teams have nemesis. Aliquippa was the team that you must go through to get to the promise land or to achieve your goal.

"Y'all going to get y'all a**es kicked," Cassie's uncle had been saying all week. "They sent seven guys to division 1A schools last year before and they just keep reloading."

"That humble pie going to be good, Mr. Charles." BJ said

while riding in Tremon's car.

"I can't wait Timmons." Tremon said. "We owe them." They had monster's every year if you let the people around the county tell you. This guy is 6 foot 6, and this guy runs a 4.3 forty - yard dash."

"Face it, you guys can't beat them." Mr. Charles said again and again.

"Man, he going to be salty when we smoke them dudes Friday." BJ said staring at Mr. Charles.

The community had zero faith in this year's team. Maybe it was because the girls were dating half of their young men and wearing their jerseys and Lettermen jackets. One time, Tremon Barksdale snatched a girl's Aliquippa Lettermen jacket out her arms and asked her why she would flaunt it in his face so much. It wasn't that the boys didn't respect their program. They did... but the disrespect from the other end went too far. Girls would say things to the Tiger players in class. Some would even try their hardest to coordinate little fights on the weekends when Aliquippa players would come down. They would instigate the boys in school by saying *I bet you can't do this and that like so and so.*

Some of their players also made matters worse by telling DeJon how they were going to purposely injure his friends and family. Some of their players would talk smack on the AOL instant messenger. Timmons father's church was threatened to be egged. Another ridiculous thing was that if the Tigers won, they were supposed to get beaten up. This threat had been surfacing since the 2003 class was in middle school. BJ, A.B. Shakes, Nate, Calvin, Regis, Fife, DeJon, Dougie and Tre had been whooping on them since middle school in hoops.

There would be a display of good sportsmanship after the Tigers won. Calvin always talked a little smack because his "Pap" lived up there. Football was a little different, though. They always had the Tigers number. "Not this year." Dougie said. "We want them."

"Remember what they did to us last year." Goosby said.

"Punch them in the mouth this week." Timmons said.

Did he mean that literally or metaphorically?

You see BJ never understood the ruckus. To him, he looked at Aliquippa like another neighborhood in Pittsburgh. Regis, Rory, and BJ all had been from the city. All parts of the Hill District, Wilkinsburg, Northside, and the West Side. Beaver Falls had a history of looking at this predominantly so - called black neighborhood as the "notorious" tough guys. The boogie man syndrome. However, the tide was turning; these group of men were different. They were fighters, alphas, and good athletes to go along with it. The only thing that could intensify this rivalry was something that happened two years before when BJ and the boys were freshmen.

A young man by the name of "Damon Grace" had a Jimmy Hart "mouth from the south" persona. Damon a.k.a. "D.G." was Jimmy Hart mixed with Lil Boosie and Flavor Flav. He was an instigator, agitator, negotiator, and gladiator if he needed to be. He had a way with getting under people's skin. He was a great hype man. The story went that DeJon and Tremon had stomped him out at a community college event for running that mouth of his. The stomping wasn't for no reason.

Before the college stomping, Grace coordinated a few confrontations with DeJon when he was by himself. One event occurred at Center Stage. Center Stage was a place for teens to go and party. There were concerts and festivals there. DeJon thought a couple upperclassmen from Beaver Falls had his back. He thought wrong. DeJon would tell you today that someone from Beaver Falls set him up to get jumped that night. From there on out, the 2003 class had an understanding to not go out with certain people. Even if they were your so-called homies. DeJon had already ensured combat would occur if anything got out of pocket while he was a student at Aliquippa high school also.

"I'm telling you right now, if you touch my cousin…" he would say intensely, "then I'm in it. I'm not going to just sit there and watch my dudes fight. This ain't no threat, it's a promise!" He would consistently say this in the lunchroom full of Quips. All this was a recipe for a rivalry on and off the field.

The night of the game, the locker room was silent. The big game was finally here. Not quite the championship but a barometer for the Tiger's ceiling. This team they were playing tonight had high hopes as usual. One would say they looked right passed these Tigers. Beaver Falls started off fast and never looked back.

Catch by Timmons for 15 yards. Barksdale 17 yards, Goosby 13 yards. Runs by Williams and great blocking by his full back, Regis Bolden. On the defensive side, big hits from Clemons, Steve, Nardone, Benson, Timmons, Regis…etc.

Everybody came to hit that night. A 48-8 beatdown. Though the Tigers won round one, they almost knew they would see the Quips again.

After the game, BJ called Cassie on her room phone.

"Good game baby!"

"Can I come up?" BJ quickly asked.

"It's kind of late, I gotta cheer at the game tomorrow." she said.

Cassie cheered for the 12-13-year-old team.

"O.K. will you be on AOL tonight?" BJ asked.

"Yeah, I will I change my screen name and info."

Her profile went from talking about her likes and dislikes to the song One in a Million by the late singer Aaliyah. Cassie had put the world on notice. The two were a couple and she wanted people to know it.

BJ laughed then prayed before he went to sleep. He realized that the eyes would be on he and Cassie Washington now. In church, school, and the community. *"Isn't he a little old for her?" "What's her mother think?" "He's just trying to get in her pants...etc."* All these statements were already in BJ's head. This was a good thing. He wanted to stay on his toes for when people made things awkward. He also prayed that he would continue to play hard and impress some school. He would have plenty of opportunities to show what he had.

BJ lived in a clergy house. Sometimes BJ wanted to get away from the choir rehearsals, bible studies, and meetings. He had to be quiet at times and not show emotions when a ballgame or favorite show was on. BJ looked at Cassie's house as a safe place… a place where he could unwind from the pressure of being a preacher's kid. Her family accepted him and made him feel at home. BJ liked to watch old school action movies and sporting events and Cassie loved to read so it worked itself out. BJ would begin practice weekly on getting his license. He wanted to take this girl everywhere. While they were skeptical in the beginning, BJ's family allowed things to play out because they could see they were happy together.

The next night, BJ would read some inappropriate instant messages from girls. Some girls would send messages on what they admired about him. Some girls claimed they were at the game the night before. He would have to get off the computer fast because he didn't want his parents to think he was a developing a narcissistic character trait. He would arrive at Cassie's house and plop on the couch in her room in her basement.

"I want to tell you something," she said to him as he was into whatever ball game that was on the tv.

"Sup babe?" He said setting up his space in her room.

BJ turned her tv off and looked at her. "Someone say something to you?"

"No. Why you say that?"

"Because I don't want nobody filling up your head with no jive talk." BJ said. "I don't want you for just your body."

"I know." She stared him in his eyes for a few seconds.

BJ began to get a little up tight.

"Just relax," she sighed. "BJ...I love you."

BJ looked up at her. "Yeah, yo?"

"Yes BJ, I have never felt like this before. I love you for real."

"Fo real, fo real?" BJ asked.

"Yes knucklehead." She said.

"I love you too."

Smiling through her glasses, she suddenly took them off. "I know you just don't want to use me. Me and my ma talk about it a lot."

"How so many girls fall by the wayside because a man took advantage of them." BJ smiled. "Men try to get women in bed before high school."

"Cassie, you know I want to take it slow because one day I'll have a little girl. *Cough.... Cough.* Speaking of that, the other night you said you wanted to have kids."

"Well, I do." Cassie said. "Who knows, maybe one day with a guy like you."

In his head, BJ was thinking or *me!*

The things men think when they cake baking.

What's cake baking? Cake baking is a metaphor for putting something in the oven. The oven is the woman's womb.

Cassie went upstairs to get BJ something for him to take back home. It was homemade rice crispy treats.

"Yo these is fire!!" BJ said when he tasted one.

"Thanks, I didn't know if you like sweets like that." She said.

"I love sweets." BJ said.

If BJ could hit the weights later with the sauna suit on, he felt like he could treat himself. When you're 16, you think you can eat anything. Tremon ate 10 Twix peanut butter candy bars every lunch. A.B. ate nacho cheese and tacos every day. Calvin ate big giant cinnamon rolls every morning with milk. One day, that dude will be a diabetic. Don't build bad habits. You are what you eat.

"Before you go BJ, just know I'm ready." Cassie said.

In BJ's head, he was thinking…. "Green Light!"

While the light might have been green for BJ, Calvin was hitting yellow. One of the female classmates of the 2003 class had missed her period. Her monthly friend didn't come by. Two words no man wanted to hear: "I'm pregnant." They weren't together, simply good childhood friends.

"Who do you take me for Calvin?" She asked with conviction.

"Are you sure?" He asked.

"Yes, and I'm keeping it." She said walking away.

Calvin was going to be a father. He was working and trying to keep his grandmother stress-free. How was he going to break this news to his family? Calvin had pride in representing his family even though people didn't think it. Calvin used to wonder what it would be like to have a father like Tremon,

Regis, Fife, or BJ. The Tigers had a lot of fathers who attended practices and critique their sons. Dougie Benson's father was laid back and stood by himself up against the fence at practice. Even he would scold his son if he missed a play or two. Calvin had just become a young man and now he was a young father.

As the regular season ended Rory would become more concerned about his future in football. Rory had an incredible run against Beaver and a huge catch in the Mohawk game. He still felt underappreciated.

"Rory…Rory……Rory Santiago," His girlfriend called to him over the phone.

Looking at the phone irritated he said, "Yeah, babe. I hear you!"

"What's with you?" Kristi-Ann asked. She had asked this question repeatedly through she and Rory's phone conversation.

"Look, look I don't got time for this tonight." Rory interrupted.

"You played a great game babe I don't get it." She said.

Doing his pushups over the phone, breathing in heightened frustration Rory said- "I got to work tomorrow."

"Work, work, work!" She said furiously. Rory's work habits had been growing on his woman. She watched him practice, then work out at home, go to work, and work sometimes on weekends part time. She was very demanding, and it was time for her to throw some salt.

"When I was with Jake….," she began.

Rory became irate. "Who? Oh, you want a thug. Check this

out girl! You starting to be salty because I ain't sweating you. Because I have goals…"

"I have goals too, Rory!"

Instead of being patient she wanted it all. Right now. She had stressed to Rory that she loved him and wanted his baby also. Rory's commitment was solid but when he felt betrayed, it was time to go.

"Rory?" Kristi-Ann hollered through the phone. "Rory…. Rory!!I know this negro did not hang up on me."

No one wanted their business in the street back then. For example, If Shakes was having an issue with his girlfriend. It wasn't BJ's job to tell everybody that there were problems in paradise. Another example, Tyler had got cheated on. When everyone heard the gossip, some men sat back and observed. Others were there if he needed to vent. What young men did not do was tell the rest of the school, because when Tyler found out he was going to confront you. Everyone was held responsible for their love life. Everyone also was held accountable if they were the culprit of gossiping. Therefore, Calvin and DeJon were important to the 2003 class. Sometimes they would overdo it, but they let you know where you stand.

Second part of the season is always more stressful. Shorter practices because of the daylight savings. Coaching schemes, scouting reports, player's health, and production. The team had been jelling on both offense and defense. The team was getting along off the field also. When you're winning, it's easy to be friendly with one another. Coach Hilton almost had a heart attack when the Tigers barely won the first round. Carlynton was tough and had a lethal passing attack. In the end, the Tigers had too much fire power. Tre Barksdale, BJ, Tyrell, and the running backs were too much. Jason Sparrow played a superb game. Following the game Goosby put the state on notice. He had an All-American game. Gaining more scouts by the dozens. He and Larry Fitzgerald (future Arizona Cardinals Wide Receiver) were 1 and 2 on some college scout's wide receiver board. Goosby was that impressive.

"Where is Tyrell looking at for college?" Pastor Timmons asked BJ the morning after the Carlynton game.

"Pitt, some black schools, Cincy, Marshall, and West Virginia." BJ said.

"Even some Junior Colleges are looking at him if his grades don't get better."

A Junior college is a college that is typically a two- year school to get you ready for your next step. The next step for some students is a four-year school. Athletes who go to Jr. Colleges go to develop athletically or have a hard time with their studies.

Tye fit that criterion perfectly. Beaver Falls had helped him a little too much. Because Tye was so likeable, he was easy to let slide through the cracks. The charisma he had on the girls, he had on the female teachers too. Don't look too far into that last statement.

"Did the mail come today?" BJ asked.

"It's Saturday, he don't typically come until about 12:30 pm." Pastor said. "Speaking of black schools, you do that paperwork for the tour in the spring?"

Lacing up his timberland boots BJ nodded his yes. BJ was scheduled to go on the black-college tour in the spring. A "black school" is predominately black school. These schools also can be called HBCU, which stands for Historically Black College University.

"You going to see some nice schools boy." Pastor Timmons said.

"Dad you know the other day I heard Cincy was looking at Andy Horn from Rochester." BJ said. "Dude ain't better than Spencer or Tye or Dougie! And his boy Jordan Moses, he's going to West Virginia!"

Looking in the mirror putting on his earring BJ heard the mail truck.

"Why you so geeked for the mail today?" Pastor Timmons asked.

"No reason…Boo yow!" BJ screamed.

"There it is boy," He replied and then added sarcastically, . "Wisconsin, Syracuse …. *and Dayton you heard of them?*" BJ heard of Dayton University, but they were not first on his radar.

"Dear, BJ Timmons we've been watching you……"

"Dayton is a solid program boy." Pastor Timmons said looking at the brochure. "That's good football." Don't be a fool and think it ain't.BJ it's probably just a questionnaire." A questionnaire was a document like an application. BJ would be reminded of this every time from here on out by both his parents. They wanted him to stay grounded.

"Michigan!" BJ said jokingly.

"Boy, please" Sabrina Timmons said as she passed him with the folded clothes.

BJ's heart was set on Michigan for long distance and Pitt for home choice. Barksdale had been getting letters since the end of his sophomore year. He and Macklin were already on a lot of radars. Tre put on such a show at quarterback and punt returner the end of his sophomore year that he was well known by the summer of 2001. Macklin was a track guy, remember? When you're 6 ft 2 ½, 220 pounds, running 100 yards in 11 seconds or lower, schools will come. BJ was kind of newcomer to this recruiting thing. Regis was a scholar athlete; he was already in certain college's database. Blaire, Dougie, and Rory were all anticipating their letters from a college. In their eyes they were as good as any of the guys on their team or in the state. Because Tre was humble, and BJ was new to the recruiting process both young men kept the news to themselves.

"Now don't be salty if someone hate on you." Mrs. Timmons said. "Some things are meant to be kept to yourself."

Later that night Cassie and BJ would go out to eat at a Chinese restaurant in a nearby community.

"Baby I got something to show you…here." BJ said handing her some folded pieces of paper.

"What are these?" Cassie asked with confusion on her face.

"Letters from college, love." He said with excitement. "What you think?"

"I'm happy for you," she said. "But Syracuse is pretty far."

90

BJ smiled, "It's in New York."

"I don't even want to think about you going that far." Cassie said.

The atmosphere was very silent for a few minutes as the two chewed their Lo-Mein and fried rice. That night, they were discussing one of their first serious topics outside of the September 11th scare. The feelings they were experiencing were not because of envy or jealousy; the "unknown" can scare the hell out of a sinner. He was only 16 and she was about to be 14. Neither had much experience in long distance relationships or any experience in relationships period.

When BJ got home after he and Cassie's date, he stayed awake tossing and turning. *"Am I being an a** hole?"* He thought. *"Am I bragging?"* *"I love that girl."* *"She's going to be my wife…"* All these thoughts ran through his head until he finally fell asleep.

Round two of the playoffs was with who the Tigers expected. The Aliquippa Quips were looking to avenge their butt whipping from the regular season game. The game was sold out at Ambridge High school.

"BJ they are coming at you tonight." Pastor Timmons yelled during pre-game. "Stay home on defense."

The Tigers were aware that the Quips would come with a different game plan, and they did. The Aliquippa quarterback overthrew a lot of balls in the first game. Second game, he was sharp and very agile. The receivers couldn't get open. Now they were faster and more disciplined on their routes.

"Damn man who got him?" Tre asked Tye in the defensive huddle following a slant route that broke the game open.

"I couldn't hear the call." Tye said.

The crazy thing was the receiver had Goosby beat by at least 6 yards. He still caught him, and it might have been the most impressive play of the game. On offense, Barksdale and Goosby both took the game over. BJ didn't get the ball that game, but he did block well. Macklin was still on crutches and cheered his friends on from the stands. He and BJ would talk when BJ came off the field for a blow which could be water or rest. Tye would come in and play tight end. If Macklin were healthy, Coach could have had a field day calling plays. The game was neck and neck for three quarters. Fourth quarter was one for the ages. After Tre had scored another touchdown, Aliquippa had got the ball and started to gain momentum for a game winning drive.

"Timmons stay home!" Carlos Clemons yelled from the opposite side of the field.

The ball was hiked, and the Aliquippa QB dropped back to throw the football. BJ dropped back in a defensive stance and started to back pedal. The play was going in slow motion through BJ's eyes. The QB threw the football where he thought his receiver was going to be. Blaire Ameen and Carlos Clemons put the pressure on the quarterback to force him to throw the ball so fast.

"*Interception!*" The announcer said over the intercom. "*Intercepted by number 84, BJ Timmons!*"

BJ returned the interception 36 yards to seal the game. All

Beaver Falls had to do is kneel or run it in one yard. BJ had become a hero! This was one of the biggest moments of his life.

"Rev, you the man!" Tyler Marx yelled from the stands.

Calvin and Allen Fife had their hands waiting to be slapped at the fence. "Timmons, you did that shit!"

As BJ was looking for Cassie and his father in the stands his night had been shot down suddenly.

"You think you did something?" Coach Hilton said. "Don't you ever act like you did something. You ain't do shit!" He continued to yell.

BJ went to grab his helmet for the victory offense.

BJ's father was infuriated. "Aye, Aye! who is he hollering at?"

The coach would not turn his head around. "

"You crazy?" Pastor asked with anger in his voice.

Pastor Timmons was nobody's punk. A man of the Lord? No doubt about it. About his children? He was a lion protecting his cub. He knew his son did nothing to deserve that humiliation. What was Coach Hilton truly trying to do? Was he caught up in the moment? Was he salty because his alma mater had been eliminated? Was he trying to humble BJ? All these thoughts rushed through BJ's head.

When BJ got home that night, Mrs. Timmons had to calm her husband down.

"You have a congregation and BJ's future does not depend on a coach." She said with at her husband with concern. "God is in control. You think that will break him, Bernie?"

"Sabrina, you know me!" Pastor said.

The two had a heated exchange about their son's feelings and how he should handle this situation. Coach Hilton may have thought the good Christian folk don't have anger issues. About their children, any parent can become dangerous. Never forget that. As BJ watched the 11 o'clock news waiting to see the highlights from the game he spoke with Cassie "Sassy" Washington.

"Baby don't sweat him." She said. "AOL is going crazy right now!"

BJ went downstairs to look at the chatroom. Some of the Beaver Falls community felt very salty after doubting this group of young men all year.

"Only two rounds left." Cassie said on AOL. *"Congratulations to my baby, BJ Timmons!!!: SassyLuv84."*

The news covered the game and BJ's interception. BJ felt uneasy watching the seniors do the interviews. BJ felt he and Tremon played a hell of game. He now had to refocus on what was important: his health, his family, and his girl!

The semi-finals of the Pennsylvania Playoffs were a breeze for the Tigers. North Catholic put up a fight in the beginning but in the end, too many athletes. Dougie Benson broke the game open with an interception like BJ the week before. Rory played more and had a key block for Williams longest run in the playoffs. Rory still was substituting in and out with the other receivers. He had even got into a fight with a transfer from Riverside. Rory's patience was running low. He still played an important piece to the success of the Tigers.

"Bibby you gotta think positive." Tye said.

"Blaire and you both, we going to need next y'all week." BJ said.

"Don't bet on it." Rory said looking away.

It was Championship week. All the festivities were heightened. This included decorations with Heinz Ketchup bottles, ketchup shirts, and signs. The Heinz Company was the reason that Heinz Field-home of the Pittsburgh Steelers, was named so. Pittsburgh was only 35-45 minutes east from Beaver Falls. All the local news stations came to cover the Tigers and their school. Photos would be flashed, and everyone was waiting for a prediction from at least one of the seniors.

"I think it will be a good game." Sparrow said.

The news cast would ask the running back from Beaver Falls what he thought.

"It's been a team effort." He said. "From all the guys not just myself."

As the team was stretching at the Thursday practice coach called Barksdale over.

"Tre, this week we want you to take some snaps at the quarterback position." He told him.

The team had faith in Barksdale. This is not to say that they didn't have faith in Jason. Jason Sparrow was a sound, strong armed quarterback. The coaches and team knew that Washington (which is in southwestern Pennsylvania) would not be expecting Tre to line up behind Big Cooper, the center.

"If they see Tre at the QB, they going to freak!" Blaire Ameen said to BJ as the two were lining up for defensive drills.

Blaire would start in the championship game in place for "Big" Steve Rogers. Big Steve would have some academic barriers that he needed to cover before the big game. There was a lot of commotion around the situation. Big Steve was important to the Tigers defense. The team didn't find out that Steve was ineligible until the Wednesday practice. He would be devastated.

"Blaire, this your opportunity to get some looks and make a name for yourself." Coach said.

Blaire was an incredible athlete for his size. 6 ft 3, roughly 260 pounds and could dunk a basketball with two hands when he wanted to. The whole thing with Blaire is you had to push him; he had a motor if you could just find the right key to start it.

"You ready big dog?" Coach Hilton asked Blaire.

"Yeah, I been ready." Blaire replied enthusiastically.

He slapped Blaire on his helmet and blew the whistle to start the scrimmages. Meanwhile, Tre looked fantastic at the quarterback position. He ran the option. He threw a couple bombs to Rory and Tye. He would pass one over the middle to

BJ. Austin Macklin was back this week too. He would play a little defensive end and some tight end.

"I think we're ready!" Tye said.

Washington had been the favorite all year to win the state title. The reason Washington was favored was because they had made the trip to the championship round three years in a row and lost to some star-studded teams. Sadly, the Tigers wanted to make this another incomplete mission for the Washington players. They had a running back on his way to Notre Dame, a corner back on their way to Kentucky, and a big defensive tackle and center on their way to West Virginia. Beaver Falls had Goosby, a senior lead line, blood hounds on defense, and Tre as a secret weapon. Let the game begin!

The game would be a fast paced one. The Washington offense starting off like gang busters. They would throw little screen passes (running back runs a short distance, catches the ball behind his lineman). They would run trick plays and a couple little misdirection plays. The Tigers would stay home and not break when it seemed like Washington was going to break loose. Interceptions by the Tiger defense and pressure by Blaire Ameen and BJ lead to the interception. BJ would make a few good stops at the defensive end position yet there would be costing blow. Mike Nardone, a senior, popped his shoulder out of place on a fumble by Sparrow. Mike would try his hardest to get back in the game, but the trainer would not allow it.

The Tigers were now down two starters. Mike and Steve were great players. Blaire and Rob Tomlin would have to step it up in the middle.

"The defense is breaking down!" Blaire yelled in the huddle gasping for water.

"You just stay home on defense ." Regis Bolden the middle linebacker, said when the defense was going over plays and blitzes.

Blaire held his own the whole game. The first real big play was from none other than Tyrell Goosby.

"Number 22 gets the ball." The announcer yelled. "He makes one guy miss, then another guy... refusing to go down he runs his own man over." Goosby was the best athlete out there.

The second half was continued fast-paced play. Both Washington and Beaver Falls would make chess moves ensuring their team would be successful. Washington capitalized off two interceptions. Spencer Wallace would break the game open with a vicious hit on their best wide receiver. In the end, The Tigers this time, made too many turnovers. In football, the team that wins the turnover battle has a good chance of winning. The Tiger offense had four total turnovers. Typically, that many turnovers will ruin your chances of being victorious. The final score was 24-14 Washington.

"Man, we had that shit." Goosby said after shaking the Washington player hands.

"Guys hold your heads up high." The coaches told the team.

"Next year, we coming back." BJ said immediately following coach's speech. It was premature, but very prevalent for the juniors to hear.

As for Tre, what happened to his quarter backing that game? No plays were called whatsoever. All he could do is shake his head in the Steeler locker room.

"We better than them bro." Tre said shaking his head.

BJ, Blaire, and Tre Barksdale were the last to enter the bus to go home. There were some tears because some men never would play another game again. Some men would never play in a game to that capacity again. Macklin said it repeatedly. "Next year man, next year."

"You going to Mr. Franks tonight?" Cassie messaged him on AOL instant messenger.

"I'm sore as hell." BJ answered.

BJ knew there was a victory party for the Tigers to celebrate their game. Regardless of if they won or lost. BJ noticed all the bruises on his arms. He was all black and blue. Not to mentioned he had a massive headache. Was it a migraine or concussion? Back then, no one even thought to ask for medicine let alone see a doctor.

"Baby my head is pounding, yo."

"I think Kristal, Bridgett and some other girls are going to the dance tonight."

"My ma will take us if you can't find a ride from Tremon."

BJ knew Tre wasn't going. Tre was going to see his girlfriend as soon as he showered and got dressed. DeJon would send BJ a message on instant messenger later that night.

"Rev, you going to the dance?"

"I heard it's supposed to be packed down there!!!"

BJ would message him back: "Yo Dmagic87 (DeJon's screenname) I don't think I can tonight man."

"I'm pissed."

"I'm tired and hungry." DeJon would message back.

"Aight man, I'll holler at you later."

Meanwhile Cassie was making sure it was cool for her to go out tonight.

"I don't really want to go...but you can," he said with no hesitation. BJ didn't like the thought of another man pushing up on his girl.

Cassie was a fast thinker, she improvised. "I'll go for two hours; can I see you tonight?" She messaged him.

"If I'm up, of course." He answered quickly. BJ would do a quick weight - lifting work out in the basement and call it a night.

The Most High has a sense of humor at times. He knew that these boys with hot tempers would not last fifteen minutes if they would have seen who crashed the party. The usual Aliquippa guys. No, the street Crips and bloods? Nope try again. The Washington football players and some of their fans! No one knew who invited them players to the dance. No one would fess up to it. If Rory, BJ, Tre, or Macklin would have gone to that dance. It would have been bad. Not because the boys were troublemakers, but they just lost. Rubbing it in their face wouldn't be cool for anyone with a small percentage of pride.

There was a similar incident that occurred like this the previous year. Only the other way around. A few guys from B.F. (Beaver Falls) would travel to New Castle (PA) for a party. In the projects, by the way. Bad move for these guys. Chairs were thrown, someone got hit over the head. One guy even got his face broke. If it weren't for Tremon's girlfriend Tracey, BJ, DeJon, and Tre would have been a part of the melee.

"I don't think you guys should go up there tonight." Tracey said that night to Tremon over the phone. "I got a bad feeling." "New Castle, tonight?" Tracey ended up persuading Tremon who later informed BJ and DeJon that they would not be going to the party that night.

Tracey was oh so right! Countless times over the years Tremon and the boys had someone praying over them. It happens like that sometimes. You never know who invited who. You can only be accountable for you. That's it.

Basketball season (2001-02) would begin with the same momentum the Tigers had from Football: rough play and sensational dunks. Tyrell would start off rough but eventually he would get the rust out. Clemons, Sparrow, and Christian would contribute. The team was led by the guards: Calvin at the point, Tremon at the two or shooting guard, and Allen Fife off the bench. Regis, Dougie, and BJ once again all played hard in practice but not quite stand outs. These guys were all varsity players, but junior varsity was where they could show most of their talent.

Dougie would find himself ineligible. During football

season, he was attentive and very cooperative. Towards the end of football season, he would be more focused on the ladies. In practice, Regis and BJ would battle Christian and Tye and Clemons Jordan Sarver and Brandon Taylor, who were both sophomores, added more length in practice also. This team had a lot of spark and hype surrounding it. Calvin was a target for one of the top guards in the state.

"This is our year fellas." he said. The Tigers were ranked number 5 in the state that year.

"Who you going to the Christmas dance with, bro?" Calvin asked Timmons.

"I don't think I'm going this year." Timmons said walking up the hill from basketball practice.

"Yo, I heard that girl Jamaica wanted to go with you." Calvin said excitedly.

"Jamaica Bivens?" BJ asked his friend, laughing and rubbing his hands together in the cold air.

"Yeah, yo! She plays volleyball too." Calvin responded with affirmation in his tone.

"I got to check with baby girl." BJ said quickly.

"Who killa?" Calvin asked.

BJ nodded his head confirming the questioning from his friend.

"She the wife now bro?" BJ nodded his head again.

"Come on son!" You got to do better than that." Calvin told BJ.

Calvin continued to go and on about BJ looking so vulnerable. "What did I tell you about moving so fast, yo?" Calvin said shaking his head with a disappointed look.

Calvin would begin his soliloquy. "Listen, if she is meant to be with you. A dance ain't going to hurt her at all. "You gotta understand, you only going to be 16 once bro".

Calvin paused and then continued his point, "Remember, she will be 16 one day and she going to want to go out. "If y'all still together, which I doubt. By that time, you'll be in college."

BJ acting like he was listening intensely looked up and said, "Who you going to the dance with?"

Calvin started laughing. "That ain't the point."

As the Christmas dance approached, Jamaica would consistently ask BJ if he was going to the dance or not. Jamaica Bivens was a tall light-skinned freshman who was interested in BJ, but aware that he had a young tenderoni. BJ didn't want to lead her on in any way.

"So yeah.... I heard Jamaica telling some girls at Athens (restaurant) she liked you." Cassie told BJ one night when he went to see her.

"Yeah, I heard too." BJ said jokingly.

"Look I don't want to think about you with no other girl, but I don't want to be in the way of your high school experience." She said indecisively

BJ put his hand in the air.

"Can I say something?" He then requested a kiss on the lips.

"Do you think I'm crazy? Do you think I'm a fool? Do you think I'm crazy, deranged...?" He quoted comedian Martin Lawrence.).

She laughed and hugged him. "I just know she like you." Cassie said. "That damn Denise too."

BJ turned up Cassie's radio. The song *"Differences"* by Ginuwine came on followed up by Usher's *"You Got It Bad."* As the music flowed through the air, they forgot about the conversation for a few minutes.

"I'm here and I'm here for the long haul, yo." BJ said. "I'm in love with you girl."

Before BJ left that night, Cassie made sure she sent him with a love letter ensuring his needs were met. BJ took his dad's Astro Van keys and kissed her good night. He looked up and reassured her, "Them girls going to be salty as hell when they see me with you before the dance."

Jamaica and BJ would end up going to the Christmas dance together. As promised, BJ took pictures with Cassie before meeting up with Jamaica. The two would dance for a few songs but not any slow songs. BJ would dance to Michael Jackson's "Smooth Criminal." and captivate the dance with some old school "M.J." moves. BJ would sit and cheese(smile). He was truly a sucker for love. He had fun with his boys. Calvin ended up taking an Asian girl from BF. Tre and Tracey looked dapper. The dance was nice, but it had to end early for BJ.

"I had a nice time BJ." Jamaica said walking up her grandmother's steps.

"Glad you did." BJ said taking his suit jacket from around her shoulders. "Well good night Jamaica, I guess I'll see you in school." He followed that up with a hug.

As BJ got ready to get in his father's van Jamaica stopped him

"BJ! she said, "Cassie Washington is a lucky girl."

He smiled. "I know, I'm headed up there now."

Cassie was asleep, BJ would tap on her bedroom slide door. Now, in 2001 you couldn't text your lady friend. You had to trust that your girlfriend or boyfriend was the person that they said they were. Keep in mind all BJ had was a driver's permit. Not the official license yet. It was very risky, but to him, this girl was worth it. So, he took that risk driving to Cassy's house that night.

To BJ "BJ" Timmons, Cassie had showed yet again that she was worthy to be in the number 1 spot.

Christmas that year was awesome. BJ got everything he wanted. More letters from big colleges and some more muscle tone from lifting weights twice a day. However, Christmas night, BJ got the stomach flu. Thankfully, Cassie was in Maryland visiting her aunt so, she couldn't catch it. She called him three times a day making sure he was recovering well. BJ would realize that this was a trait of a good woman. Back then conversation and anticipating conversation was just as important as facetime is today.

The Tigers were ready to open against the teams in their division. They had lost to New Castle in a Christmas tournament but that was it. They were ready to play their rival. Aliquippa had a good team and were ready to avenge their football season that had been cut short. Calvin was nothing short of breath taking. There was a rumor that he feared playing against "black" teams. However, this was nothing further from the truth! Calvin had already dropped 25 points on Oliver. A city school, Oliver, was in the same neighborhood where BJ and his family were from. Against Aliquippa, Calvin dropped 37points in an overtime loss.

"Who called them dumb a** defensive zone plays?" Calvin said on the way home. "Who said number five can't shoot?"

Calvin was irate.

"Chill, we will get them next time," someone said in the back of the bus.

"See that's that dumb Shit I'm talking about." Calvin fired back.

Calvin's temper was still an issue with his teammates. He lost his cool in the Christmas tournament in front of Gannon University and Miami of Ohio University. The schools came to see Jackson from BF and Jackson from Monessen, PA. Calvin was being looked at by several schools, according to Pastor Timmons. Who was informing Calvin about his conduct on the court? Who was allowing Calvin to process that a school took interest in him? This information could have empowered Calvin or could have created a bigger monster, too. Despite it all, Calvin would continue to dominate on the court and in practice.

In basketball you play your division opponents twice a year.

Beaver Falls had been crushing teams the rest of the season. They had destroyed New Brighton, Center, Beaver, Shenango and Riverside. Aliquippa and Beaver Falls were ready for a rematch. Before the varsity game both Allan Fife and BJ would put on a display of playground basketball against the Quips. BJ finished with a game high 17 points and 8 rebounds. He would later be speaking with two football coaches from Aliquippa. They had told Coach Demona that he was the most improved Athlete in the past year. The coaches mentioned his movement on the court and the failed attempted slam dunk on the fast break. It left some folks laughing but scouts could see BJ coming.

BJ's parents sat next to a couple parents from the team.

Mr. Cooper, one of the parents of the Tiger's football team tapped Pastor Timmons on the shoulder and said "That kid has changed so much in one year. I watched him pitch in baseball, make catches in football and now he trying to dunk. He's only a junior, wow!"

BJ left the junior varsity game early to get dressed for varsity. Later, he thanked Mr. Cooper for those kind words.

In the varsity game, Beaver Falls started out strong and finished strong. The standout player of this game was Tyrell Goosby. He would produce rebounds, put backs, foul shots and two fast break thunderous dunks. Carlos Clemons also had a thunderous dunk on an Aliquippa player which made the crowd go went crazy. Tremon and Calvin were too much on the perimeter. BJ was waiting for his opportunity in the varsity game. 0.7 seconds would be all he played before the 1st half ended. Humbling moment for a guy who was just told he was the most improved athlete. In the moment of frustration BJ thought about two individuals.

Rory and Regis: Rory because BJ watched him go through his own humbling taste test. Rory had been better than what he could show the Beaver Falls fans. Regis who had been a captain of the 2003 players had also been taken in and out of the basketball game for the past three years. Everyone had a test to take. It's tough when your ego is up in one instance and down in the next.

"I'm going down there and telling Damona how I feel." Mrs. Timmons said that night before BJ went to bed.

"I bust my tail at practice man." BJ said to his parents."

"He's trying to break you BJ." Mrs. Timmons would say to her son. "You stay strong. You just stand."

BJ was very embarrassed. He was also confused and ready to quit. Who else went through something like this?

Rory "Bibby" Santiago. He had to go through these growing pains to become a man. BJ would swallow the humble pie, but he would gain more stripes along the way.

The remainder of the season BJ would wreak havoc at practice. Hollering on rebounds, dribbling when he wasn't supposed to and shooting when he wasn't supposed to. Tye Goosby would call him "Rasheed Wallace" (Power Forward for Portland Trailblazers) because his fiery spirit on the court. In all reality, BJ was more of tweener. He wasn't 6 ft 5 or taller so he wasn't a big man. He also wasn't a shifty guard like his friends Tre, Calvin, and Fife. He was a 6ft 2-inch wrecking ball. A football player who happened to enjoy basketball. He grew up watching his father play so much and then to top it off his father always had the NBA on TV.

Sometimes BJ wished he were lean and fast like his father. They were two different athletes. Pastor Timmons played corner back for South Catholic and shooting guard in basketball. He also played baseball growing up. BJ wanted to be like his father, but he had to be what God made him. He did have his father's personality: when he felt he was being done wrong, he had a way of letting you know it indirectly. BJ would argue with the J.V. head coach so much that they wanted to throw him off the team.

BJ saw Brandon McDowell and Regis both get looked over daily because they were good humble young men. BJ was also but he wanted you to know that he knew that you didn't like him. No matter if you were quiet and a good teammate like Regis or confrontational like BJ, you would still get dogged, in BJ's mind. So, he felt he had to add some spice in practice. His teammates laughed at BJ's antics on the court, but they understood where he was coming from.

Coach Jamison, an assistant coach for BF, would tell BJ, "I see you and I'm going to tell Coach Demona he should be playing you more."

Coach Jamison had played Division One basketball for Tennessee Chattanooga and had come from a basketball family. He knew talent and he valued young men who had heart. BJ knew he wasn't going to go but so far in hoops, but he also knew he could add some flavor to the team.

As the basketball team kept rolling closer to the playoffs, Tye got more questions about school.

"Tye, I got Pitt on the phone." Coach Hilton said. "Did you take the Scholastic Assessment Test (S.A.T.)?"

Tye would shy away from the question.

"We need you to take this test, Tye so we can get you into a good school."

Tye would hear a lot of noise surrounding his colleges choices. He would work out with BJ at the YMCA and try not to answer everyone's questions. He wanted to focus on hoops and lifting for football. Tye knew he could go anywhere, but he wanted to go to the University of Pittsburgh to stay close to home.

While Tye was busy being occupied by college scouts and filling out college applications, Calvin "Hollywood" Jackson was now on the minds of some local college coaches.

"What's his attitude like?" Coaches would ask the guidance counselors. "How does he like to be coached?" "What's his grades like?"

These were all the questions the colleges would ask consistently after watching Calvin put on a show on the basketball court. Calvin would use the court to block out the problems in his personal life. Calvin was on his way to being a father. He was still working on his temper and feeling the pressures of being a son without a mother. Calvin loved his mother, but he needed her now more than ever. Junior year is supposed to be your most important year. Getting ready for senior projects, proms and making college decisions. Calvin shouldn't have been worried about if his mother would come home or not. Now being a father was his doing. Who was telling him about responsibility? Were Beaver Falls administrators more worried about basketball games or Calvin getting the proper education to be a father?

The playoffs had begun, and the Tigers were on their way to playing in the championship game. The Tigers would play Sto-Rox. Sto-Rox was a suburb of McKees Rocks, PA which is right outside of Pittsburgh PA. It had a rich tradition in winning championships. They too, felt like it was their year. The Tigers played lights out for three quarters but fell short of the Gold. Calvin and Tyrell played very well. Allen Fife added stellar play off the bench., however, this game slipped through the Tigers hands.

After shaking the Vikings hands BJ found himself arguing with a BF manager.

"Pick up that medal." The Manager said.

"Why? I ain't play." BJ said getting on the bus.

"You got no class Timmons." The angry Manger said grabbing BJ's arm.

"You better get off me man!" BJ said to the manager, yanking his arm away.

On the way home the coaches had a discussion on kicking BJ off the team once again. BJ wasn't upset that he didn't play; it was the substitution rotation. BJ felt he was better than a couple seniors who he believed played because of merit-- not Clemons or Goosby, but some other seniors.

BJ had listened to coach Jamison before the game. "Your time is going to come, be patient." Coach said.

The season ended disastrously against Mercyhurst Prep. In high school basketball there is a division playoff and a state playoff tournament. The Tigers played a team with less talent and no reputation. They were outrebounded and outsmarted. Embarrassed and discouraged Calvin lost his cool.

"They suck period." Calvin said about the Mercyhurst players. "No way we should have lost to these bum ass white dudes."

"Calvin, watch your mouth." Coach admonished him.

"Nah, they waited until the fourth quarter to start playing with some emotion!" Calvin said about this in the visiting locker room.

BJ and Regis would sit at the end of the bench in disbelief. Coach did not play neither boy this game. A teaching lesson or a panic button? No one was inside the coach's heads. It just seemed like everyone wanted the season to end. In four months, the Tigers had lost 3 championships: one in football and two basketball championships.

"Next year, this shit is ours, Tre." Calvin said. "We lost to these.... bums."

These boys from the 2002 -2003 classes had played together their whole lives together. This would be Tyrell and Carlos's game playing together. No one said a word on the bus home. The bus driver let the slow jams play the whole way home. and sadness was the vibe. Tye knew he had another chance to bring home state gold in track. He was a high jumping machine. Time was running out for this fantastic Tiger's career.

March Madness or March Sadness?

After the 2001-2002 basketball season ended a good bit of the Tigers ran track but the majority needed that time to rehab and heal from nagging injuries. Tye, BJ, Macklin and Calvin would go right into training for track. Macklin and Tye would both stand out above the rest. BJ's friend Tyler Marx would also stand out in the triple jump.

"Tye what's the deal with school man?" BJ asked one day after track practice.

"Still waiting to hear my scores from the S.A.T.'s." Tye said. "I asked Holton everyday if he heard anything."

Tye would do the same regime daily. Track practice, YMCA for weights and then restless nights of thinking. Tye knew he had a lot of people in his corner. Tyrell the "Goose" Goosby had been the man for so long and been a leader for many men.

As Tye, Tyler and the boys tried to make the best out of track season. BJ had to get ready for the college recruiting season.

"Running track looks good on a college application, BJ." Pastor would tell his tired son when he came in from practice.

"I ain't got no chance of winning no races, but I'll try." BJ said.

BJ's father was right. Colleges love to see all the activities and sports you participated in while you attended school. BJ sang in honor's chorus, was in Spanish 4, played football, basketball, and baseball. For three years he had been going non-stop. Now track? He wanted to take a break. The only break was the Black College Tour coming up. He would miss one whole week of school and track practices. When he came back, he would also have to get ready for prom... if he wanted to go, that is.

BJ and Cassie also had to prepare mentally for being away from each other that long.

"Tell your mother I said thanks for buying those pizzas." BJ said. He had to sell pizzas and sandwiches to raise money for the black college tour.

"You ready?" She asked BJ as he scarfed some chicken nuggets down that she made.

"Yeah I am." He said wiping the crumbs off his face.

Cassie settled in to reading her book, which was part of the *Babysitter's Club* series by Ann M. Martin.

She would continue, "There's going to be a lot of girls there... college girls, too. They won't even know how old you are. I trust you though."

BJ smiled.

Cassie finished, "I support you in everything you do."

He nodded his head "Mm hmm."

She looked a little harder at BJ.

"Will you be able to call?" She asked.

"I will…. I'm mean I better." BJ said.

As soon as BJ got home, he asked his dad if he could use his cellular phone. His dad said he would think about it.

"I might give you a calling card." His father said. Calling cards were cheaper than using a hotel phone.

The closer the tour came the more BJ would press about making a junior. year highlight tape and statistics sheet. The Stat sheet had all his accolades and his stats from the year. BJ "BJ" Timmons, Tremon Barksdale, Dougie Benson, Tyrell Goosby all made all conference that year. Tre Barksdale, big Rob Tomlin and Goosby made all state. Because of the team success BJ would be able to spring up on the recruiter's list. BJ made 10 stat sheets and some tapes to send out to the colleges on the tour.

BJ and Tre both signed up for different camps to show case their talent. They would discuss it later that day in Communications class.

"I'm going to Virginia this summer and Maryland for camp." Tre said.

"Pitt for me this summer." BJ said.

He then turned to Rory.

"Hey, Rory what's up with you man? What's your plans when school lets out in a couple weeks?"

AB, Tre, and BJ all wanted to hear their friend's future aspirations.

"I honestly don't know no more man." Rory said. "Right now, we just need to complete this project."

Rory's friends could hear the uncertainty in his voice.

"It's late March and I ain't getting no shine. Some little schools and some technical colleges." He said shaking his head.

"At least you're getting looked at by someone." AB said setting up the camera equipment.

AB, Tre, BJ and Rory were doing a public service announcement commercial for their communications class.

"Let's do a football commercial." Tre said.

"Too easy boys, I need you all to challenge yourselves." Ms. Marion the communications teacher said. "How about a drug free commercial for kids?"

As soon as she said it, Ascheley Brown a.k.a. AB a.k.a. "A-beezy" ran with the master plan.

"I'll be the coke dealer; you and Tre be the cops." AB said. "Bibby, we need your beamer to be used as the ride."

Laughing, Rory put his hands over his mouth. "I'll be using my own whip (car)!" He said.

The four did a low budget after school commercial about drugs in the projects. One day of filming, Tre left the camera recording on the tripod. Another student that the boys were acquainted with stop by to add his own two cents in.

"Is that camera still on?" He asked AB.

"Yeah man, why?"

The young man investigated the camera and had a message for Bibby Santiago.

"Rory Santiago! Aye Rory, eff you man! You're a sucker and when I see you, I'm kicking you're a**!"

Little did they know, Mr. Santiago was pulling up to hear the end of monologue.

"What the hell he say?" Bibby said rolling his car windows down.

The young man turned and fled south into the projects. BJ and AB could not stop laughing.

"Tomorrow I can't wait to see that fool." Rory said.

BJ and his friends all enjoyed challenges in school. Sometimes they just enjoyed the thrill of a teacher saying they couldn't do something. For instance, both Rory and BJ took college prep English 11. This was the hardest class taught by arguably the strictest teacher in the school. Regis shockingly also enjoyed the mental challenges from Ms. Salem daily. The three of them would sometimes brainstorm before class started on how they would get around a certain activity or exercise.

Rory had a lot of pride but didn't mind asking Regis for advice. BJ also would ask to see Regis's notes or note cards for book reports. Regis was the go-to guy when it came to the college prep classes. BJ took other classes like Culinary Arts with DeWarren Ford. DeWarren or, "Pong," as the boys called him loved to cook. He also was another go-to guy for basic food questions. Little Nate and Darren "Shakes" were artists. Paul Joseph was a mathematician. Paul came into the circle of Tigers BJ's freshman year. He was a Catholic school kid. He grew up partially with Nate and Allan. He was discipline one minute and totally insane the next. Not unstable, just a typical teenager. He added more mental ammunition to this army of young men. Tyler Marx enjoyed working on cars and doing things with his hands. BJ knew he could go to any of these young men for assistance. Thank God the 2003 class was full of gifted men in a variety of subjects. It just so happens that they enjoyed competing in sports too.

Everyone knows junior year is the year that you grind out all the hard classes and start to fill out college applications. In the spring, future college students take the A.C.T. (American College Testing) and S.A.T.'s (Scholastic Aptitude Test).

"You sign up for the test yet, Bibby?" BJ asked Rory in study hall.

"Nah I got to find a tutor first." Rory said. "I heard that computer teacher will tutor us for fifty bucks."

"That ain't bad man." BJ said.

Both Rory and BJ would sign up for tutoring that next week.

How did these guys find all this time to do so many things? The more you stay busy, the easier it is to dismiss foolishness from entering your life. Because Rory worked full time between the two jobs, he used some of the money he made to pay for tutoring.

Rory was feeling pessimistic about his chances at getting a scholarship, but he knew he couldn't give up. In his mind, if he would have blown off the S.A.T.'s, he was giving into the naysayers. Rory didn't want to be a statistic. He had come up in the crack epidemic. He saw junkies, pimps, and dealers his whole life. *It's easy to be those guys,* he thought. The challenge is going through the gauntlet of cynical people.

"You got to let me know about that tour too bro when you come back." Rory said.

"I need a decent score on the S.A.T.'s to get into the majority of the schools on the tour." BJ said. "I'll fill y'all in though." BJ, Calvin and Tre would all take the S.A.T.'s the Saturday before he had to leave for the black college tour.

Towards the end of March into early April, BJ would finish up selling all the fundraising and he was set to go on the tour. BJ would see Cassie a few hours after church and then he had to leave to head to the meeting place. BJ's father looked around at all the other parents and chaperones.

"I don't care what them other kids do. You be on your best behavior." He said. "You represent this family."

BJ looking at all the teens board the bus nodded his head.

"Yes sir." He assured his father.

The Omega Psi Phi tour began with a trip to King's Island in Ohio. However, this would be no warm spring fun; even though it was early April, it felt like December. The chaperones insisted that the teens get to know each other and wanted them to have fun before the tour officially began. BJ "BJ" Timmons noticed all the letterman jackets on the bus: Woodland Hills, Penn Hills, Schenley, Gateway, Perry, Westinghouse, Peabody, and other schools. He realized he was the only person from his county on the tour.

"Where's Beaver Falls?" A few girls asked BJ as he walked around with a stuffed bear, he won shooting hoops.

"About 40 minutes west from Pittsburgh." He said.

"Oh yeah, y'all was on tv the other day," one girl said.

"Y'all lost to Sto-Rox in basketball," Another girl said.

Most of the teens came in small groups. A few Woodland Hills football players would introduce themselves to BJ when they left the park.

"Hey man, a few of us going to smoke tonight." One of the guys said to him.

"I don't smoke, man." BJ said.

The chaperones made it noticeably clear that if anyone was caught smoking or breaking curfew this was an automatic termination being a participant on the tour.

"What, you a square or something man?" The young man asked.

He started laughing when BJ kept pushing his hand away.

"Ok man, I can see you going to be on your own."

The young man had a couple other guys with him. One of them had even whispered the word *lame* in BJ's direction. Even though BJ was from Pittsburgh, he felt like an alien. He recognized one girl from elementary school, but she also was with a different crowd now. BJ Timmons was no stranger to weed. He sat thinking over the encounter with the guys from the other schools. He thought even if he did smoke why would he smoke with some boys he doesn't know? Also, if they got caught the first person they would blame, would be him.

These cats ain't going to make it, He thought to himself as he checked in to his hotel.

BJ ended up bunking with two guys that were also "weed heads" and they were wrestlers.

BJ made it abundantly clear, "I ain't going down for nobody!"

He demanded their respect, and they chose to smoke outside.

BJ would make a phone call home and a phone call to Cassie.

"I hope I don't have to kill nobody up in here." He said to her on the phone.

Taking a deep breath full of thought she said- "BJ just try to relax and get ready for tomorrow. Where y'all going first?"

"Tennessee State, Jackson State, then off to Atlanta." He said with a tired undertone. He was fully exhausted from helping carry young women's luggage and also his.

The first day BJ noticed a few girls who had taken a likening to him. He would try his best to sit by himself at restaurants and diners. -- not because he was anti-social. He knew that he wanted to stay focus on what the schools were offering. He would go site seeing, and...some of the girls would miraculously end up also site seeing. Then one night, one girl had to see if the discipline was real.

Madeline Robinson was a cheerleader and 4.0 student who also happened to be dating a Michigan University football player. She sat next to BJ at the Jackson State visit, the Tennessee State visit, and tried to sit next to him on the bus to Atlanta. The few boys who were smoking the first night ended up getting sent home and because of that there was more room on the bus now.

Madeline made her way to the back of the bus to sit next to BJ.

"So, let me ask you something."

BJ opened his arms up like he wanted her to spill her thoughts in his lap.

"Do you have a girl?"

BJ nodded his head and looked up at Madeline with conviction.

"Oh...ok that's cool, I got a man so we're even." She hesitantly said.

The two talked about their relationships from Tennessee to Georgia. BJ had nothing but sweet things to say about his woman. Madeline not so much. BJ knew that when a woman starts to trash her boyfriend, she normally is working getting her next boyfriend. She complained about him never being there and how football was like a fulltime job in college.

BJ practicing active listening and started to think about Cassie feeling that way one day in the future. After about two hours of looking at this 17-year-old girl trash her boyfriend, she asked BJ if he would be joining the group to watch a movie that night.

When BJ checked in his room, he would call Cassie.

"When I go to college, I hope you're patient," he told her. "Some nights I'll be practicing three times a day. I don't even know when I'll have time to call you."

He would go on and on about how hard it is to be in a long-distance relationship.

"But we're going to make it." Cassie said.

BJ knew that Madeline's negative view on college boyfriends would be the cause of his passive aggressive approach towards his own girlfriend.

"BJ you tired?" She asked him as he took longer and longer to get his sentences together.

BJ was deep in thought.

"I might be baby." He said with a nervous look. He knew at any moment someone could bang on the door or shout something that would trigger Cassie's emotional state of mind.

BJ was interrupted by the two clowns that were his temporary roommates. BJ was invited to a party in the rec room.

"Nah man I'm going to chill." He would tell the two young

men. BJ was able to get rid of them by constantly saying no and singing listening to music wearing headphones.

Eventually BJ would fall asleep, he would be awakened by hard pounding at his hotel door. BJ's intoxicated roommates ignored his orders about bringing up unannounced strangers to his door, but the roommates had a special guest: Madeline.

"Mind if I come in?" She asked curiously.

BJ knew if he let this girl in the room many rumors could be started. He also knew if he allowed Madeline in, it could spark a possible misunderstanding.

"What's up? Come... Come in." BJ stuttered knowing he was uncomfortable.

Madeline who was already dressed in her night attire sat at the edge of the bed. There was a sequence of sexual poses and then the questioning.

"Why won't you look at me? Am I ugly? How long have you and your girl been dating? What grade is she in?" She would ask all these questions in the matter of seconds.

BJ would make sure he didn't sugar coat his plans for Cassie Washington. BJ was adherent to the idea of monogamy. Spiritually, he knew he wouldn't be right. He would also be adding on one more distraction while trying to train for college ball.

"Look, you know I been scoping you since day one of the tour." Madeline said. "Let's cut the bull. You been looking at me too."

"I ain't never say I wasn't." BJ interrupted. "You ain't ugly at all."

"Then what is it?" Madeline asked angrily. "What? Your girl going to find out?" She continued to press up on BJ. Kissing his hand and rubbing his shoulders. "I ain't no hoe either."

BJ started laughing and gently replacing her hand on her own lap.

"Who said you was? Better yet, who's to say if something went down tonight you wouldn't tell everyone that I raped you?"

Madeline starting to become hostile. "Hold up, you think I'm leaving my man for you?" She said with a denying tone. "No disrespect, he would kill you. Then my dad would resurrect you and kill you again."

BJ stood up and made the two thumbs up gesture with his hands. "Then we have an understanding. Babe, have a good night."

As she fixed her lip gloss, she started to cry. "You think it's easy for me?" She asked.

"What, getting a fixing while your 200- pound wide receiver boyfriend is away in Michigan?" He said with conviction. "Yeah, I do. You been giving me crazy rhythm and now you want to put me down because I don't want to jump your bones?"

Madeline became ticked off! "Stop it! Don't judge me! You don't know me!"

She went into her day-to-day routine. How she was a girlfriend who everybody looked at as a gold digger or a trophy wife. She was unhappy with her life and wanted to create her own path.

He eventually asked. "Why you on the tour then?"

Wiping the tears from rolling down her face.

"Because my parents want me to." She said with a face full of tears by this time.

She would later state that she admired BJ for not just diving on her and quenching her thirst. He talked to her about her worth and what it means to be valued. Sure, she was gorgeous and on paper, she had a lot going for her. Madeline just wanted to be loved in the right way using the wrong tactics. She wanted to sleep with BJ, he wanted her to feel valued. In another world or another time, he would gladly grant her wish. He sensed something was off. Madeline Robinson's father did a disservice with showing her how to be a princess. She had a big-time football player as a boyfriend. She was daddy's little girl who spoke had the right etiquette yet, she was lacking in self-awareness.

As the tour went on, Madeline would try to make a few more attempts to get BJ to change his mind on being with just one girl. BJ remained focused and would end up passing his tapes to several coaches. Virginia State, Norfolk State and Hampton all told him they liked what they saw. BJ even took a private tour with some of the coaching staff at North Carolina A & T. He almost blew his chances with John C Smith when he and some other students got into a fight with college students. He broke curfew a few times looking for snacks at night. Overall, BJ felt like he could compete both academically and athletically. He also knew Cassie was ranking higher on the priority list.

When the tour was over, there were a lot of hugs from the girls and some numbers were passed out, But BJ just wanted to get back to his girl.

His father picked him up, "How was the tour man?" Pastor Timmons asked.

BJ would fill in his father bit by bit. He could tell his father anything.

"Your mother is going to be glad to see you."

"I missed mom too." BJ said. "I'm starving, did mom make some parmesan chicken?"

His father began laughing hysterically. "Is that all that's on your mind?"

"Actually, nah." BJ said with a smile on his face. "After I eat, can I use the van to go see killa Cassie?"

Pastor Timmons nodded his head. "Yeah man, don't crash my ride. Before I forget, you need to take your driver's test next Saturday."

"Yes sir." BJ said.

Most people would think, why would he let him do that? He trusted his son to drive six minutes up the road. Was it a risk? Yes, but Pastor Timmons felt he had to give his son a rope to either hang himself or help himself. A true test of manhood. This driver's license was for BJ to appreciate having a license and having two great parents who trusted him. If he were to take the van and run around crazy, he would blow future opportunities to take the van further. He would also lose his privileges to go to places like Kennywood Park and other events that teenagers like to participate in.

BJ would make it to Cassie's in a flash following his dinner discussion with Sabrina and BJ Timmons, Sr.

"I missed you so much." Cassie said. "I even wrote you every day."

BJ started laughing. "Babe you didn't have to do that."

"But I wanted to." She said as she walked towards her dresser. "Here you go."

She passed him the letters. She brought him some snacks she made. BJ was so tired he passed out on her lap before she was able to give it to him. Cassie would stare at him as he slobbered on her lap and listened to the NBA game in the background. She would wake him up at 11. He had been sleeping for over two hours.

When he finally awoke, he asked her, "What you been doing this whole time?"

"Just being thankful." Cassie said smiling as she sat a plate of snacks down on the table. "Thankful for you."

BJ smiled because he knew he was faithful. He had dodged a couple bullets. He avoided speaking on his gratefulness and decided to change subjects to avoid anxiety between the two. "This week I got to get with Regis and Rory and see how much work I got to make up in college prep English."

When BJ went to the school the next day, Regis would inform his friend about all the make-up work.

"Man don't trip I got you if you need help." He said after class.

BJ felt overwhelmed with all the work and telling his boys about the tour.

"Timmons you lying!" Tremon Barksdale said when BJ was giving him the juicy gossip about the tour.

"Nah man, swear." BJ said.

"My girl supposed to be going on a similar tour in two weeks!" Tre said.

Coach Holton interrupted BJ, Tremon and Rory's conversation.

"Timmons, see me in my office after lunch." Coach Holton said.

BJ and Tre would go to the coach's office following lunch. Purdue University (IN) was in Coach Holton's office.

"Coach Bennett is here, and he wants to talk to you." Coach Holton said.

BJ shook Coach Bennett's hand.

"Son do you think you can play at Purdue University?" Coach Bennett asked.

BJ coughed and stood up straight. "Yes sir, I do."

Coach Bennett would measure BJ's arms, shoulders, and his height. Following the meeting with the two coaches BJ couldn't help himself.

"Thanks, Coach Holton." BJ said.

"Son, you earned it." Coach Holton said with his hand on BJ's shoulder. "I know you're going to Pitt this summer and Dayton has been calling and calling."

BJ cracked a smile.

"Now don't get big headed. There will be other school's baby." Coach Holton had that 1980's cop slang with the "baby talk".

"Wisconsin has been sending me a lot of mail." BJ said with a confident mug on his face. "Coach, I want Michigan."

Coach Holton started laughing. "You got a lot of work baby. You got to get faster and stronger. I want you and Macklin to go see a guy in New Brighton. He's a weightlifter and trainer Here is his address."

Tremon was in the hallway meeting with another school.

"My dawg!" Tre said walking up to BJ. "BJ Timmons, number four…"

"Tre!" BJ hollered. "Don't say nothing man, you the only person that know right now."

BJ didn't want anyone knowing outside of his parents and Cassie. The reason was because the same coach who just brought him Purdue, also belittled him a few months back. BJ hadn't forgotten that and neither did his father. He didn't want the upperclassmen knowing because some of them had not chosen a school yet. Rob Tomlin was on his way to Indiana of Pennsylvania. The star running back chose Howard

University. Some other guys chose small Christian schools and Ivy league schools. Coach Holton threw Cincinnati out his office for saying they had no more scholarships. Cincinnati University was looking at Spencer Wallace, who was a senior, and Douglas Benson, a junior. He cursed those assistant coaches out from Cincinnati so bad, they probably scratched Beaver Falls off their recruiting list. Cincinnati gave a young man from Rochester their last scholarship and Coach Holton ripped them a new one for passing on Wallace.

Now what about Tyrell Goosby? He was still struggling with coming to the realization of not being college ready. Who was telling him which way to go? Tyrell was an 18-year-old young man who needed to be the assurance of his family and friend. Tye started to put extra pressure on himself. He was pressing so much that it was affecting his track performances.

"Tye what's with you man?" One of the track coaches said.

"I don't know." Tye said.

He knew that he had a couple months to choose a school. Junior college or four year? What about S.A.T.'s? Tye had a million questions running through his head. The magical question was *"will they remember me?"* Everyone always asked, *"Will you remember me when you make it?"* No one ever asked. *"Will you remember me if I don't?"*

Pressure from All Directions (Spring 2002)

It was the spring of 2002, and the schools were all getting ready for Prom. Beaver Falls had no shortage of single girls who needed a date. BJ Timmons had no plans of going to the Junior Prom. He aspired of taking Cassie the next year before he left for college. He had it planned out. Take Cassie to Christmas formal and Prom.... marry her in 2008. It was all mapped out. At that time, Cassie could not go to the prom. She was too young. It didn't bother him; he knew everyone knew the deal. Everyone except Alexis Wingate. Alexis had notice BJ at a few basketball games and gatherings. She had a cousin who went to BFHS. Her name was Dana.

Dana approached BJ one day in the hall in between classes.

"Hey BJ, do you have a date to the prom?" She asked.

"Right now, I don't think I'm going." He said.

"Aww come on, you gotta be kidding." She said with her

arms open like she was selling illegal toothbrushes in a trench coat.

BJ thought she was asking for herself.

"Do you know my cousin Alexis?" She asked.

BJ nodded his head. "From Beaver, right?"

She smiled, "Yes, her."

BJ told her he would get back to her. He had to think about it.

Calvin would come up the stairs with "Shakes" behind him.

"Yo, she is *bad*!" Calvin said. "You better get on that."

Calvin knew the deal. He wasn't disrespecting Cassie. He wanted his friend to live a little and not miss out on the fun.

"I'm going with this Candy babe from Aliquippa."

BJ looked at Calvin with a cautious look. "How you hook that up?" he asked.

"Come on bra, I told you! I don't discriminate." He said cunningly. "I date them all."

"Black, white, Asian." BJ said, "His sister, her sister, her mom!"

Everyone started laughing.

"Well, I'll just tell Lexi (Alexis) that you said you'll think about it." Dana said going to her class.

"Man, I don't know how Cassie going to take this cuz." BJ said to Shakes.

Shakes gave BJ a smile and said, "Good luck, man."

That night was one for the ages...and not in a good way.

"How did she even know you?" Cassie said with anger in her voice.

"Let me explain--" BJ said.

"Nah, check this out." She said cutting BJ off. "I don't like that. She knows what she's doing. She could have asked anyone, why you?"

BJ thought to himself: *why not*?

BJ and Cassie would go back and forth like a married couple, or a great one-two punch on a team like Shaq and Kobe. They needed their space in Cassie's basement like two NBA players, too. She would then hit him with the million-dollar question:

"And what did you say?"

BJ knew he had been matched.

He paused and said, "I told her I would get back to her." Cassie, for the first time in their relationship, started to yell.

"Let me see that girl at the Elks! I'm going to slap that b**tch!"

BJ had to calm down his other half. He knew he should have just alleviated his woman from this pain. She had to put up with the dumb stuff before they got together. She had been silent for Jamaica's request to be BJ's date at the Christmas dance. She also had no idea about Madeline and the crazy dames on the college tour. Now she had to be this meek, calm, withdrawn mute. She had had enough. In time BJ would realize the drama she had to put up with. Not to mention his ex-Denise had it in her head that she would someday get him back. How much can a girl take? Being 14, she had her own insecurities. Daily, she had boys coming after her and older ones pursuing her. She worked on the weekends and had her own life to worry about. In a way, BJ was being selfish.

Ms. Lisa, Cassie's mother, had a way of checking BJ. She would typically get BJ's attention with empathetic examples: *"How would you feel if you were Cassandra??"* Depending on the subject.

She would say "Her time will come when you have to trust her."

"I see your point" he would say after going back and forth.

He was unaware that he would be leaving for college next year. Caught up in the moment. He would foolishly think in the moment when the two were arguing. If BJ and Cassie were Kobe Bryant and Shaquille O'Neal, then she was Phil Jackson. She made the mood calmer. She allowed the two to get their frustrations out and then she offered solutions. Because BJ was the male and older, she put more responsibility on him. Ms. Lisa knew the man that BJ patterned his life after and what his expectations for his son were.

BJ's parents were big on solutions.

"All that arguing ain't necessary," Mrs. Sabrina Timmons would say.

The mothers of both Cassie and BJ were vastly different

in their parenting but also similar in some ways. They both wanted their children to be safe and make the right decisions without sacrificing their own happiness. They both depended on the strength of the Lord to guide their children. When you allow your daughter to start dating an older boy and vice versa that's the only solution: *Train up a child in the way he should go and when he is old, he will not depart from it.* Holy Bible, Proverbs 22:6

"Don't she have a man?" Cassie asked BJ before he left her home.

"I honestly don't know, babe." He said back to her. "I really don't care, it's just a picture."

He realized he had to place himself in Cassie's shoes. Shortly after he got home, he called her. Cassie already prepared to make her apology. She was going to swallow her pride once again and say sorry. She stated that she had put herself in his shoes and wanted him to live out his final years in Beaver Falls with his friends. Once again, Cassie made a power move. She would do her research on this Alexis person. If she was going to be silent and watch her man go out with another girl. She wanted to make sure this girl understood her role. What was BJ's way of showing his appreciation for Cassie's patience? He would continue to make her proud by staying committed and spending more time with her to ensure her needs were met.

While BJ and the gang were getting ready for their Junior/Senior prom, DeJon was getting the 411 on Alexis's boyfriend or ex-boyfriend Tyler Wilkerson. Tyler was a running back for the Aliquippa Quips. He had started dating Alexis after she broke up with Andy Horn from Rochester. Andy was a well-known athlete in the area also. He had gained some notoriety for getting a scholarship offer to the University of Cincinnati. DeJon overheard the boys from Aliquippa talking about Tyler's relationship with Alexis.

"BJ, some of them is still hot over you punching Tyler on the sideline." DeJon said.

BJ and Tyler got tangled up on a punt return play. BJ punched Tyler in his helmet. Tyler got caught retaliating and was thrown out of the game immediately.

"That's her dude, yo?" BJ asked DeJon.

"I believe so man." DeJon said. "Just watch yourself."

"She asked me man, I ain't ask her." BJ replied shaking his head.

Later that evening both DeJon and Alexis confirmed her new relationship on AOL instant messenger. Cassie also found out she was dating someone through a Beaver Falls cheerleader she was close with.

"That's Kylee's cousin, she said the same thing I said. Why she ask you? Knowing she got a boyfriend?"

BJ became frustrated. "Look man, I don't know."

Cassie started to grill him a little harder.

"Do you even know who her boyfriend is BJ?"

BJ shrugged his shoulders "I don't know, I don't care!"

Even though he knew, he still didn't care. Cassie would warn BJ again about this Alexis Wingate.

The day had come finally: The 2002 Beaver Falls Prom. Calvin and Candy. Tremon and Tracey. Shakes and Leah. Nate, Allen Fife... Everyone looked great. BJ had to meet up with Alexis's family before heading to the middle school for pictures. He had a nice talk with Alexis's parents and when he and Alexis finished taking pictures in her living room, the limousine pulled up.,

BJ and Alexis talked very little in the limo.

"You look nice." BJ said to Alexis.

"I know." She said back to him.

*Ok, BJ I know how this is going to go.*BJ said to himself. He was already tapped out. He wanted to take the pics at the school and get it over with.

When the two arrived at the school, BJ looked for Cassie immediately. The middle school is where couples gather for the Grand March. Tickets are passed out and all the families pack the school to see their children with their dates.

Alexis had some strict rules.

"When we get up there on the stage don't act like an idiot."

BJ looked over at her with a devilish look. "What you mean by that?"

"You know all ghetto and stuff." She said with her hand covering her mouth.

BJ couldn't wait to get up there.

The announcer's voice blared over the mic, "Coming to the

stage BJ Timmons and Alexis Wingate."

BJ made sure he would do everything possible to make this girl uncomfortable. He stood up and did the Heisman Trophy pose.

She immediately said under her breath. "You a** hole."

He fired back at her. "This is my school." In his mind he was thinking *"you asked me!"*

After they came down the steps off the stage everyone could feel the tension between the two. She may have thought BJ's nerves were due to the atmosphere, but he was trying to spot Cassie in the audience. After everyone was announced and the Grand March ended, BJ made his move through all the parents and family members.

"You look nice!"

"BJ, smile!"

"Tre and BJ look here."

"Regis turn here, look here!"

"Tyrell... Tye... smile."

All the young men had to display respect even though they were ready to go to party. BJ finally found Cassie and they took some pictures together. Some folks needed another reminder who his actual girlfriend was... even Alexis. She was also taking a lot of pictures, but she and BJ didn't really want to take any pictures together. Her immature behavior would eventually leave her alone.

As BJ and Cassie finished up discussing their after-prom plans, he heard a yell.

"BJ, the bus is leaving!"

It was Alexis.

"BJ Timmons!"

Cassie even thought it was funny. "You better hurry… your girl is ready!"

As the busses pulled off to go to the Marriott for the dance and dinner, Alexis was livid.

"Why would you do that BJ?" She said rolling her eyes.

BJ began to chuckle.

"I mean where is your discipline?"

He started to laugh harder.

"And who was that girl?" She asked.

"My girl Cassie." BJ answered.

Alexis was starting to present herself as a curious girl. BJ tried to ignore the sincerity in each question. She even had the nerve to become irritated. Her communication skills weren't the strongest to say the least. She was vain and had little to no interest in BJ's relationship. She was just being plain old nosey!

At the dance BJ would sit mostly with Calvin, Tremon, and Tracey who was Tre's girlfriend.

"You don't mind me asking Alexis to dance, do you?" Calvin

asked BJ when he was in the buffet line.

"Shoot your shot man." BJ said.

Calvin and Alexis would go and groove for a while. When Calvin came back there was a pause in his report.

"Yo... something is living foul over there." He said drinking the punch at the table. "I think her arm pits need some freshening up."

BJ made sure he wouldn't make it obvious they were talking about her. He watched Alexis's dance with other guys, everything looked fine. He knew how Calvin liked to joke. He also knew how serious Calvin was with his pursuit for females.

The rest of the night BJ made sure to stay clear from Alexis. Eventually everyone would go back to the school and then to Eat-n-Park for breakfast. Following the prom there was no rap between Alexis and BJ. Alexis was with Rob Tomlin and his date Dana, who happened to be Alexis's cousin. Rob would drop off BJ at Cassie's house.

"Thanks for the ride, big homie." BJ said.

"No doubt man, you going to Kennywood tomorrow?" Rob asked.

"I don't know man I'm tired as hell." BJ responded as he tapped on Cassie's glass door to her bedroom/basement.

Kennywood is an amusement park in West Mifflin, PA. All the area schools go there the next day following their proms or formals in the spring. Alexis noticed how antsy BJ was at Eat-n-Park and she may have developed a complex because BJ never even turned to look at her. She was a beautiful girl who typically got hit on daily. She made sure she showed that she was unimpressed by his neglect during the night.

"BYE BJ!" She yelled as Big Rob, Dana and she pulled off.

"That girl is off BJ." Cassie said opening the bedroom slide door. "I'm telling you she's up to no good. I overheard some grown folks talking about her and some "Andy" boy from Rochester."

BJ fully dressed and all plopped on Cassie's couch, shaking his head. "Babe I'm tired." He said.

Cassie continued, "She still talks to him and that Tyler Wilkerson from Quip! She going to round up some shit!"

"Babe I don't give a..." BJ cut her off.

"But she does." Cassie went back at BJ.

The two would argue 20 minutes before BJ fell asleep and walked home. Cassie was very appreciative for BJ coming back to her for her security. However, she couldn't let go of her gut feeling. Cassie knew it sounded fishy for her to want to go to the prom with BJ. She knew about Tyler's ejection from the regular season game against Beaver Falls due to BJ's sneak punch to his helmet. She also knew Andy Horn was headed to Cincinnati University and he was a sought after by a lot of the girls in the county. Was she right about her feelings towards Alexis?

Over the next few weeks all the guys would continue to go through their spring routines. BJ would continue to study for the S.A.T.'s. He would bomb three times. He also failed his driving test. Rory Santiago would also study for the S.A.T.'s; he would do well enough to enter the NCAA clearing house for schools to recruit him. Virginia University and Richmond University would take notice to his 6'1" frame and his grades. His patience and hard work were noticed. Finally, Rory got the match to light his fire.

Austin Macklin healed up and started to train with BJ daily after school. Tremon Barksdale and Calvin both got invitations to basketball camps and would secretly work on their basketball skills. Tyrell and Tyler Marx would make it to the State Track meet to compete. Both boys made their school proud but fell short.

Tyrell's high school star stellar career was coming to an end.

"What will it be Goosby?" Coach Holton asked.

Tye would be invited to several track invitationals, all-star basketball, and football games. He needed to take the college test and to focus on his future. He was able to goof around far too much his senior year. It was time to decide: junior college in Kansas, Valley Forge Military School, or community college in Beaver County? Truthfully, Tye should have gone away to school. He needed to experience life away from his family and friends.

The pressure he faced the last two years was overwhelming. He had been dominant since the 6th grade. His whole life he beat the odds of the community. He didn't sell drugs. He didn't do drugs. He was faithful to Tara when they were together. When he was single, he made sure he was courtly to any potential girlfriend. He never got into fights and displayed respectful behavior for his teachers and coaches. But how would he tell his supporters that he wasn't going to Pitt, Syracuse, Miami, West Virginia, or Penn State? No matter what he chose Tye was in good graces from his peers. But did he know that? He watched a couple of his classmates sign with some decent size colleges. He knew his talent, he had belief in himself when it came to athletics. Football and Track were easy targets for his success at a college or university.

What was the holdup though?

Were his socialization skills at risk?

Was he feeling apprehensive because the school system of Beaver Falls kept him socially enslaved?

Did they hold Tye accountable for communicating his college aspirations with his family?

Did the school system or coaching staffs contact Tye's mother and father?

His parents were incredibly supportive but maybe behind on the college documents to get him on the right track. Tyrell Goosby should be held responsible for not being college ready. Tye had all the right tools to become a successful collegiate athlete. He was polite, humble, and coachable. However, being a stud since grammar school made him lazy with being committed to the most important thing in his life. The man in the mirror. His unwillingness to detach from Beaver Falls emotionally caused him to not see the vision of a promising collegiate career.

Pressure can eat away at all of us, whether we are girls or boys. We all at some point or another face peer, intellectual, parental, systematic, educational, and political pressure. There are many other types depending on who you talk to. Cassie faced pressure of pushing away a young man that she had no clue how to articulate her or his feelings at times. It had to be tough to hold in frustrations and to be misunderstood due to being a young female.

Regis had the pressure of continuing his excellent streak of good grades and adding to his educational accolades. He would potentially have to narrow in on what he wanted to do following his days of being a Tiger. What about Calvin, Blaire, DeJon, and Rory? All four of these men had different challenges at home more than their peers. They were raised by mothers and strong grandmothers' part of the time. They had to be the men in the home on days they wanted to be a kid. Guys like Ascheley Brown, DeWarren and Darren Shakespeare had to come to realization of leaving behind athletics to concentrate elsewhere. No matter who you are, you will face pressure. It's how you accept it and eventually deal with it, is what's important.

Tyrell Goosby was not the first to deal with pressure on choosing a college and he wouldn't be the last. Beaver Falls was rich with talent but poor with preparing their Tigers for the wild. The "real world."

"When you need a recipe for success make sure you find a good "pressure" cooker to fix your meal. "- BJ Tench

McDonald's Beef

Towards the end of the school year most teenagers start to get the summer feeling. Classes start to lighten up with schoolwork and weekends tend to be longer. Graduation parties and planning for vacations go on in some households. Depending on your family's financial status, summer trips could be exciting. As the countdown to summer break began, invitations to parties increase in most towns for the weekend. Beaver Falls was no different. Beaver Falls had two weekend hangouts during the school year for teens: The Elks or "Mr. Franks."

Sometimes the local radio stations would come and host or the local Disc jockey (DJ) would come by and play some music. Beaver Falls D.J. was future star quarterback Dom Henson. He would come and play what the kids were into. He was also one of the water boys for the football team. All the kids knew every weekend was two things: there was a dance somewhere and Dom was going to be disc jockeying somewhere.

As the word traveled in Beaver Falls, it always found a way

to travel to the surrounding towns such as New Brighton, Center, Rochester all the way to the Pittsburgh. For some odd reason other teens would manage to make it to the dances. One town always showed up and couldn't keep their words to themselves: the "Quips". Aliquippa boys normally would come down and hang out with some of their family members or girlfriend's. Sometimes the Aliquippa young men would make their way to see both. A lot of the Tigers were related to the Quips. Even Calvin had a pap who lived there. At this time, DeJon was a student there and lived with his father. Carlos Clemons, Bullet Pitts and Goosby also had family there. Their communities were correspondence between the communities and family ties.

There was some tension between the two towns due to sports and the mouths of some young women. The "beef" was thick between the communities, and it was starting to smell. It needed to be seasoned and served!

The beef included Damon Grace getting stomped out by DeJon and Tremon, then DeJon being set up by whoever at Center Stage. It touched BJ Timmons when he was running his mouth being an antagonist at times punching Tyler Wilkerson in the helmet. And finally taking Tyler Wilkerson's now girlfriend to the prom unapologetic. Don't forget all the side conversations of all the jealous girls who the boys of B.F. didn't pay attention to. There were some scorned past lovers who wanted to see justice served. Some girls were tired of all the hype and wanted to see who was tough. To some of the girls at BFHS, they believed because Aliquippa had a rougher reputation then they could exercise their right to walk over the B.F. boys.

Outside of the field and court, Aliquippa had typical "black" issues that needed to be resolved. There was poverty, there was gang violence, dope dealing and crooked politics on all levels. There were also successful black folks who went to work every day and wanted to see their community flourish. Like all communities there are people who want to have a good time. There are also people who want to conquer every land they step foot on. The night came when both groups of young men didn't have time to figure who was who.

That Saturday night, BJ was on the computer getting the head count who would be at the Elks. DeJon would message BJ on AOL messenger

Dmagic87: "Yo, you going to the Elks tonight?"

BJ would message him back on his name.

Timenator (Tim~ in~nator): "Who all going?"

Dmagic87: "It's supposed to be packed yo."

There would be a chatroom full of details and filled with the screen names of all the guys. Tremon was Nijenix, Goatfacekilla26 was Austin Macklin's, Rory Santiago was Bibby2Nyce, Calvin "Hollywood" Jackson was Dadimedropper23 the chatroom was full of teenagers the afternoon of the dance.

DeJon would call BJ later.

"When you going down there?" He asked.

"Eight thirty, nine o'clock."

"BJ Schroeder, I'll be down there my brother."

That was another nick name BJ had. Only DeJon called him that.

"I'm going to let you know now, Tyler going to be down there. So, watch ya head man." DeJon cautioned him before getting off the phone.

DeJon wanted to keep it cool between the two communities, but he also knew there was tension. He didn't want to start up nothing, and he didn't want no one to be caught off guard. He had warned a few of the Aliquippa boys that there would be no threatening his friends or family. They had laughed at him and sarcastically promised not to touch Barksdale or anyone else. Cassie also said she would be there at nine with her girls. The night was set.

Once BJ got into the Elks, he noticed everyone on the dance floor. His brain was like a computer that never turned off or caught a glitch. His senses and system started to function immediately following the metal detectors. Mission one: find Cassie Washington, execute hugs and a potential kiss if necessary. Mission two: find DeJon Alford, Rory Santiago, Calvin Jackson, Tremon Barksdale, Austin Macklin, Regis Bolden and any other 2003 graduates from Beaver Falls. Tremon and Rory were not present. Tremon was waiting for Tracey to get done modeling and Rory was handling some business in the city. Mission three: find out who is a potential perpetrator or predator.

Tyler Wilkerson was present and full of animosity. He was sitting in the dark on the opposite side of Cassie, Tori (DeJon's sister), and Kylee Wesley-- a girl Cassie cheered with. BJ's senses started to detect harmful words and fire in the eyes from some of the Aliquippa boys. DeJon spotted a few guys he was ok with from school. Unfortunately, he also spotted some of the same threatening body languages; point of fingers, stares and sucking of the teeth.

"Man Timmons, don't do it." He said waiving his hand rapidly. "Tyler is over there, stay over here man."

BJ was full of pride that night and fed up with the talk of a possible ambush.

"He over there?" BJ asked.

"Yeah man, he's over there and he got some back up too, so don't do it." DeJon quickly responded.

As the song *"Always on Time"* by Ja Rule featuring Ashanti played loudly, the two would go back and forth about the cause and effect of BJ setting off the moment. Dom Henson the DJ that night would change the song to Lil Jon and the Eastside Boyz ft Mystikal and Krayzie Bone ***"I Don't Give a F**k!"***

"*Wrong song to play, Dom.*" BJ said to himself.

Cassie would come over to BJ and try to talk some sense into him.

"Move out my way babe, I gotta say something," he said moving Cassie's body out the way.

He would make his way over to Tyler sitting next to his boys. DeJon grabbed a few folks to let them know what was about to happen and to move out the way.

"Aye, Tyler!" BJ yelled over the music. "You got a problem with me dawg?"

Tyler, with quick reflexes, stood up and took a fighter's stance.

The lights turned on and some of the chaperones and security yelled, "The dance is over!"

DeJon and Big Brian a.k.a. Bullet Pitts would hold BJ back.

"You just had to go over there, didn't you?" DeJon yelled at his friend as teens would exit the dance floor.

Tyler was also grabbed by a couple cordial young men from Aliquippa.

"Chill out Rev!" Bullet yelled at Timmons. "You gotta chill that Shit out man!"

Cassie was furious because she predicted it.

"It's that broad man!" She said to her friends. "This is over her, where is she?"

The crazy thing was that Alexis *was* there! Did she fuel this man's hostility? Was he really that mad over a sucker punch on the field several months prior? Did the Aliquippa football players hype up the situation and make it worse? No one really knew what this beef was over. BJ knew that in his brain, he had to set the tone for not only Tyler, but whatever fools in the future would step to him. All Cassie knew was her man was about to fight over another woman.

"How whack is that?" She exclaimed.

As adults and teens filed out of the building after the dance, someone yelled "Let's take it to McDonald's."

Now why Mickie D's? Who knows, but it was a dumb thing to say to BJ. Rory's senses also must have gone off and told him to hurry. He pulled up like he was a superhero coming to save the day." By 2002, cell phones just started to become more popular. Tremon had a cell phone and so did Rory. BJ could use his dads on the weekends. Rory and Tremon both came at the perfect time.

"It's on now." Tremon said pulling up with Tracey.

Tracey tried to get Tremon to realize what was at risk. She knew about Tremon and DeJon jumping Damon Grace. Everyone got into their vehicles or ran seven blocks to see the second part to this drama.

Rory would tell BJ to get in the car.

"BJ don't do it!" Cassie said to BJ as he got ready to get in Rory's car.

"Yo, you coming?" BJ asked Cassie as she contemplated on going or not.

As the two teenagers got into Rory's Beamer, he made sure he set the tone with a certain song. "*Fight*" by Project Pat. He would blast the song to make sure that BJ understood what time it was. The speed limit was 15 but Rory had to be clocking 70!

"We gonna fight up in this b***h" –the lyrics blasted through the air and kept on playing in BJ Timmons head over and over.

Did rap music cause any of this behavior back then? Does it now?

DeJon rode up with Stacey, Austin's sister. Austin made sure he rode up under his own influence.

"Who called the white boy?" Someone from Aliquippa yelled.

Tremon and Tracey arrived in his dad's gray Honda with the bullet holes in it. When he pulled up, he went around the back where no one could see him calm his lady down. Some of the 2002 class was present also; Spencer Wallace, Carlos Clemons, and Bullet Pitts were all there. Someone had mentioned Deon Winslow (who was a Beaver Falls running back) was there. He had gone into the McDonald's to get something to eat. Calvin and Regis were also in the McDonald's.

Now keep in mind, no one was officially ready to throw down until BJ and Tyler Wilkerson met in the middle. Even if those two would have met man to man in the middle, it wouldn't have lasted-- no way, no how. Not with these Tigers. There were years of Beaver Falls guys running from Aliquippa guys. In Barbershops and at every barbeque there had been several urban legends of Tigers wimping out. The two young men of color were ready to meet in the middle of the McDonald's parking lot over.... what?

"We're not on the football field now Wilkerson!" BJ step in the middle first.

BJ would do a shimmy or shake to make fun and egg on the Quip. As soon as Tyler got ready to proceed with the confrontation, Pastor Timmons entered the scene. Austin Macklin also tried to reason with some teens from Aliquippa.

"BJ, let's go!" Pastor said to his son as he scoped the scene.

BJ looked at Cassie with suspicion. "You called him, didn't you?"

As Cassie Washington got ready to plead her case, there was a pack of females surrounding Macklin with adult size males walking closer to him. BJ knew his father and Cassie were in the right. He knew that if he fought and won, it wouldn't be over. If he lost, some folks would be in the glory saying, *"He finally got his a** kicked!"* When BJ got back to the van, a classmate of his ran up to him.

"They are jumping your dad!" He said running up to BJ.

The moment BJ Timmons heard this his system finally got fully activated. He had turned into the wild animal his parents wouldn't allow the public to see. Five girls dove onto Macklin, and he took three punches to the face before throwing them off like a lion does to hyenas. DeJon and Rory ran around like martial arts video game characters, one punch knocking out people.

Tremon would also jump into the action. He would knock down a man and stun three more. One boy fell under a Cadillac bumper because of Rory's punch! The young man had a seizure . Towards the southern Part of the parking lot, The Pastor kept pushing away a couple grown men. Later he would tell BJ there were at least four grown men there. These grown men were zeroed in on DeJon and BJ. DeJon for his betrayal and BJ for being BJ…

Jake Jones and Vince Moses who were both graduated, jumped in. Jake would zero in on a young man from Aliquippa who had tried to sneak his woman away a couple times. Vince would get in on the action also. Another young man known as

"Dre Lee" from New Brighton also got in the action. He sided with the Beaver Falls boys that night.

BJ would be picked up by one of the Quips who played tight end. He used his body weight to fall on the young man and took a chunk out of his chest. The anger he had inside was almost demonic. His adrenaline also was increased when he thought someone tried to hurt his father. When the young man rolled over in pain, Cassie jumped in like a dirty wrestling manager. She would stomp on his head with her heels that she was wearing. The fight lasted for over 10 minutes. Some of you readers may think that's short. Don't think that for one second! Every second feels like 40 seconds. Keep in mind eight boys from BF were fighting and Aliquippa had over twenty. The fight ended by the police coming to break up the brawl. When it was over the only people who got pulled over was Dre Lee and Vince Moses: the two that got injured in the fight.

What about the teens who were in McDonald's? There were three stories surfacing around the community that night. One was that Calvin and a couple other boys tried to come out and defend but the managers locked the door. Calvin made sure he let his boys know that this was false. You can lock the door so that no one can get in, but you can't lock the door for the guest not to be able to leave.

Another story, from a senior who shall rename nameless, said "I had y'all, but the manager grabbed me."

DeJon and Rory called out his bull shit.

The third story was that Calvin said, "Look at them fools outside fighting! Them negroes is crazy!"

When everything came to the light about who was where and who said what, BJ believed his friend Calvin. Calvin would fight you if he had to. There were other spectators there that night also who said they were involved in the fight. Andy Horn, from Rochester who happened to be Alexis's ex, was also there. He was watching the whole time with her in the Wendy's parking lot. Alexis knew she had a lot to do with it. Here is a trick question: did Tyler Wilkerson know that Alexis was shacked up across the street watching he and BJ fight? Did he know that she was with her ex-boyfriend? If so, would those two men had even got into the fight? That night the Tigers may have won the battle, but the war was far from being over.

When BJ and Pastor returned, both men had to share the story with Sabrina Timmons.

"Brina, I've been alive a long time, I ain't never seen nothing like it." Pastor said to his wife. "Them young boys was down there rumbling."

BJ couldn't figure out if he were in trouble or not. He also couldn't figure out if his dad were proud or not. Now some "holier than thou" folks will assume Pastor shouldn't have been happy at all. However, though BJ's father was a pastor, he was a man. As BJ's parents talked in the bedroom. BJ slipped downstairs and got on the computer to see the gossip in the chatroom. BJ would read a few statements from some Aliquippa girls. Some threats were made, and one girl even set up BJ in conversation to brag. He would end up getting into a verbal fight with her because he knocked out her brother. She promised him a butt whooping the next time she or her brother saw him.

The following Monday the guys who weren't there wished they were.

"Man, if I was there." "Why ain't y'all call me?" "When is the next fight?" was all BJ heard that Monday.

The Beaver Falls boys who were in the fight were rock stars. They were celebrities in the school. BJ, Tremon, Rory and Macklin all enhanced their profiles. There was some seriousness in some statements that were given during the day. Tyrell Goosby really would have made matters worse for some of the Aliquippa teens. Aliquippa probably had a few boys that wanted to be there also.

If you were to ask them about that night, they would probably say, "If so and so was there someone would have got shot... etc."

God was on the Tigers side. The numbers favored the Quips. All the boys who took part in the fight would be in good spirits that week. There was one minor problem: DeJon still had to go to school there. He was a Junior at Aliquippa High School. He played football there and developed some solid friendships there even though his loyalty laid with the Tigers.

That following week for him, was not too welcoming. He had put his life on the line. It was a badge of honor from his BF boys. He was marked for death from some of the Aliquippa citizens. He was threatened so bad that the principal told him that it was best if he went home. When he returned his father could not understand why he wouldn't go back. The principal and DeJon both told him, he was a dead man walking basically. He couldn't go back, or he wouldn't make it through the day without being jumped, stabbed or worse.

BJ's father said following the fight, "If this was in the city, someone would have got smoked."

BJ Timmons father didn't know that a situation almost happened like that a few months back. BJ and DeJon met up with some guys from Coraopolis (PA) outside of the Elks. There was a conversation and the Crips (or so-called Crips) from Coraopolis left after BJ demanded respect from them. The young men had disrespected him over the internet. It's amazing how young men run to go fight over internet threats. Back then it was dumb and it's dumb now. DeJon would echo that line later in life. There was a price DeJon would have to pay for fighting. He would have to go to night school or go to summer school. Or the worst-case scenario, fail the rest of the year. Please remember everything at stake before you get involved in any fight. DeJon would pay a price for something technically he had nothing to do with. Yes, he chose to fight, in some family's that goes without saying. Especially in the black community.

Coach Holton, an Aliquippa native, would state his frustration with his future seniors. He ripped into Macklin and Rory for jeopardizing their futures. Tremon and BJ would get a lecture on being stupid. In the end, all four boys knew they had to do it. Whether you blame BJ or Tyler, it was coming eventually. Hell, even if you wanted to blame DeJon and Tremon for kicking it off by stomping Damon Grace, it was still coming. No one wanted to acknowledge the elephant in the room. Aliquippa met a group of Tigers who didn't care about reputation. These 2003 Tigers were on the prowl for respect within the county lines.

All the adults took heed to the commotion that took place

the previous weekend. They would shame the young men and let them know how fortunate they were for not getting shot. In 2002, Timmons and his friends were not trying to hear that. Now looking back, they were right. This could have been resolved with men of color sitting somewhere neutral and getting the logistics down. Tyler should have checked his woman and demanded an apology from Timmons. Timmons wouldn't have apologized in the moment, but who knows what would have happened in the following months. Cassie Washington was right, and BJ knew it. This was another notch in her belt. No matter what, this fight brought the brothers in the 2003 class closer and would set the tone for loyalty with their circle for the rest of their lives.

Boys II MEN

The Beaver Falls 2002 class would leave a strong legacy. They had made huge strides to putting the "Falls" back on the map. The last time Beaver Falls was ranked in both sports was 1994 when they won the basketball state championship. They had won in football in the 1980s but nothing to scream about. Jason Sparrow, Deon Winslow, Brian Pitts, Rob Tomlin, Spencer Wallace would all make huge impacts at their college campuses their freshman year. Carlos Clemons would choose a small school in Pittsburgh to go play basketball. Tyrell Goosby would choose to stay home and go to the community college. He would transition from being the big fish in the little pond and become the man who continued to make the world around him more peaceful.

He never stepped back on a college football field. He would go play semi-pro football and work with kids. The Lord makes no mistakes, Tye had a time and he made it work. Did he make the best of it? Would he look back and say, *"what if this or that happens?"* Sure, he did but he would pass off the baton to a young 14-year-old man- child by the name of Lance Jamison, "Sir Lancelot". He too had been dominating his class his whole life and he was ready to become an apprentice to the

2003 class.

The summer of 2002 was the time to take a victory lap. It was also a closing act, the last dance, and transitioning from being a boy to becoming a man for BJ and his friends. Before leaving to Atlantic city and Philadelphia with Cassie and her family, he went to the University of Pittsburgh's seven-day camp. He would compete and try his best to impress coach Harris and the other assistant coaches. He was able to see the country's top football players. Guys came from all over the country. Ted Ginn Jr., a future wide receiver for the Ohio State Buckeyes and later the Carolina Panthers, showed out. Some other prospects also put on a show. BJ gave himself a B- when he reported back to Coach Holton. He spent most of the camp studying different linebacker moves and watching the 2001 NBA championship when he got back to his dorm room.

Tremon headed out to the University of Virginia camp. He too would compete and get his name out there by running and catching everything. He slightly injured his hamstring. The report was given when he came back from camp. Tremon would push himself to the limit making sure he was the top receiver in the State. His teammate Rory wasn't too far away. Rory was not as highly recruited and started to gain weight and some height. Coach Holton would explain to him that there would be some competition for receiver with DeJon, Cameron Mosby, and Dre Lee who was moving to the community from New Brighton. There was a new quarterback, also, who had a good rapport with everyone. Jordan Potter was a big strong kid who had a lot of heart. He would make sure he would continue the tradition of good quarterback play. Tremon also would be asked to play some QB if Jordan got overwhelmed with offense.

Austin Macklin would gain more recognition from scouts following his results from track. He gained good weight and continued to get stronger with his personal trainer. Off the field, he would battle with the pressure of being top dog. Everyone knew that he and Regis would be the middle linebackers heading into the 2002 football season. Regis made the tough decision to turn in his cleats in for pencils and note cards. His academic excellence would have to supersede his position with the team. Regis could have gotten a scholarship somewhere for football. Football was in the beginning of the school year, so more than likely he wanted to start off on the right track.

"Man Reg, we need you." Macklin said.

"I thought about it long and hard man…." Regis said to Macklin and Tremon when they met with him. "It's best if I don't play this year."

BJ knew that Regis's speed and power were essential. More importantly that senior leadership and continuity would be missed. Regis wasn't the toughest blow to the team for next year; there would be several disappointments. Regis's early retirement announcement was just the tip of the iceberg.

New blood would enter the Tiger's locker room. A six-foot-two sophomore stud named Cameron Mosby would add on to Jordan Potter's arsenal. Jordan Potter would be awarded the starting quarterback. He was a hard worker and great leader on and off the field. Reshaun Taylor, Shawn Curry, Seth Williams, Tye Jackson, Kevin Barksdale (Tremon's brother), Brian Trevor, Josh Whisenhunt, and Kyle Watson would all be the future. They were cocky just like the 2003 club but with less action. They were cool cats and would rather chill than rumble. They were ready to compete and didn't mind telling people.

Dougie Benson would be up against some academic barriers. Some of the barriers were self-inflicted. Dougie, now a three-year starter, was able to hold on to his place on the football team and had to make up some grades. Did the school tell Dougie all the requirements he needed to be eligible to play? Did Dougie assume he was in good standing? He would continue to show up for passing camps and some work outs. He like Calvin, was a brand-new father. He had new responsibilities along with his studies and his placement on the team.

DeJon would transfer back to BFHS. He followed option three and failed the rest of the school year. He was able to sign up for summer classes that would be offered at the county college in Center Township. He would carpool sometimes with other "03" classmates. The aftermath from the fight had trickled into DeJon's plans of focusing on bringing up his grades. . One gentleman who DeJon had a close eye on, rode to school sometimes with the same driver. The gentleman had some animosity because DeJon and Tre had put a beatdown on his older cousin following a family reunion. "Seis" was a young man who threatened Tre's younger brother Kevin. One thing leads to another and Seis met the Barksdale family.

The McDonald's beef was still on the grill cooking. It had a Death row records versus Bad boy records smell to it. DeJon noticed Seis' cousin on campus. They would see each other, but nothing was said. One afternoon, DeJon got a ride from one of his Beaver Fall's classmates that he played youth football with Brian "Red head" Summerville. Brian and DeJon not only played football together. They also played basketball together and they were in a couple homerooms together coming up in junior high.

Brian would take DeJon and Cedeno Seis' cousin, a different route that day. Because of the summer fun, DeJon stayed up late the night before and fell asleep on the ride home from summer school. When he woke up, he noticed the street but didn't understand why they were stopping.

"Brian, where we going man?" DeJon said to Red-Head from the back seat.

Brian would pull onto a side street. Cedeno started to look mischievous and moving quickly gathering his bag and ready to bolt.

"D, I had to!" Red said back to DeJon as he looked suspiciously back at him.

"Yo, Brian, let's go." DeJon said to him. "You had to what, man?"

Brian became frozen in the moment, full of shame. Cedeno turned around one last time to make sure DeJon didn't try to bolt. Over ten boys with sticks and knives came towards Brian's vehicle. DeJon angry now, started to choke Brian "Redhead" Summerville. The men started to tap the car and even tried to get Brian to unlock the automatic doors. Brian kept repeating himself.

"Sorry DeJon I had to!" Keep in mind, he had DeJon's hands wrapped around his neck.

"Start this goddamn car up or I'm f***ing you up!" DeJon

said with fury in his spirit.

DeJon was terribly upset, frustrated and afraid that he may have to seriously hurt someone. Brian and DeJon weren't necessarily homeboys but there were supposed to be a code of respect. Or at least DeJon thought so. Who were those boys, you ask? They were Seis' boys, but they were also from Quip. Who would take all that time to conspire against a 17-year-old kid? They would. Seis' pride was killed that day he got mashed out. He wanted revenge and he knew that Cedeno moved down to Beaver Falls because his father took a position with his cleaning company.

"This is jacked up Brian, take me to Tremon's crib." DeJon said looking at Brian like he could rip his head off.

"DeJon, they threatened me and offered me fifty bucks." Brian said.

"Fifty, huh?" DeJon said back at him.

When Brian dropped off DeJon, he made sure to get the heck out of dodge. He knew the ramifications of crossing someone like DeJon. No one was killers in DeJon's camp; however, Brian didn't want to take a trip to the emergency room. Brian knew, DeJon knew, if DeJon told Tremon the story while Brian was sitting there. It would have been bad. DeJon knew he couldn't trust anyone now.

"This shit starting to go too far man." He said on Tremon's porch.

Tremon couldn't believe it.

"They ain't letting it go man." DeJon said.

Now another barrier would get in the way of DeJon focusing. Were the group of young men going to try to kill him? Would they try another act of violence soon? These were all the thoughts in the 17-year old's head. Once again, the most high has a way of keeping young men on their toes. D almost got caught sleeping officially! How would DeJon's family and friends respond? Would someone get shot? Would anyone guarantee DeJon's protection? Would he allow it? DeJon wasn't going to go to the police to report a potential slaying. Whether you're in the city or the suburbs, snitching wasn't going to happen. He also wasn't going to keep going to summer school. How would this help him bring up his grades? A lot of questions, a lot of distractions, a lot of setbacks. He put his blood, sweat and fears on the line for his boys. Would those fears become tears one day?

Calvin would be concentrating on his own safety by practicing and temporarily detaching from his toxic family members. Not all his family was toxic, however the ones that were, could become a test of patience for him. A few nights a week Calvin would find himself arguing with his child's mother, his mother, or someone else's mother was coming for his neck by prejudging his character. The drama would come to a high sometimes and he would be kicked out of his grandparents' house.

Calvin generally had respect for his grandparents and for the most part he followed the rules. The older he got, the bolder he got because he wasn't conveying his frustration with becoming a man. When he got kicked out, Calvin would meet an older woman who would prey on him. He would take a likening to her, not realizing that she was 10 years older than him. She was

27 which was awesome to him and his boys. He didn't find out she was 27 until he stayed the night and met her children. Guess what? She was a married 27-year-old. In Pennsylvania, the crime of passion states: *A person who kills an individual without lawful justification commits voluntary manslaughter if at the time of the killing he is acting under a sudden and intense **passion** resulting from serious provocation by: the individual killed.* (Pennsylvania Voluntary Manslaughter Laws – FindLaw)

In other words, if a man comes home and sees his wife being toyed with sexually, the alleged perpetrator can be killed on the spot due to the man of the home being in his feelings.

Calvin listening to his lower head, was in dangerous waters. The woman, Bianca, had a husband named "J.T." who wasn't ready to let her go. He was from Florida, and he didn't play fair. Calvin was used to taking risk and taking people's girls if need be. This time, he may have met his match. She was a woman with three kids, Calvin had one himself. This young man was about to be "step daddy" and "baby boy".

The young men were all facing their own trials and tribulations. Drugs were on a personal high both figuratively and literally. Fife, Paul, and Dougie would be tempted daily to put off their daily summer duties to go get high. Some men were falling deeper in love like BJ and Tremon. Some young men were just becoming antsy and wanted to get out of school like Shakes and Nate Lewis. They were great students who enjoyed hanging out with their boys but wanted to get out of school to experience new things.

BJ's summer schedule was already filled up with camps and

plans for starting his senior project. He knew he wanted to do something with kids. He would volunteer helping with his Father's church youth group by volunteering with the little children at Vacation Bible School and passing out treats to the preschoolers. Later, he would volunteer to play Jesus in the Christmas play. Before all the stress of being a senior, he wanted to go away. Ms. Lisa, Cassie's mom offered to take BJ with she, Cassie's father Iman, her other daughter, and Cassie to Atlantic City.

Before they stopped in A.C. they went to Philadelphia to visit with Cassie's Uncle. Mrs. Lisa was a Philly native, and she needed to see her side of the family occasionally. They would go site seeing and visit some malls. At night, BJ and Cassie snuggled up and watch scary movies. They watched the whole *Halloween* movie series up to *Halloween H20*. They ate Chinese food and all kinds of goodies. Afterwards, BJ would go to a guest room and sleep in another room.

Mrs. Lisa and Mr. Iman trusted BJ. BJ secretly knew that he offered a balance to his girl's family. Cassie had a big family, but she didn't have any brothers. Her male cousins were close with her but had their own lives. They were in committed relationships, and some were in college. BJ was her boyfriend, but he displayed older brotherly advice at times. When Mr. Iman was gone, BJ would add a balance in the home. A good percentage of the time it was just Mrs. Lisa, Cassie, and her younger sister. Cassie and her sister would get into arguments like sisters do. BJ brought different energy into their home. His casual demeanor was just the right fit for their family.

Mr. Iman Washington was a sports fanatic and loved Penn State football. The two could talk sports and sometimes he liked to crack a beer or two. Cassie knew that BJ didn't drink, and she would try her best to make sure BJ was comfortable. Mrs. Lisa echoed that sentiment, letting Mr. Iman know BJ didn't drink. If Mr. Iman became a little tipsy, BJ would talk to him until he fell asleep. Everyone's family wasn't like BJ's; BJ knew that, but he wanted the Washington family to know that. All in all, the family and BJ enjoyed themselves. BJ's family also trusted Cassie's family with taking their 17-year-old son with them. When they came back, BJ knew that it was all business from here on out.

Tremon and Tracey also went away with Tracey's family to Bermuda. The 2003 senior group felt like they could take a snapshot of life one last time being a child. Because now they were about to turn into men. Was this unhealthy to go away with Cassie and the family? Was BJ setting up Cassie for disappointment? The boys all knew their lives would never be the same. When you're a senior, that last summer before school starts is supposed to be memory making; looking up at the stars on summer nights, whether you were partying too hard, vacationing with the fam or girl, or going away with your friends. For BJ and the boys, it was time to cap off the good run from the mid-1990's to the early 2000's. They had been good since the sixth grade. They were the group that everyone was waiting for.

"When they are in high school, they going to win like every year!" the community would say.

The truth was they had fell short and underachieved. This was the year to bring it all together. If they were healthy, they would win. Health is particularly important in sports. The cubs had turned into handsome Tigers on the prowl. The boys had become men.

The Chrysalis Stage

In nature, the chrysalis stage is the transformation of a caterpillar to a beautiful butterfly. The butterflies go through a unique cycle of five stages from the egg all the way to the caterpillar's old body which dies inside the chrysalis. A new body with beautiful wings appears after a couple of weeks. With other animals such as the male lion, he starts to grow a mane. The deer or moose start to grow antlers. When it comes to human men, they start to play with the idea of independency-- wanting a challenge, needing a challenge, or becoming the challenger. Going back and forth with adult men, women, or sometimes family members. When boys turn into men, they start to believe they are ready to fight grown men. Some young men even flirt with the idea of being intimate with grown women.

BJ Timmons and Calvin Hollywood Jackson were dealing with different roles in the homes they lived in, but the outcome was the same. They would both start going to anger management. BJ was having some problems with adjusting to the new priorities in his life. He couldn't run around and play the hunk all day. He had to worry about passing the S.A. T's, getting that driver's license, and finishing strong this football season. He would constantly get into arguments with his father about BJ's priorities. Sometimes the arguments would get intense, and BJ would find himself outside the house. His father was trying to save his life and his son's life. He didn't want to kill BJ for that mouth of his. BJ had started to buck up against the system.

"I'll do the dishes later," he would say.

He would question his parents, *"Why this? Why me? How come this... and how come that?"*

BJ would constantly try to test his father, not realizing his father was once 17.

One night, BJ went too far.

"You got to go!" His father said. "Get out, or I'm going to put you out!"

Keep in mind, his father was a man of God but a *man* first.

Sabrina Timmons BJ's mother would step in between them.

"You going to get enough!" She said angrily. "He will beat you down BJ!"

Sabrina knew BJ's father before he was a pastor... before he gave his life to Christ. He also had a temper. That's where BJ got his temper from. This was the man who showed him how to throw a curve ball, shoot a jump shot and wrap up in football. He was also the man who gave him the nerve of never feeling intimidated from another threatening male. BJ had to go to Cassie's house to let get his mind right (thank God for Cassie's parents!). Even if they assumed something was wrong at home, they stayed focus on what they thought he needed. An active listener can sometimes be as effective as a motivational speaker. His parents wanted the best for him and sometimes the best meant tough love. All in all, tough love was still love. The chubby boy he used to be was gone. BJ was a weightlifting, handsome, boisterous, hot-headed jerk!

Calvin had been also going back and forth with the adults in his life. That short tempered, slick talking, basketball dribbling a** hole had finally crossed the line in his grandmother's house. Bianca, the cougar (an older woman who dates a younger man), had her eyes on the homeless tiger. Calvin had been to detention centers and many other scenarios were painted for him if his behavior didn't shape up. He had enough. Bianca would allow him to stay the night and one night turned into some months. In a strange way, Calvin had the maturity to keep a woman like Bianca. The only problem was her husband who was abusive and still didn't get the memo of Calvin Jackson being the new producer in the crib. Both Calvin and BJ would go to anger management once a week for different reasons. Their tempers hadn't caught up to them just yet. If they didn't get it checked though, they both were in jeopardy of losing potential athletic scholarships.

Two men with different upbringings, both struggled with managing their anger. BJ had the supportive family who would bend over backwards to ensure their son's future was prosperous. Calvin also had two supportive grandparents who were losing their grip on their grandson's life. The misplaced aggression towards BJ's family was from the false sense of self-awareness. BJ thought being tough meant always being the toughest idiot in the room. He had to go above and beyond to move away from the passive church boy way of life. The fights were one thing, but he didn't understand that true strength meant knowing thyself. BJ wasn't a thug; he wasn't a bad boy. He was running away from the humble character that he once was.

Calvin was looking for intimacy in a proper manner. He had love for his child's mother but knew he couldn't stay committed. Their lives were just too different. His mother had been in and out of his life. She would take jobs and leave jobs; live close then move away. This was a pattern in Calvin's life. Who would really take time to listen to Calvin if he started to vent? He never really trusted any woman except his grandmother. Would the lack of a mother really change a man? The first relationship you have in this world, is your mother. Before a child enters the world, he spends nine months with his mother. If she is loving and nurturing, then the first 10 years can be a smooth educational program for young boys. If she is in and out, then there could be some delayed emotional responses.

No matter how much a mother is in or out of a child's life, the child continues to grow and develops his or her understanding of how the opposite sex behaves. Rory and DeJon both struggle with these same delays. The ladies misunderstood them at times. Rory's mother also had jobs and they would cause him to move or stay. DeJon's mother would made the conscious decision of letting him stay with his paternal grandfather and his dad. She unselfishly allowed her son to see other men live their lives. DeJon's father and grandfather were both hard workers. So, every now and then teachers would see small periods of maturity, then larger periods of frustration. No one was taking the time to examine these boys home lives. They were phenomenal athletes, yes, but they needed some guidance on women. If it weren't for their grandmothers, all three of these men could have been criminals with no heart for anyone.

Blaire Ameen was also starting to leave his old image. He was starting to feel the need to have respect from his mother's boyfriend. He would grow some in height and grow some in wisdom. He was no longer the passive, silly, boy. He wanted respect and he wanted acceptance. He tried to hang with the smokers and found out that they smoked and that was it. He hung out with some of the small street gangs. He found out how to hustle a little. He started to hang more with his football buddies. He wasn't sure about the college football thing, but he knew he could go somewhere and play. All these avenues lead to somewhere. He wanted love and wasn't necessarily getting it.

Blaire was raised by his grandmother, and she happened to be experiencing some changes due to her age. Who was talking to Blaire about all this? How do you approach a young man about his grandmother experiencing life changing events? The community first noticed Blaire changing when he pummeled a young man on the basketball court who took horseplay too far. He had always been overlooked by his family. The Timmons family always liked Blaire, but they were unaware of his anger accumulating at a rapid pace.

Heading into the football season, all these young men would be experiencing changes, however, the right coach would recognize the spirit of the 2003 seniors. They were all solid in their young manhood. Tremon had a solid girlfriend, a good arm and full of college scouts coming to see him. He drove and he was a four- year starter. Austin Macklin also drove and showed the commitment to himself by putting his body first during the hot summer days. He battled with partying hard but knew how to put football first.

Rory, DeJon, and BJ all had a chip on the shoulders always. BJ Timmons made up a lot of those chips. One day it was because people were doubting him. Another day because he was chubby. The next day, he could have chip because someone made fun of a special needs or crippled child in his mother's classroom. He would find a way to light his own fire. By any means necessary!

Rory had waited two years for this moment. He felt Coach Holton overlooked him the previous year. He knew Tremon would be the go-to receiver, he wanted to be a go to also. The theme that year should have been "execute the hunt." Would these Tigers come back with prize possession? Or would they come back empty handed? The militant but strangely compelling spirit went through the locker room during the summer work outs. These young men fought and clawed constantly. With sports, lovers, previous coaches, and neighborhood gangs. They wanted to leave BF with solid reputations.

Tremon and Calvin would have one more battle on the blacktop. They would battle fist to cuff back and forth in the championship. Calvin held the trophy, but Tremon had the scoring accolades. Tremon would score 67 points in one game. He held a single game record in the "Tiger-Pause" basketball tournament. It was one last time that the two would play up against each other in that capacity. Tremon and Calvin battled in everything since the 4th grade in Ms. Rawlings class. Hopefully, one day these two will look back and laugh at the rivalry. In a couple months, they would share the same back court in the regular basketball season; one last time, they could go for the gold together. The hostility towards each other at times would be transferred to the surrounding schools. So much was going to change in the matter of weeks. One thing that would never change was these two trying to out-do one another. It was healthy competition for the most part, but sometimes it got crazy.

Full beards, chin strap beards, braids and full of attitude. Their bodies had changed and their way of looking at men and women had changed. Coach Holton was an authoritative figure in these boys' lives. He could be imposing at times but for the most part he was very unpredictable. He made sure to let the young men know that he would do his part with getting them looks by colleges. Other times he would make sure to let you know he had the power to tell a school if they should take your or not. "Power trippin" is what they call it in the hood.

Coach Holton had different relationships with different people. BJ and Tre didn't mind because they had fathers who were incredibly involved. Rory, Austin, and Blaire not so much. Their dads were either not interested or not there at all. DeJon had a unique way of looking at "Holt" or Coach Holton. DeJon knew Coach Holton for years. Holton was unaware that though he knew DeJon's grandfather, he didn't have the slightest idea of all the crap DeJon had to go through. Coach Holton had his hands full of college letters for his seniors. He also had his head full of questions about coaching all these egos.

"Military Captains"

Captains are normally chosen by the coaches. The coaches typically choose by who has the most on the field experience and who displayed the most leadership. On and off the field, a captain displays self-control along with the charisma to captivate the whole team. Sometimes, he or she will yell and scream to gain the attention of the team. Sometimes he or she has the right attitude during practice and in the game. Beaver Falls in the 2002 was rich with captains. As stated before, Tremon was a four-year starter and the number 14 recruit at the wide receiver position in the state. Austin, BJ and Dougie were three- year veterans who worked to get their names out there. These four were the first to be handpicked by Coach Holton.

Right before the two weeks overnight camp began the young men would head to Youngstown State University. Tremon went away and had let the coaches know that this trip was already planned. With Tre gone, the main target had to be Rory Santiago. DeJon, Dre Lee, and Cameron Mosby would all inform young Jordan Potter that they would be open. Jordan had big shoes to fill as quarterback play was always important on any football team... especially when every year a passing record seemed to be broken including Joe Namath's. BJ and Austin were more focused on defensive coverages and learning the play book. Austin would move to fullback and some running back.

When the boys got to YSU's (Youngstown State University) passing camp, they competed hard and continued to gain the attention of college coaches. Rory was levels above the competition. He and Jordan would put on a passing clinic. Like years before with his counterpart Barksdale, he would be the epitome of graceful. DeJon would collide with Reshaun Taylor, and he would suffer a concussion. BJ and Seth would make some defensive stops. When it was over, the coaches from Youngstown State wanted to talk to three people. Tremon who they thought it was, BJ and Austin.

"That's Rory Santiago, are star receiver." Coach Holton said to a YSU assistant coach.

Rory with a puzzling look, shook the YSU assistant coach's hand.

"Hell of a day for you, young man." The coach said. "We like what we saw today so much that we would like to offer you a scholarship."

Rory thanked the coach and walked off trying not to gain the attention of other young men. While Rory was talking to the coaches on one end, BJ and his father Pastor Timmons spoke with Bowling Green and YSU.

"There is his dad, talk to him." Coach Holton said sarcastically.

BJ really didn't do much offensively, but his size and

lateral movement gained a position coach's attention. Coach Holton seemed irritated with Pastor being present at the camp. Maybe Coach Holton was still feeling the vibe from Pastor Timmons wanting to address the embarrassing moment from the Aliquippa playoff game. Even if Holton let it go, Pastor Timmons wouldn't forget it.

Rory was mistaken for Tremon, and this was a blessing in disguise for Rory. The way he caught the ball and ran after the catch would make you think he was the go-to guy. If Tre was there who knows, Rory might have not got the same looks. Or best-case scenario, both young men would have put on a clinic like they did the previous two years. Rory might not admit it, his life was about to change sporadically. God has a way of putting the pieces together in your life unexpectedly. A few months prior, Rory was ready to quit. He was tapped out from the foolishness that coach Holton put him through substituting in and out, working countless hours at his McDonald's gig just to play eight plays a game. He worked hard for years; it was his time. His grandmother would have been proud of him. She taught him patience and she challenged him daily.

"The Lord makes no mistakes" BJ used to say.

Now keep in mind, Tremon was away and unaware that his buddy Rory put on a show. If this were 2020, there would be social media. Tre could have Facetimed his boy and congratulated him on the spot. However, this was 2002 and word of mouth was the gospel.

When Tremon came back from vacation, all he heard was they had mistaken Rory for him. The coach could have sat Tre down and explained to him that his teammate would help him get more touches because Rory showed he could be a number one target. He could have brought Jordan and Tre in along with Rory and thought of a way to insert Tre's play making ability. Tre was a competitor, all he wanted to do was win. When he came back, it seemed as if Holton put Rory and Tre against each other. Tre would start to fill the pressure of being a multi-talented athlete on the football field. He would go from quarterback to receiver. With athletes like Tremon, Calvin in basketball, and Goosby the year before or a young phenom like Lance, all you must do is make them see your vision as a coach but make them think that it starts and ends with them. If you look over them or dismiss their talent you're asking for problems!

Coach Holton would experience these weeks to come. Tre was a bold 18-year-old with a lot of confidence. If he felt slighted in anyway, he was going to let the coaching staff know it. He had been making the crowds go crazy since he was a freshman. "Holt" or Coach Holton was not going to get in the way of his success. Rory was an innocent bystander who just wanted to win also. He wasn't worried about Tre getting the ball or not. If Tre were open, Rory would have been glad for his partner to get the ball.

There were other receivers and running backs who were waiting their turn in the pecking order. DeJon a first -year starter, was the fastest on the team. In any other school in America, you get the ball to your fastest player. DeJon didn't help his case with running at the mouth every chance he got. However, he was an important piece that the Tigers needed. His grades would put him on hold. Dougie, Reshaun, Mosby and Macklin also wanted the ball. Lastly, there was BJ. He noticed an ache in his foot, but he chose to ignore it. He thought it was from the spikes he wore. Nevertheless, the pain would worsen. It slowed him down and he started to become less of threat on offense. He knew his ticket was defense-- or at least he thought it was.

It was time for the overnight camp and the team had to mesh. The underclassmen would test the patience of the older teammates. BJ and Cameron Mosby would fight over Mosby's complaining about running sprints. DeJon and Reshaun would fight over Reshaun's late hit on him. DeJon would fight his cousin Tremon also. It looked like the Deion Sanders and Andre Rison fight from 1994. DeJon would be sure to let him know he wanted his respect on the field. BJ and Blaire would go back and forth about water bottles. It was all about hard hits, smack talk and full of testosterone.

There were a couple surprises during camp. Shawn Curry and Brandon McDowell were two impressive underclassmen. Brandon was a rookie as he never played football before. He made a couple hard hits and didn't mind getting hit. DeJon leveled him a couple times. Tremon would hold a meeting at night with the future stars of the team, Reshaun Taylor, Shawn Curry and Cameron Mosby. Tre had let them know he noticed their talent and he wanted them to take the program to the next level. One thing led to another and Tremon was shirtless ready to let the hands fly! He was ready to knock Reshaun's head off for saying he wasn't afraid of him in an argument. Macklin, DeJon, and BJ would tell Tre to chill.

An assistant coach came outside to check on the boys. The coaches probably saw a potential slaughter about to occur. Reshaun was DeJon's cousin also. He wouldn't have let Tre beat him down like that. Tremon was irritated of his young teammates. He was tired of the horseplay and giggling every night. Tre had enough the last night of camp. The radio was playing too loud when he was trying to talk to Tracey on his cell phone.

"Aye! Turn the radio down before I come over there," he said.

Some of the underclassmen thought it would be funny to keep Tre getting up. He would go over to the sophomore side of the gym where they were bunking.

"Give me that." Tre said taking the cord out the wall.

A couple boys said somethings under their breath, but no one pressed their luck.

Tre earned the right to make the decisions. Even though Austin and BJ were the biggest along with Blaire Ameen. Tre had been a Tiger varsity player the longest. He was the kind of captain that was the "silent type." He was everyone's older brother. He made you feel stronger when he was by your side. BJ was the roaring alpha. Every now and then he would become silent like a Green Beret waiting for the mission from his commander. DeJon and Rory both were moody and were like strong commander sergeants. They would let you joke around but at any moment they were ready to rumble, but they were more patient than BJ and Tre.

Dougie Benson and Blaire Ameen were Lieutenants. They liked getting dirty and loved making the opposition feel helpless. Austin Macklin was the president. He liked making everyone feel at home... even to a fault. He would make sure that no one felt left out. In times of chaos, he would put on his own hard hat and by force he would demand respect. Even off the field, he loved to party and wanted peace. You need people like that in your circle. No matter who the war was with, all these young men were prepared to win every battle. All they needed was the right coaches to put it together.

"A Foggy Start" (Fall 2002)

BJ and the boys began their senior year full of excitement and big expectations for the sports seasons. BJ's schedule was light with schoolwork but full of amazement. With one hour in a half period his schedule was perfect for napping until practice time. Block One: Gym with Lance Jamison, Dom Henson, Kevin Barksdale and Ascheley Brown. They would throw the football, play a lot of basketball, and argue about everything. Lance, the new cat in the jungle, would show his time was coming soon. BJ would challenge him and encourage him later. BJ had watched the young lad destroy his age group. He wanted to see if this cat could really ball.

He would tell Cassie after class. "Lance, he got next, yo. That boy strong man."

"He got next" meant he was the next great athlete to take the athletic program to the promised land. Lance would play fight with BJ and challenge his seniority. Dom also displayed a cannon of an arm, and he was very scrappy. It would get intense daily.

Block Two was Basic Foods with his boy DeWarren a.k.a.

"Pong." Pong was a nickname given to him from the south. Pong was from North Carolina. As mentioned in the book earlier, he was the guy who would take his God gifted talent in the kitchen to the next level. BJ would not only take the class with Pong, but also with Angela Corbin and Kyle Watson. Kyle was a sophomore football player who made a huge impact in the class. He would add ideas and challenged the young substitute teacher, who was fresh out of college, to give better cooking ideas. BJ's cooking group had big appetites for food and bigger appetites for drama occasionally.

Block Three was Study Hall following lunch, so he would either hold up Cassie and make her late to class or he would try his hardest to go home and take a nap. Sometimes he would go to the weight room and lift, other times he would go and ice his foot. That foot continued to nag him. Tre's hamstring, Rory and Macklin's shoulders were both slightly dislocated. The young men felt pain but ignored it because in football, you always play with pain. Right?

The last block was very fitting for BJ: College Prep English 12. There he and Rory Santiago would both exercise their brains before heading to the school to prepare for football. Rory already signed with Youngstown State University. He still needed to complete some assignments and needed to turn in his senior project. He and Nate Lewis would work together on their projects. Rory was equally competitive off the field as he was on the field.

BJ would make sure his gal had a great first week in high school. He would try to protect her from the rolling of the eyes, the slick comments, and the boldness of the ex-girlfriend, Denise. She was on the prowl, and she made sure she let it be known that she was still available. BJ wasn't worried about falling for her silly antics. There was only one problem, she was his senior cheerleader. A senior cheerleader makes sure that her senior player's life is much easier. You see for seniors it's a curtain call for the young men, so they needed their roses while they were still in the school. Denise brought Snapple tea and his favorite snacks: Rice Krispy Treats with a side of Hot Cheetos. Thank God Tremon Barksdale sat next to his boy, or he would have easily been wrongfully accused of flirting.

BJ, Shakes, Tre, and Denise were all in the same homeroom. She would keep her comments to a minimum. Tre and BJ would talk normally about a game plan for the week or something sports related as the news came on the tv's in the classroom. Shakes would draw or make sure his homework was done from the night before. All in all, the year looked promising. BJ was happy he could see Cassie more and he just wanted her to adjust to her schedule.

"I ain't worried about these girls." She said the Friday morning of the Blackhawk game.

"The Pep rally is fourth block, here." BJ said giving Cassie his double xx-large number 84 jersey. "Now don't get no ketchup on my shirt!" He said jokingly.

She wore that jersey with honor. She should of wore a bullet proof vest because there were verbal bullets coming at the girl all day.

"*Look how big that shirt is!*"

"*She knows she ain't right.*" Some of the senior cheerleaders said.

Bad enough her freshman class also made corny jokes too. She had some loyal supporters, who loved seeing her glow when she walked to her classes that day. Having haters builds character when you're young. It teaches you how to ignore people, also helps you build an emotional wall if need be. Cassie had a wall: BJ. He knew he had one year to mark his territory. Not that he looked at Cassie like property, but more like the "promised land". For that land, he would fight. In his mind he already planted his flag and had the future planned out. Yeah, it was like that.

Game one, the Tigers played the Cougars who were a school size bigger. Despite all the seniors playing a solid game they were crushed. Coach Holton took out the seniors towards the end of the third quarter. The score was 42 to 0, but the coaches knew it was just an exhibition. The Tigers had scrimmaged Westinghouse and Sharon (PA) two weeks in a row and performed very well. That night, they ran into a more seasoned team. Macklin wanted to show his old school what they would be missing. He was disappointed but not defeated. He knew the Blackhawk cougar football team very well. He grew up with them and played sports all year round with them also. One last time, he would share the field with them.

BJ had more than 10 tackles, but he noticed something towards the end of the game. He had felt an increase in pain in the foot. That night after he shared his frustration of losing with his family, he called Cassie and started to moan about the pain.

"You need to get it checked out now before it gets worse." she said.

"The trainer said to ice it." BJ replied with discomfort in his voice. "If I got to miss a game because of this…"

Cassie instantly tried to give her advice. "Better now than later, right?" She asked quickly. She had the awareness that BJ was starting to get self-conscious about his so-called reputation. Low self- esteem turned outward looks like rage at times.

"Man, I got schools looking at me babe!" He yelled.

The misplaced aggression was received well that night, but eventually Cassie would have to defend herself. She was just trying to be supportive. BJ had a way of taking out his anger on the wrong people. Due to the fear of being left out of the recruiting process, he lashed out. He knew he was wrong for yelling and throwing a tantrum. His pride would get in the way of admitting he was wrong.

A few days later the x-rays came back a hair line fracture in the foot. Cynical thoughts started to enter his head. To detach from the negativity of not playing 100 percent, BJ would work out before school to ensure his strength would increase sense his speed would decrease. BJ's parents, Pastor and Sabrina Timmons would push BJ to fight through the pain and wanted him to stop feeling sorry for himself.

"Poor you, boy you better go head and play the best you can!" Pastor told him that night.

BJ was upset because the work he had put in leading up to this point. Lifting weights twice a day with Austin Macklin, running the steps with Cassie and more importantly, trying to lead the younger troops. Barksdale would make sure his friend felt that he would step it up. He would go back to receiver for week two. Potter would go back to the starting quarterback and BJ's tight end duties would be reduced to more blocking in the run game. In his head he was thinking: *what now*? The offensive coordinator wanted to run, and pass based off he and Macklin's strength. How would he lead not being a 100 percent? Would Coach Holton try to empower his wounded warrior or push him off to the side? Not on BJ's watch!

Week two, BJ played a solid game against Shadyside but had to leave with a walking boot on his foot at halftime. The pain would not ease up. He sat on the bench with tears in his eyes. Rory and Tremon put on a show, Blaire and Macklin anchored the defense, Dougie and DeJon were still patiently waiting to be eligible to play. On the bus ride home BJ listening to his headphones started to zone out and lash out once again. Selfishly he argued with a couple of the sophomores and even threatened one to a fight. Misplaced aggression at its finest.

Michigan, Syracuse, Pitt, Wisconsin all was going to leave him high and dry. Is what he thought. Macklin had West Virginia in his back pocket if he played well. He too was secretly in pain. His shoulder was constantly nagging him and kept coming out of place. Hypothetically, if Regis and Calvin were playing, BJ's injury and Macklin's pain would be bandaged up by the play of their teammates. Macklin was the strongest on the team and was an important piece to both offense and defense. Injuries were apart of sports, you just had to have the right timing when they occurred. Rory's shoulder would eventually become a problem. He would have to be taken out more than he wanted on defense. Coach Holton was an offensive genius, he really didn't liken to spending a lot of time on defense. The severe injuries were yet to come. It was only week two and the Tigers were looking like a snake bitten team. Dougie and DeJon were not due back until weeks four and five.

Week three against the old rivalry New Brighton looked easy in the beginning of the game. Reshaun Taylor and Macklin were both running all over the Lions. Blaire Ameen the lead linemen was whooping their star linemen "Big C!" He was no match for Ameen. After Halftime there was a shift change: The Lions got stronger, and the Tigers got very frustrated with the play calling and the referees. Macklin was ejected for fighting and the Lions capitalized on his absence. This would have been the perfect time for Dougie Benson and DeJon Alford to step up, but They weren't there. As a result, the final score was New Brighton 28, B.F. 19.

Dre Lee who transferred from New Brighton took the lost the hardest. He like Austin Macklin, grew up with another community. He had been misused by the New Brighton coaching staff and he wanted to win at all costs. When the game was over, he became emotional. Coach Holton with a defeated look started to give a heart filled speech.

"Guys we played hard."

As he continued to try to motivate the team for the following week. Someone must have informed the Geneva College fireworks crew that the Tigers had won, because the fireworks started to go off.

Holton was heated! "Who did this?" he said. "Who the hell did this?" He yelled.

When the Tigers got back to the locker room, he demanded

to speak to someone. He felt that the school had showed him up. Almost like a sarcastic joke or a big eff you! That night, BJ felt sorry for his coach. He knew that whoever gave the go ahead for fireworks didn't care for Holton. Even though Holton gave BJ a hard time, he was still a man of color, he was a so called "black" authoritarian. Because of his title, BJ knew Holton had to be perfect and to maintain the image. Holton also had to play the game, or he would be fired. What game you may ask? Holton had times where he wanted to snap out and call out foul play or politics. He thought that because he knew how to talk the talk of the higher ups, he would get a fair shake. Coach Holton had gone to the championship and sent off a good number of seniors with scholarships the previous year. However, he was still on probation. He had to win and there were starting to be rumbles of his intelligence for his questionable play calling.

After the Tigers fell short to Quaker Valley, they knew their backs were against the wall. BJ had played another solid game, but the foot was still broke and wouldn't be healing anytime soon. On top of the foot, BJ was still having some stress about the test he had to take to get into college. Tremon and BJ both had been scheduled to take the S.A. T's at the end of the year. Rory and BJ still took the tutoring for testing with the computer teacher after school. The two seniors that had been watching on the sidelines were just about to be inserted into the lineup. Dougie and DeJon had patiently waited for the moment to come back to the team.

The assistant principal Mr. Mendoza came into the room and met with both seniors.

"DeJon and Dougie come back here I need to talk to you."

He said knowing he had to break the news to the two seniors. "DeJon your eligible to play this week against Ellwood."

DeJon was ecstatic! He walked out with a face that was full of relief.

"Dougie, I need to talk to you." Mr. Mendoza said. "You're not going to be able to come back this year."

Dougie's eyes were starting to turn red, and it look like he had to throw up.

"What you mean?" He asked Mendoza.

"You missed too many days." Mendoza replied. "I'm sorry Doug."

Dougie Benson looked around in the office as if he knew it was his last day in school.

"If I'm not playing then I'm out. He said looking in the eyes of DeJon and the principals.

Mr. Mendoza and DeJon tried to stop him. It was too late. Dougie's spirit was broken. He couldn't show his emotions in front of everyone. Coach Holton got the message and he to became angry. In his mind he was thinking, *why didn't they tell me earlier?*

"I got a three -year starter coming back that would help this team," Coach Holton couldn't believe it.

When BJ heard the news, selfishly all he thought about was how it would affect the team. Never once did he ask how Dougie was feeling overall until he went to Cassie's house that night.

"That dude might not come back to school babe." He spoke.

"Why didn't he just go to school?"

BJ new she was right, but he had to defend his boy's position.

"It's bullshit! They don't want us to win!" He yelled.

BJ would go on and on about how the system was against Coach Holton and Dougie because they were black men. When you're 17 you lead with your emotions more than you should. Patience is an expression of wisdom. BJ wasn't trying to wait to see how Dougie's senior year would turn out. He thought there were puppet masters trying to damage Coach Holton's record. He also thought that Dougie would become a statistic to the Beaver Falls streets... 7th Avenue University, or Johnnie's Bar's (which is Beaver Falls Bar) newest regular attendee! He thought Dougie's departure was based off racism instead of looking at Dougie for not coming to school. He had watched Dougie get the girls Monday thru Friday and Friday nights he would get interceptions.

"It's not over for him though babe." Cassie said back. "If he wants it, he'll try to get his grades up and go to college."

She had a point. Coach Holton had a job to do. It was his job to persuade Dougie not to give up and to come back and try to get into a college. Dougie had enough footage of him playing his junior year to get into a two-year school or a small four-year college. He had decent size and he had the heart of a great-white shark. Dougie had a lot of Tyrell Goosby in him-- meaning he was naive to the fact the world was much bigger than the Falls. There was a whole world waiting for Dougie Benson's gifts. The community and the program had fattened him up socially to get slaughtered.

Dougie was a great English student who didn't mind reading and writing. He also had the street smarts to mingle with college kids. Was he ready socially? We knew academically he was behind, but he was far from slow mentally. What was Dougie going to do now? What was the team going to do with his absence? Austin played running back temporarily since Dougie was out. His 220lbs. frame was hard to tackle but the team needed more speed to hit the outside. Now his running back position seemed permanent. That night BJ cried in Cassie's arms was because he realized how Dougie would not be a part of his last days as a Tiger. Dougie Benson was a huge part of the boy's growth on and off the field. He added life to the locker room and wisdom on the field.

"Sometimes the signs for our paths to greatness or failure are side by side. You have to look closely because they look similar when you're moving fast."- B.J. Tench.

When DeJon Alford came back, he assumed his starting position in the defensive backfield was a given. He had shown repeatedly he had all the gifts to be a great high school corner back (which was a defensive back position). He was the fastest on the team, one of the hardest hitters and had great instincts. It didn't hurt that he was 6 ft. tall. In 2002 defensive backs were typically 5'8" to 5'11". It was his time, right?

"Alford you're playing junior varsity this week." One of the assistant coaches said.

"Who playing J.V.?" DeJon replied.

"You DeJon…." Coach said unapologetically.

"No, the hell I'm not!" DeJon said back. "What the hell is wrong with y'all?"

DeJon was livid. He dropped a couple "F" bombs as he became belligerent.

"Is this the shit I came back for?" He said pacing back and forth outside the locker room.

DeJon and the coaching staff would go back and forth for about 10 minutes. The word got back to his grandfather. DeJon's grandfather was a huge supporter of the Beaver Falls football program and a good friend of "Broadway" Joe Namath. His grandfather wanted to punch Holton and his staff in the mouth. DeJon and his grandfather knew that he came back to Beaver Falls due to the bounty that was out on him. He couldn't go back to Aliquippa now. He didn't want to either. He wanted to play with his childhood friends. He went to camp and completed all the requirements he needed to play the rest of the year. In his mind, he should have been a three - year starter. He had proved he was worthy to see the field by the end of his sophomore year. He left went to a rival school, had some setbacks and--- boom! Back to square one again! His last name should have been Adversity instead of Alford because he couldn't escape it. If he got on the field immediately it might have ruffled some folk's feathers. The Tigers needed to win to get in the playoffs. It's not like DeJon missed four weeks and didn't show up to practice. He paid his dues, and he wasn't getting his chance to showcase himself for colleges. Like Dougie, he had the perfect size and speed to play college ball. He also was highly intelligent… just uninterested in the education system at BFHS.

The Tigers ended up whooping the Ellwood City Wolverines. DeJon ended up playing. He played out of position. He was a linebacker. Austin had to catch him up to speed by helping him understand the defensive sets and calls. DeJon was a football player. He was ticked off that he wasn't one of the safeties or corners.

"If you're an athlete you know how to make adjustments." BJ told Tremon after the game.

"DeJon played very well." Tremon said.

Potter connected with both Tremon and Rory for big plays. BJ, DeJon, Macklin, and Blaire Ameen anchored the defense. The sophomores also stepped up. Shawn Curry and Reshaun Taylor both had game changing plays on offense and defense. This was a good conference win but the big one was next week. Next week was Homecoming and guess who was invited to dinner?

It wasn't the Brady Bunch or the Jacksons... it was the Quips. All week the hype had been once again leaning more towards the Quips. They were the number two team in the state this year and they had a few bones to pick with the Tigers. The two losses from the previous year and the McDonald's brawl. This was perfect propaganda for a homecoming game in the fall. The boys had to get clean before they could get dirty on the field. What's that mean? In some neighborhoods, young men of color like to dress up if their families have the financial ability. There are other times when an older male in the family may give his family member a suit or tuxedo. We call them hand-me-downs. After that, some guys go get their haircut at the barbershop, or they do it themselves. Calvin, Rory, and

Darren Shakespeare all could cut hair and didn't mind shaping up BJ if it was an emergency.

Sabrina Timmons could also cut a little bit. He even had a loyal barber Ms. Susanne at Jackson's Barber shop on the main avenue: Ms. Tricia Keaton who had been cutting his hair since he was a child. Beaver Falls was full of barbers. When the haircut is done, the suits come on. Hopefully, you showered, and you are officially clean! That's what getting clean meant to the boys in B.F.

The homecoming court was set. BJ, Tremon, Regis, Rory, Darren, and Macklin were all chosen by some of their senior female classmates. Calvin Jackson was chosen last year by one of the seniors. BJ was blindsided by the idea of going because he assumed no one would ask out of respect for Cassie and his relationship. BFHS was considered on the small side for school sizes. People knew who was dating who. There were enough lids for every jar, so he assumed all the gals would find a nice escort.

Lisa Teflon had not asked anyone to be her escort. She was a straight A student who had just lost her mother a few months back. Knowing her, she was probably more focused on her future and masking the pain of losing a loved one. All the guys loved Lisa. She was soft spoken, slow to speak, even keel, and very humble. She was always willing to help the next student. She, like Regis and Darren were teens your parents would want you to hang around.

"Hey, BJ." Lisa said one day in the hallway before fourth block. "Can I talk to you after school?"

BJ nodded his head and said "Sure."

BJ thought it was going to be about a fool trying to push up on her. He started to game plan early on who it could have been and how he would handle the situation. After school, the two met in the lounge area of the school.

"Would you be my escort to the homecoming formal?" Lisa asked.

BJ cracked a smile and started to laugh.

"Why are you laughing?" She asked him as he looked up at the banners being hung for homecoming. "I know you're busy and it's a late notice."

BJ cut her off with a look of relief on his face.

"Lis, yes of course!" He exclaimed. "I thought I was going to have to kill somebody."

Lisa thanked BJ for his concern. Sometimes girls have struggles with self-esteem and confidence due to their counterparts not ensuring their safety. Beaver Falls was small in stature, large in character...especially the 2003 class. From the most-mute soul to the largest ego, bullies, antagonists, and school terrorists were very silent that year. Not quite Utopia, but far from disorganization. If someone was getting mistreated, it was in the dark or kept secret.

When BJ told Cassie the news that night after practice, she had mixed emotions. It wasn't that she wasn't happy for BJ being selected. She just had to put her emotions in neutral due to the circumstances.

"Didn't her mother just pass away?" Cassie asked.

There was a pause and then a deep breath. "I like her, she's sweet." She persisted in her thought. "It's just every time I turn around, you're going to another dance, or dinner, or formal with someone else."

Cassie was right for feeling that way.

BJ had to think fast on his feet.

"You don't think she trying to make a move, do you?" He asked.

Cassie shook her head. "Nah, it's not that, it's just... damn, man!" She said.

"I'm trying to talk to Principal K to see if he will let underclassmen go to the Prom this year." He quickly said back to her.

He could see that she was using discernment in BJ's endeavors. She didn't want to seem jealous. She also didn't want to ignore the fact that in the past two years she has had to be the trusting girlfriend that seemed like a push over. BJ had to ensure that Cassie's understanding of her role was illuminated.

"I promise, I'm not trying to walk over you or make you mad."

In a sense BJ looked like a sucker. In another sense, he looked like the captain who wanted a co-captain soon. That night the two talked about kids, marriage, college and roles being reversed.

"One day I'm going to be away, and God help me!" BJ said.

"What you mean?" Cassie asked.

"I don't know how I'm going to hold it together." He said back. "It will be your turn to exercise your right to be the upper classmen, the big dog--"

"And B.J.'s girl!" She said with a smirk on her face.

Cassie Washington was very analytical when it came to dissolving the possibility of breaking up. There were several times they wanted to face the music of ending their run at being high school sweethearts. One of the two would ensure that would never happen. *"I'm not going anywhere,"* would be said by one of them. The crazy thing was, at that time they both equally meant it. In B.J.'s mind, he believed God would pull a chess move and get him into a school that had a great holiday schedule. He would travel to and from school to see her. In Cassie's mind, she would continue to study hard, pray hard, and grow as an individual.

While BJ and Cassie's handprints were drying on the school's Hollywood walk of Fame, Rory, and his new girlfriend Sharice Winters were the new hot topic. Sharice was a 4.1 gifted student who turned heads. She was humble and naïve. Rory would challenge her to use her common sense more than her book smarts. Rory knew how to use his smarts in both areas. Rory Santiago was the course she couldn't study for. He kept her thinking 24/7. Sharice was also more secure in her character than Kristi-Ann. She had typical high school girl issues at home but in school she was more focused. She understood Rory had his priorities in line so, she didn't mind him going to the homecoming with another girl. She wasn't on the court anyway, but she could have caused a scene. She didn't... she played the background and she played it well.

The homecoming court was set for the evening. The game had yet to be played. BJ Timmons had a metaphor that would shock the world that afternoon at the pep rally. He would hype of the student body by guaranteeing a hard-hitting game, but it was what he said to end the rally.

"We're going to take them to IRAQ. (I. Run. All. Quips.)!"

The children went bananas, the teachers were looking around to make sure their ears weren't failing them. Keep in mind at that time, terrorism was in the front of everyone's brains post 911. BJ's metaphor was risky. "Let's take them to war!"

The theme song Eye of the Tiger from the epic film *Rocky III* played and the students were dismissed early.

After the ceremony in school BJ took pictures with Tremon, Cassie, Lisa and a couple other students.

"You're crazy!" Cassie said to BJ when he finished taking the photos.

"I'll see you tonight babe after the game." BJ said back to Cassie.

"It's kill or be killed." Dre Lee interrupted the two from talking.

Everyone was just so hyped for the game. Dre Lee was a transfer, but he already understood the climate of that rivalry.

When it was time for the game, all the Tigers patiently waited to begin. Coach Holton had done some pep talks before the game. The seniors had been zoned out since Wednesday. When the bus arrived at the locker room at Geneva College, the Quips were already getting dressed to take the field for stretching. The problem was, they were in the wrong locker room. There was some woofing from both teams and the coaches made sure the Tigers stayed on the bus. Not that there would have been a brawl, but hey-- anything could have happened!

The captains for the game were BJ, Blaire Ameen, Tremon and DeJon. It was as if time was suspended when the referees brought the players to the middle of the field.

One of the Quip players stated, "It's just a game."

BJ waived off the handshakes and said, "Let's go."

It was very immature looking in hindsight. In the moment, BJ wasn't focused on looking foolish. He was more focused on intimidating the opposition. The rain started to fall, and the Tigers took advantage of it. Tremon and Rory both tore into the defense with tremendous wide receiving plays and running after they caught the ball. BJ, Macklin, and Blaire had two strong stances on defense. Jordan Potter, in the rain, was on fire. The Tigers were up 14 to nothing on their way to score another touchdown. Between DeJon's kick off returning ability, Tremon's dangerous play making ability and Rory's leaping ability, the Quips had no answer. The Tigers were on the Quips three-yard line. If the Tigers would have scored another touchdown, the game would start to seem out of reach, especially with the October rain coming down.

The Tigers had big strong running backs to punch it in for the death blow. Austin Macklin was 6 ft 2" 220 lbs., Shawn Curry was 6 ft 3" 210 pounds, Reshaun Taylor was close to 190 pounds, Jordan Potter was over 200 pounds. BJ was a Tight End next to Blaire Ameen. *Just run the ball* Is what most people would think. Coach Holton called a slant pattern to Rory Santiago and the shifted change following Aliquippa's 107-yard interception returned. The whole Beaver Falls crowd section had become silent. The Aliquippa side erupted. They had built momentum. The Tigers made a couple crucial mistakes on their own side of the field. Tigers fell short with a score of 30-14. The number two team in the state knew they ran into a tough Beaver Falls team. When BJ came home, he was detached emotionally.

"If my foot was healthy, we'd win easily." He said firmly.

"No doubt, why would he call that play? Pastor Timmons asked BJ before he went to bed.

"I don't know honestly." BJ said.

The Tigers could not afford to lose any more games, or they would possibly be bounced out from playoff contention. The following week, both Tremon and BJ were players of the game against the Center Trojans. Tremon on offense and BJ on Defense. Macklin and Blaire made BJ's life easier. The two seniors quietly were having a tremendous defensive year. Blaire wasn't the hardest worker in practice, but he was coachable. Since grade school the only thing you could criticize Blaire for was lack of hustle at times. Macklin's shoulder was heeling slowly but his name was becoming more noticeable to the recruiting circuits due to his track accolades on top of his weight room numbers rising. He was one of the top recruits and never really comprehended the fact that his ceiling was raising.

"Senior night baby, one last time at Reeves!" He said to BJ the Thursday morning before senior night.

Senior night and the last time the 2003 class would ever take the field at "Reeves" Stadium (Geneva College). Tremon, Rory, BJ, Blaire, DeJon and Macklin would all join hands in prayer before the game against Freedom. BJ Timmons led the team in prayer and Macklin gave a heartfelt speech heightened the moment. The team trashed the home locker room. Macklin broke the black board and front door. Full of excitement, DeJon and BJ threw garbage cans and broke one of the lights. There would have to been some explaining after the game.

Following the internal mosh in the locker room the seniors lined up to walk out with their parents. It was a time to reflect on the journey and to be grateful for the loved ones who walked aside of your journey. The parents were full of emotions. Some of the boys had been playing organized football since they were six. Players like Tremon and DeJon had played together since they were pee-wees. Macklin and Rory did not start their journeys with the Tigers, but they had represented the orange and black to the fullest. Dre Lee was a first year Tiger, and he put his blood, sweat and tears into the year.

One last time to take the field at Reeves stadium and to keep their playoff hopes alive.

The Game would go back and forth with the Freedom Bulldogs. Tremon and Rory for the most part dominated. Potter looked dapper and had put on a clinic for patient quarterbacking. He was precise and full of confidence. On Defense Blaire Ameen was "lights out." Between he and Timmons the Tigers were anchored by stellar play. Towards the end of the fourth quarter, the Tigers had a ten-point lead. Freedom was on the charge and was gaining momentum. Austin Macklin would come into the huddle and call the defensive play. The play was designed for

DeJon to drop back into coverage, Shawn Curry was supposed to blitz one gap and BJ was supposed to slant the opposite way.

To the reader, it sounds simple... but between the crowd, the band, the coaches, the opposite team yelling and your nerves. The speed of the game for a sophomore goes so fast. Shawn Curry was an explosive six-foot three monster who depended on his athleticism to get past his opponent. BJ had a broken foot and if it were not for his experience and upper body strength, he would have been a half step behind his opponent.

The Freedom quarterback would holler the cadence behind his center. The ball was hiked, and the chase was on. BJ would grab a hold of the quarterback along with Macklin. As BJ got ready to swing around the quarterback for the sack... *Boom*, then a *crack!* The boom was Curry's helmet hitting the back and side of BJ's knee.

The crack was the BJ Timmons's ACL/MCL.

"Aww shit!" BJ yelled. "No! God no..." He screamed through his helmet rolling around on the wet field.

Player after player would get up as his parents watched from the top row.

"I know that ain't BJ." Pastor Timmons said to his wife. "Get up BJ!" Pastor Timmons called to his son.

In denial, BJ's father thought his son was probably just cramping or a little stinger. Players would start to surround BJ. The trainer would attend BJ. Blaire Ameen, Tremon and Shane would be the three players BJ notice in his agony. Shane's face was speechless, and he became tearful.

Blaire Ameen started to tear up also. "Timmons man…" He said with puzzled look.

It was as if Blaire saw more than just a bent-up knee. Maybe he had been stunned in a trance. He saw his middle school rival, his teammate, his friend, his captain, and his brother hurt. BJ's eyes started to close in disbelief. The foot in his mind was bad enough and it was even starting to heal… now this? Where was Cassie?

After the coaches and the training staff took BJ to the sideline. Rory came up to BJ as his head was down and said, "We got this for you. I promise bro!"

The amazing thing about that moment was Rory was on the sideline at the time cramping up in his legs. The trainers had given him some bananas to help. Rory would deliver his promise. He caught the pass to seal the victory. As BJ started to rap his knee with ice, he heard a mob of teens behind him. Cassie's cousin Marco would get into a fight with a freshman. She was caught in the middle trying to calm him down. She didn't notice who had got hurt until the busses started to load to go home. BJ didn't even go back to the locker room. He went home. He would sleep in the basement watching the local news.

The cordless phone rang, and it was Cassie. That night, the girl who barely made a mistake through their two years of dating, the one who recorded BJ's games and was his biggest fan, had no answers for her not attending his aide during the game.

"Where was you?" He asked her.

"Marco and Chuck started arguing and one thing led to another." She quickly answered. "I had to break it up or at least try to! They almost knocked me down the steps."

BJ became furious. "You mean to tell me that's what stopped you from coming down to check on me?" He said pounding his chest.

"Babe after I saw your dad down there, I didn't want the coaches and police to stop me."

She was right but BJ wasn't hearing now. BJ was scared and mad. He didn't want to admit he was scared, so he doubled down on the mad.

"Bull!"

The two began to fight so bad that he couldn't make out what she was saying because she was crying so hard. Ms. Lisa would intervene between the two and advise the two to end the night and cool off. She insisted BJ charge Cassie's inexperience to her age and not her heart. She reassured her daughter loved BJ and he needed to relax. BJ went to bed that night full of questions for God.

"All that work. all that work!" He continued to repeat to himself. He cried himself to sleep.

In life, there are no guarantees. We all expect to have happy endings with no roadblocks. It doesn't work that way. In this instance, BJ was being unreasonable with himself. Yeah, he had a broken foot and now an injured knee. How could he question God? Look, his friend Dougie didn't even get a chance to showcase his talent. What about DeJon who had been bumped

208

around all year and overlooked? Injuries and pain are a part of football.

Rory and Macklin both had been in and out of the training room. Who did BJ think he was to question The Almighty? He needed to be reminded like Job in the Holy Bible (JOB chapter 38:1-18). Better yet, here's a question for BJ: what about all the young men and women who suffer from head injuries or were paralyzed? In his homelife, he never went a day without a home cooked meal, fresh clothes, and parents who gave a damn. He had a great young girlfriend who recorded all his games, so much so that colleges were still contacting him with the broken foot. The Freedom coach would turn his name in for player of the game and honorable mention for the All-Star games following the football season. He had a lot to be thankful for even in a time like this. Yet, you're 17 you don't always see it that way.

BJ would eventually see a doctor and his football season was cut short. Coach Holton never called to see what the status was. He assumed that BJ would risk his future by playing in the Beaver game. If the Tigers won, they would go on to play South Catholic in the first round. If not, their season was over. Pastor Timmons, the athletic director at Beaver Falls and Coach Holton would have a meeting. Pastor Timmons let Holton know he didn't appreciate him not checking on his son. He also let him know he didn't appreciate him trying to belittle BJ last year in the playoff game. Finally, he assured him that he had no way of getting in the way of BJ's future.

"You think you going to break my boy?" He said to Coach Holton. "You can't stop what God has already done."

Holton would say back to him, "I thought you were a reverend. Why are you so hostile?"

Pastor Timmons would let him know. "I ain't Jesus."

BJ had been a four-year member of the Tigers program. He had busted his tail trying to improve his talent. Holton looked at him as a cash cow who he no longer needed. Therefore, it was time to move on. Later, Calvin Jackson, Tremon and many other men would come to realization. Very rarely do high school coaches care about their athletes after their last game therefore, the family dynamic is so important.

The Tigers would fall short against Beaver. DeJon played lights out on both offense and Defense. BJ observed his classmates and teammates from the sideline with crutches. He hugged Rory, DeJon, Blaire, Macklin and Tremon. He told them he loved them and boarded the van with tears coming down his face. He knew that the coaches gave up on the season too soon. One may ask, how do you know? The previous week DeJon had been singled out during practice for not going 100%. The coaches told Macklin to run him over as if DeJon didn't hear them... or they thought he was that weak. DeJon ended up being the aggressor and was kicked out of practice for it. The hit was so hard that Macklin wanted to fight him following the practice. If it weren't for Tremon and BJ they wanted to kick him off the team. Tremon informed the coaches that they needed DeJon to win. Tremon also thought the coaches wanted to go to the playoffs and win it all.

He was sadly mistaken.

The week before that, Macklin, and BJ both said they would go play the line for the sake of the team. The offensive coordinator shut this idea down. Why? Because they were done with this 2003 class. They came in cocky and brash. They left out just as cocky and now they were men. If these boys weren't raised right, a few times they may have assaulted some of these young assistant coaches. They were in their 20's and some of them hadn't ever achieved what these young teens would later achieve. No matter what, these men would look at this year as a disappointment however they passed their test. They were all college bound if they handled the off the field stuff. In theory all they had to do was come to school and not get into any trouble. For these young men, it was only one season ending and off to another.

"A New Life"

"Little Moses Jackson is so cute!" Cassie said as BJ entered the slide door with a slow limp and crutches.

"That boy Calvin is a father, yo!" He said back to her. "Can you believe it?"

She nodded her head. "Where's Calvin going to school?"

BJ shrugged his shoulders with a look of discernment.

"I believe he's looking at Robert Morris, Temple and some other small division one schools." He said reading a "Sports Illustrated" magazine with Reggie Bush on it.

"Robert Morris is close, isn't it?" Cassie asked as she helped BJ Timmons elevate his gimp leg.

"Yeah, it's about 25 minutes up the road. It's in Moon township."

"So...How's that knee feeling?" She asked.

"You really want to know?" He asked back abruptly.

Before Cassie could answer, her statement was intercepted.

"It sucks!" BJ said.

He would later complain about the feeling of being unbalanced with the knee and the fractured foot.

"So, what now?" She asked.

"What you mean what now?" BJ began to get antsy with his answering.

"Have you heard back from any schools?" She said with a concerned look.

"Syracuse, Wisconsin, Purdue and Pitt all said we will keep you in mind." BJ said. "Politely, they all said have a nice life."

BJ would make the rest of the evening uncomfortable. His freshman girlfriend had felt the level of comfort becoming more and more unsure. BJ would become difficult to be around the next few weeks. His basketball hopes were down the drain, and he wasn't being honest with Cassie about feeling broken emotionally. He was angry that he couldn't have one more crack at a championship with his boys. His junior year went fast, and it was unclear how good he could truly be. BJ wanted the challenge of proving Demona wrong. BJ felt he and Regis could duplicate what Carlos and Tyrell did the previous year. Nothing against those two because physically they were more imposing and appeared to be better, but with Calvin and Tremon's leadership those two along with Allan and they thought would be DeJon. Demona could have had a great senior line up. Good- byes are a part of life. If BJ wanted to have a head start on his college football career, he would have to face the music and walk away from organized b-ball. He would have to rehab that knee and start a new life.

As for his childhood buddies, Allan Fife, Regis, Tremon and Calvin they were getting ready for hoops. Between BJ's injury, Dougie, A.B. and Shakespeare's early retirement, DeJon's reputation from the coaches and Rory's unwillingness to try out. The Beaver Falls basketball team went from a senior led team to a new breed of Tiger starters. Jordan Potter and Brandon McDowell would become key pieces. The newest acquisition was probably the best one. Lance Jamison the freshman man-child. He was big, strong, fast, and very crafty with the ball. If it weren't for Tremon and Calvin, he probably would have been the go-to player as a 14- year- old.

If BJ wasn't hurt and Dougie didn't withdraw from school. If it were a perfect world, Coach Demona would have eight seniors that had been playing together for years. Can you imagine 8 seniors at practice working hard? Calvin who was a natural floor leader could of have been able to utilize his teammates. He could have been the kid that was spoiled with too many gifts. Tremon was also a natural leader being a safety and quarterback in football. Man, it could of all been so simple! Life has a funny way of seeming perfect at one point. Then a sudden change of direction happens.

Regis would become more comfortable with the understanding that his athletic catalog was ending, and his academic excellence was beginning to become more advance. "Man-Man" (Regis) would be the utility guy of the Beaver Falls basketball team. He wasn't the same player he was in his younger days, however his basketball IQ. was still there. The only problem with Regis was balancing his time between band, National Honor Society, president of this, president of that, and basketball. Coach Demona didn't seem understanding. On paper Regis was the perfect scholar. However, coach wanted more of his athletic attention. Regis was fully aware that his bread was buttered through education. Reg would put up with the sarcasm and passive aggressiveness from the coaches. Regis a.k.a. "Man- Man" was named this for a reason.

Calvin and Tremon would dominate the headlines for the first few weeks. Coach Demona knew this backcourt could take them all the way. All they had to do was focus on making each other better and stay out of trouble! Avoiding trouble was simple. Staying out of it was another. Calvin was on the *"Players to Watch"* list in both The Pittsburgh Post-Gazette and Pittsburgh Tribune for the pre-season. The newspapers Came to Beaver County to take pictures of him and interview him for his upcoming season. Tremon had just came off a tremendous football season and was highly considered for all state recognition.

During the pre-season Calvin "Hollywood" Jackson rolled through teams with his floor general characteristics and his athleticism. Off the court, he was working part time, learning how to cope with an older woman, trying his best to deal with the reality of being a father, and still maintaining healthy boundaries with his mother. She was proud of her son. He could have taken a couple quicker paths to make money. He could have been to juvenile hall or in someone's court room several of times. He wasn't-- he cut hair on the side, cut grass, and almost never cut class. He was still a lady's man who had a way with women. However, his way with words would catch up with him.

One Friday afternoon, Calvin came to see his Algebra teacher about a misunderstanding. He was having a hard time understanding his grade on his report card. Ms. Fieldsman, the Algebra teacher, was wondering why Calvin's attitude was in rare form this afternoon. Could it have been something home related? Was it his woman friend, Bianca? Maybe he was feeling the weight of being a senior point guard with little time left on the recruiting timeline No. Calvin was angry for Ms. Fieldsman giving him a C instead of the B he had been promised. Now, BJ was not there. However, he had heard Calvin's voice yelling some curse words and saying he didn't care, from his last period theater class. "

"Yo!" BJ said from the third floor. "What happened?"

A senior classmate came up to BJ and filled him in.

"He wrote on the board, 'I'LL BLOW THIS BITCH UP!'

"No, no, no!" BJ said to the girl.

The local news stations fled the lounge. There was talk about Calvin going to jail and being expelled from school the following Monday. All the male teachers and administrators were waiting for the Beaver Falls Bomber to arrive at the school. The climate in 2003 was too hot for terrorist talk. Bomb threats and school shootings started to become more and more popular. This was a profoundly serious offense. Calvin being a man of color and a star athlete would become public enemy number one.

"What the hell is wrong with him?" DeJon said.

Cassie came up to BJ as he walked closer to the commotion in the hallway.

"Go back to class, I don't know what is about to happen!" He yelled, pointing towards where her next class was.

She put up a little argument, but she could see that the tension thickened. There were too many men lined up to talk to one teenager. Lance, the freshman superstar also had no clue what was happening. Regis and Tremon would get the news later.

"His mouth finally got him into some real mess." The principal said.

When BJ Timmons got home, he shared the information with his father.

"I got to go see that boy." His father said. "He probably thinks the whole world is against him right now."

His father was right. Calvin had blown a fuse. It was very necessary for BJ's father to go see a young man who was truly at risk. Calvin knew he had made a mistake. No one knew the root of his frustration that day. Pastor Timmons met with Calvin at his grandmother's home. Calvin needed all the support he could get. When Pastor came back home, and BJ came back from Cassie's house they discussed Calvin's plan.

"They are probably going to try to kick that dude off the team indefinitely." Pastor said.

"Nah, it wasn't that serious!" BJ said.

"BJ when you say you'll blow this B.I.T.C.H. up..." his fathered interrupted him.

"But dad!" BJ said.

"Look man, I'm just telling you how this thing goes." His father replied.

"They been waiting for the day they could tell Calvin, 'YOU'RE DONE'." BJ became emotional, like Calvin had been sentenced to life in prison. It might have well been the sentence that he feared for his friend. Time wasn't on Calvin's side at all.

The Devil has a way of putting roadblocks on your path to greatness. For some people it's sex. Others it may be alcohol, weed, coke or worse. For Calvin it was the man in the mirror chained with the favoritism of being an athlete. Calvin was favored by God initially when he came from the home he did and maintained to fly straight this long. He was able to stay drug free and thug-free for the most part. However, he couldn't see the tokenism that some of his classmates put on him. Calvin had a way as mentioned before to sit with anyone. He chose some days to sit with the athletes. Other days he would sit with the "sistas" from the hood. Most of the time he said with upper class white folk during lunch. It wasn't like he thought he was better, right? Regardless how he felt, it was time to put him in timeout and the official game would restart, the game of life. In hindsight, Calvin was competing with himself because he wanted that B. He had the smarts to get an A. He didn't like being shown up by anyone. Dougie had the same mentality, and Rory, and DeJon too. They may have not always articulated it well. The guys all wanted to prove their critics wrong. So now the Tigers had to wait to see what the verdict was on "Hollywood Jackson."

The ruling from the school board was 30 plus -day suspension. He would miss some important games in the next few weeks. Including the away game at Aliquippa. Tremon who enjoyed competition, took on the challenge. He, Allan, and Regis would take a lot more shots in the offense. The man-child known as Lance Jamison started to rise to prominence. The night of the Aliquippa game no one anticipated what Tremon had in store. He would score 41 points and lead the Tigers to victory. There was some buzz around town that the Tigers would lose because they had two stand out guards that had division one potential. That night, Barksdale with a side of Jamison and Fife was all the Tigers needed. Tremon played the game of his life. It was after the game the Tigers had to be worried about.

"They are talking about rumbling if they lose." DeJon said to BJ in the stands.

BJ responded back to his friend, "Like they always said they are.

BJ knew his knee was still being rehabbed and had the thought of being jumped in the back of his mind. "

If they play it cool, then I'm going to play it cool."

"As long as nobody don't come at my cousin!" DeJon said.

Following the game there was some mean mugs and some few harsh words thrown in DeJon's direction but thankfully nothing jumped off.

Cassie's aunt Virginia was BJ's ride home.

"That damn DeJon is always in some mess." Her Aunt Virginia said.

"What you mean?" BJ said in the front seat.

"BJ, he's bad news."

BJ started to turn around and look at Cassie, he was shaking his head in disappointment. She was prejudging him because her husband and in-laws were all from Quip.

"Why can't he be like Carlos and Bullet?" She continued.

She went on and on until BJ snapped. "We ain't like them niggas!" BJ yelled punching the glove compartment. "Maybe that's why!" He said adamantly. "Everyone is scared of them, not us!"

She cut BJ off. "This is my car, you got to control your temper! You see, those boys in Aliquippa they have it rougher than you. You and Tremon, and DeJon…you guys got it good!".

"Aye, I'm not from Beaver Falls." BJ said. "You think they the only black folks in Pennsylvania that got issues? Where I'm from they're domesticated... and never forget that Ms. Virginia!"

There was little conversation the remainder of the ride home. When BJ and Cassie got back to her house, BJ continued to vent.

"Who the hell she think we is?" He said to Cassie. Cassie tried her best to stay out of it. BJ was livid. "She loves them dudes. I bet she want you to be with one of them." He turned the argument on her. He was wrong, once again.

Dealing with your girlfriend's family can be challenging at times. There are ways teenagers must navigate through unnecessary arguments. That night, BJ was supposed to thank Cassie for remaining silent and be grateful they didn't tag team him in the car. BJ wouldn't have been cool with that, but she could have. She loved that man, and it was another lesson for BJ to realize who was risking turmoil in their own family and who had his back for real. BJ hated the way some adults looked at DeJon. By this time, DeJon and BJ were on their way to being grown men. He had been cool with this man for years now. Who were they to judge him? And if he were that bad, wouldn't his parents be the judge of that?

DeJon's reputation might have been misunderstood by some, but he had a lot of genuine friends. Regis and Darren Shakespeare were two of the most trusted young men in all the land. They rode with DeJon through the good, the bad, and the ugly. If he were that much of a criminal, he would have been in someone's jail cell by now. The boys in BF knew some young men who had already had a crime resume. Their paths were already leading them to prison. Not DeJon-- not yet at least. He was loved at the same time as he was feared. Tremon was his cousin, and he too knew that his cousin was getting an unfair story behind him. Hopefully, his story would continue to be written and narrated.

Calvin would go to open gym and work out with Carlos Clemon's college teammates. LaRoche college was a small Pittsburgh school with some decent athletes. Calvin would come back home and admit the competition was too easy. Question, did anyone offer to have him try out bigger schools such as Pitt University, Temple (Philadelphia) or a private work out with Duquesne? Sure, he was banned from going to practice and his name had soured in some college circles. However, there were some notable black men who had been to bigger schools and had some pull. You would have to ask Calvin to see if they reached out.

"Hell, Nah!" Calvin said to his buddy afternoon when Calvin was shaping up BJ. "Ain't nobody said shit. They happy man, it's Tre's team now. I wish them boys the best. I'll be back."

BJ asked him one night, "What do you want to do with your life when this thing is over?"

Calvin said, "I want to take up accounting or business management."

For Calvin to already know what he wanted to take up was levels above the average teenager in his quote-on-quote condition. He already knew he was good with numbers. He wanted to be great. He knew when he came back from suspension, he would have to take a new approach with school administrators.

As for BJ, his knee was still dislocating as he walked on the regular. He would discuss, his future with Austin Macklin. Austin was also rehabbing a messed-up shoulder.

Macklin asked him one morning. "What was CJ thinking? I wish I was there. I would have erased that crap! I don't want that dude to end up in Falls …"

"I think he knows he messed up bro." BJ said.

"What schools is looking at you still?"

"Me and my dad going to Dayton University Saturday for an official visit." He answered. "Then next month, I'm going to Massachusetts and the Shipyard in VA."

"The Shipyard?" Macklin said.

"Yeah, it's the Apprentice." BJ said. "It's like a smaller version of the Navy. They pay you and everything."

"You know Cassie ain't going for that." Macklin said. "They barely come home, bro. "What happened with Youngstown State and West Virginia State?"

"If I went to Youngstown, they want me to walk on first because of the injury." BJ said. "I would obviously be up there with Bibby (Rory). West Virginia Tech is looking at Dre Lee."

"Holla at ya Boy!" Macklin said. "I think I'm going to Youngstown State."

"These S.A. T's. are killing me right now!" BJ said. "If I keep bombing these tests, I'm going the junior college route. There is one in Arizona, Kansas, and New York. Coach Holton wants Blaire (Ameen) and DeJon to go."

BJ continued to go on like a nervous wreck. "Dejon needs to go! That dude got speed, he just got to beef up and put some muscle on. Blaire can go anywhere." He said. "Blaire been hanging with Toni Byers lately."

BJ changed the subject. "Blaire ain't never hang with them dudes."

"A.B. said he been hanging with them dudes heavy lately." Macklin said. "You know how Blaire is, he just wants something to drink and chill. He used to hang up Bibby's spot, but now Bibby got Sharice and Youngstown on his mind."

Blaire and DeJon had to find out how they were going to spend the rest of their Beaver Falls High School days now that they didn't decide to play basketball. They both should have met with Regis to see how they could enhance their study habits. Both these young men were lost in their new lives. Blaire was already 18 and DeJon would be 18 that upcoming Christmas. Darren "Shakes" could have met with them and told them how he was looking into Edinboro University in Erie, PA. It was close enough to home and far enough to build your own identity.

Both these brothas were in contact with A B (Ascheley Brown) on the regular. Blaire received some paperwork to look at Thaddeus Stevens near Philly. Instead of working on his body and getting ready for collegiate football, Blaire would start to learn the streets more. DeJon would also become more accustomed to being alone. Both these young men were always keeping the lonely feeling inside. They would release their anxiety on themselves by constantly being on the wrong side of the tracks. Blaire didn't have the strongest support system. He was like a big foster child in a sense. He had a home, but he didn't. You could find him just about anywhere. Men gravitate to who helps them best to survive. It's the way of life. For Calvin it was being out of school where he would gain some new stripes being around college kids on weekends.

For DeJon, he had just come off an ok year in football-- but let's face it, he got screwed in the end. Blaire had a good year but no real encouragement to go to the next level. For BJ it was his injuries, he had to get ready to move on mentally from feeling sorry for himself for getting hurt. Rory had his own issues at home. Macklin was the fun guy who buried his own disappointments in partying and detaching from society. Tremon, Regis and Allan Fife had to maintain their stewardships on the basketball team as the new year approached. 2002 was ending, 2003 was coming down the pike. It was time for a new year. For these Tigers, it was time for a new life.

"Calvin The Bomber"

When Calvin returned to school, he heard every joke in the book: The Beaver Falls Bomber, Osama Bin Laden, and other similar terrorist names. No more than three days back, he found himself being tempted once again. Reshaun Taylor, a sophomore and Calvin started joking with each other. In Beaver Falls, they called it ripping. Some folks call it ragging, ranking, depending on where you live. Ripping was when you told jokes about some one's ears, hairline, beat up kicks or shoes. If the recipient of the jokes didn't take it too personally, it was all in fun.

That day Reshaun knew that Calvin was fresh off suspension. Calvin wasn't innocent he started to call out Reshaun's initials in acronym form. Reshaun Antonio Taylor was his full name and that day Calvin kept calling him "RAT" From there, Reshaun took the rat jokes personally. Reshaun would approach Calvin and sneak punch him. He knocked off Calvin's glasses. Calvin was restrained by DeJon and a couple other people who didn't want to see Calvin, "The Beaver Falls Bomber" blow himself up. This would have been his third strike for sure. He got into it with a girl during the ethnic relations day. She became overly emotional, and Calvin was the culprit for the commotion. The bomb threat and now this? He had to walk away. Was he mad? Surely, he had to be. Calvin wasn't a fighter, but he would fight you. If this were two years earlier or even a few months ago, those two would have tangoed. Calvin was deceptively strong. You don't jump that high and run that fast for no reason. He had man strength. His pride was hurt but he had to move on. Principal K would praise him for showing some self-control.

Speaking of control, when Calvin came back, he would gain back control on the court. He went back to throwing bombs on the court and blowing up the opposing team's defense. Lance and Tremon would be relieved to have their back-court mate back. Lance was enjoying being the second option in Calvin's absence, and he would continue to blossom as a player. Calvin who was a natural point guard had no issue with getting him open shots where he felt comfortable. He and Tremon would be a little rusty at first, but once the two started clicking, so did the team. Calvin would end his senior season averaging a triple double. That means ten or more points ten or more rebounds and 10 or more assist.

The playoffs would begin with Tigers blowing out a Shenango team who was intimidated by the Tigers defense and Calvin's two thunderous dunks. The Tigers would blow out the Freeport Yellowjackets also. Calvin would find himself up against another opponent that was typically indefensible: the injury bug would strike again. This time it hit Calvin right in his big toe. Anyone who knows basketball, knows feet work is arguably the most important part of hoops. Calvin's toe was questionable for the next game. He had to have a cortisone shot to ease his pain. They had one more game to go before they reached the Western Pennsylvania championship. They would have a rematch against the Sto-Rox Vikings. The Tigers fell short again to a crippled Calvin- led team. Tremon and Lance played great, but the Vikings were more efficient that night. The good news was Calvin, Tremon, Regis and Allan Fife had one more game to lose and it was all over. They were eliminated from the conference playoffs but qualified for the state playoffs. This was their last dance.

"Rev, you going to the game tonight?" DeJon called BJ the night before the big game against the Quips.

"Yeah, they better come with it." BJ said to DeJon.

"I'll be honest, Calvin's foot is serious, DeJon His toe is jacked up."

"Tre and Jamison (Lance) going to have to take them shots." DeJon said.

"Hold on D, I got an incoming call." BJ said.

BJ greeted the other caller.

"Hello?"

"May I speak to BJ Timmons?" The unknown caller said.

BJ asked discerningly. "May I ask whose calling?"

"Yes sir, this is Coach Strong from Dayton University."

BJ asked the coach to hold as he ended the conversation with DeJon.

When he returned to the line, the coach went on to say. "We are extremely interested with bringing you on board with the

Flyers. Have you retaken the S.A.T.'s?"

BJ stated that he was waiting for the results to come in the mail.

"We were very impressed with you and your family when you came to visit." Coach Strong said.

BJ and Pastor Timmons went to the Morehead State (KY) versus Dayton game a few months back. They showed BJ the dorm rooms, cafeteria, weight rooms and a chance to sit on the sidelines. The suspense of college football is amazing. The speed of the game and the impact of the hits is thrilling!

BJ wasn't star struck though. He believed in himself and told his father. "I could definitely play out there with those guys."

Now what about his injury? Did he tell the Dayton defensive coordinator or head coach about his knee? He didn't. he was still optimistic in the rehab and in denial that it would take some time to heal.

"Well, it was good hearing from you and were glad that you still have us on your radar." Coach Strong said.

"Yes sir, I'll stay in touch." BJ said. Now BJ had two things on his brain: the injury and the test results.

BJ's knee, Rory and Macklin's shoulders, Tremon Barksdale's hamstring and now the most prevalent: Calvin Hollywood Jackson's toe. Injuries are a part of sports. Setbacks are a part of life. No one wanted to see him injured right? Calvin had put himself behind the eight ball many of day just due to his attitude. There were other times adults held him back by not scolding him or assisting in molding him. Like a lot of cases in some neighborhoods, Calvin had no father. He had a daddy which was different than a father. You see, a father takes time to raise his children. A daddy takes little time; he just helps making them. He also had two trying grandfathers. Calvin wouldn't admit it back then, but he was grateful for them. Yes, he was hardheaded and very disrespectful at times, but he also shocked people when he showed up ready to do yard work, cook, or shovel neighbor's sidewalks for money. He got that from someone. They were old school and Calvin was new school. A father in his life would have been so helpful during these final moments of high school.

The physical injury was just one issue. The internal strength is more impactful for later years of a man's life. Some hurt and pain help men to shape their character. Calvin had the foundation of work ethic, some faith and foolish pride at times. But now, He was a senior who had waited for these next few weeks his whole life. This included the state playoffs-- a chance to win the championship with his friends. Regis Bolden, Jordan Potter and Allan Fife... he played everything with them and for the most part he had a genuine relationship with these guys. The friendly rivalry that wasn't always friendly with Tremon Barksdale. These two competed at everything. Calvin and Tremon fought, argued and in the end loved each other for who they were. They had different outlooks on life. Calvin being flashier and more outgoing; Tre being more silent and conservative. They both loved ball and equally loved the Falls. It was time to take the court possibly one last time together. That warm night in March came when the Tigers faced the Quips.

The 2002-2003 Beaver Falls Tiger basketball team had their

ups and downs all year. They had lost to the Sharon Tigers, the Quips, Blackhawk, Sto-Rox twice and that was it. They had won 20 games. This game was one for the ages. Calvin, with a messed-up toe and all, put on a show. He was in noticeable pain and was wincing a little, however, he did everything he could to push through.

Regis, Jordan Potter and Brandon McDowell battled with the Aliquippa forwards for rebounds and positioning in the paint (colored area on the court). Lance Jamison the young gun would score over twenty points and played stellar defense. Tre Barksdale had the worst game of his life. He could not buy a bucket. He scored 41 points the last time these two teams squared off. This time he fell well short of that. It wasn't that he was scared. Tremon didn't fear anything, it wasn't even in his vocabulary. Just one of those nights where the ball didn't agree with him. During the game, guess who showed up to gain some star power? Tre and DeJon's good friend Damon Grace. He was yelling absurd comments at half time and the whole second half.

"They going to have throwback Beaver Falls Jersey's with Barksdale and Jackson on the back of it."

"Aye yo, I got a number ten Beaver Falls Jersey with Barksdale jersey for fifty bucks.... "Going once, twice.... Sold to the bums over there!"

BJ and DeJon sitting side by side was anticipating shutting up Mr. Grace if something popped off. Once again, the Beaver Falls student body was full of wimps and the Aliquippa side had a lot of grown men sitting around them.

"Man, I'm sick of this dude." DeJon said. "He's always

running at the mouth!"

One of the Aliquippa parents got into it with BJ about Coach Holton.

"If it wasn't for Holt y'all wouldn't be getting no letters!" The parent shouted at him.

BJ would waive off the parent and began to eye up Damon.

"Aye y'all, the Tigers fitting to lose again!" Damon screamed as time expired in the third quarter.

As the fourth quarter started to wind down, BJ and DeJon started to ponder what life would be like if this group never held up the gold medals? What would the future BF teams think of them? All that talent these past three years to only pull out a whole bunch of second place trophies.

"Two minutes left Rev; they better not lose this." DeJon said to BJ. C

Calvin and Tremon would take the court after their last timeout. Tremon and Calvin would look around at the Beaver Falls crowd. They cheered for the boys, Allan, Regis, Tre, and Calvin all hugged the coaches as the Tigers would fall short and lost by three. DeJon and BJ would make their way down to the court as Calvin started to cry. His tears were contagious. BJ and DeJon would walk through the heckling fans and made it to the locker room to hear coach Demona's good- bye speech. BJ couldn't believe it. It was over, this long line of expectations, just evaporated like that.

The Irony of that rivalry was Aliquippa had more fans in Beaver Falls than most people thought. Most of the cheerleaders for BF were happy to see Calvin, Tre, and the boys lose. The pride of these Tigers, the unblemished character cards of these young men, finally had a stain. They never got it done. Yeah, they won during the regular season, they had a lot of good to border line great athletes, but they still fell short every year. Not one first place trophy and for a short period of time, the people could call these 2003 Tigers "losers" ... but were they losers? How would this group of men move on from team sports? How would the community remember the great number 23 and number 10? Lance Jamison was now the man. It was time to move on from Calvin and move towards Lance.

Calvin was easily the best basketball player on the court 100 percent of the time. Tre on most nights, was easily the most skilled shooter on the court. Both these two men had battled against each other. Calvin knew Tre could play better and he knew his toe was the key factor to the loss. Regis Bolden also known as Man-Man. He two had tears in his eyes because he knew how special this group was. He couldn't believe it went that fast. He had mixed emotions due to the unappreciation the coaching staff showed him at times. Still all in all, these were his boys, from south school. More like his brothers! Calvin's explosion of emotion and tears displayed his disappointment to the outcome of his senior season. He missed so many games and didn't capitalize on his opportunity to put the country on notice. Calvin was a once in a lifetime talent, not as flashy as Allen Iverson or MJ. He was CJ: Calvin Hollywood Jackson. From his first dunk in 7th grade to the final two points that night in Ambridge PA, he was nothing short of breath taking. Hopefully, he knew he had more work to do, in life, right?

ARE YOU ON OR OFF THE RIGHT TRACK? (Spring 2003)

Following the loss to the quips in March. The boys had to change their mindset to the finish line. The finish line of high school. Calvin, Rory, and Austin Macklin decided to run track. Rory Santiago passed all the test he needed to move on to Youngstown State University. He had the quickness and the work ethic. He wanted and needed to get faster for the next level. Calvin still undecided about college, also wanted to get faster. Calvin may have been running from the realization of some school backing out from his off the court attitude. An assistant coach used his connections and had some schools contacting the athletic director. Did the assistant coach bother to tell Calvin? Calvin needed to concentrate on finishing strong.

Austin Macklin had a name in the county for his shotput throwing. He also ran the 200- meter race. His study habits weren't the greatest and his partying started to increase towards the spring. He needed a few yellow lights to slow him down before he crashed. He was a social drinker who had the occasional uncomfortable conversations when he became a little tipsy. He was a truth teller when he was sober and when he was tipsy, he was a straight shooter-- meaning, he would come right out and tell you how it is. That was ok for the most part but towards the end of the school year it got a little out of hand with some of his classmates. All three of these men along with Young Cameron Mosby and Reshaun Taylor would all excel on the track. What about the "fastest man" in the school, DeJon? Why didn't he run? He was eligible, he was willing.... why not him?

DeJon started to fill the pressure of becoming a man. He was dealing with some issues at home, and he started to ponder on making money to provide. Not necessarily illegally but he needed to find himself in the "real world."

"I ain't got time for that shit." He said one early March afternoon. "I got to figure out if I'm going to school or job corps."

"Job corps?" BJ asked with a confused look.

"Yeah, this school shit might not be for me." DeJon said.

"Did you see Jimmy Nardone's face when Waynesburg came to visit us?" DeJon started to laugh hysterically.

Waynesburg came to talk to Tremon, BJ and DeJon.

DeJon asked the golden question. "What's the African-American ratio on your campus?"

The football recruiter responded back, "Two percent right now."

DeJon asked to go to the bathroom. He never came back.

"Man, Coach Holton, Nardone, and the recruiter was pissed!" BJ said.

DeJon started to nod his head in agreement. "Yeah man, football might be a rap for me." He said with conviction. "Especially the way they skunk me at the end."

DeJon was bitter and exhausted with the politics in sports. He would have been a great addition to the track team.

"Just think about it man." BJ said to his friend.

"Plus Mr. Kemp be tripping." DeJon said.

Mr. Kemp was the track coach along with Coach Holton. Mr. Kemp was also the African American History teacher and history teacher. He and DeJon didn't mesh. BJ and Mr. Kemp also didn't have the best rapport between teacher and student. Something about non- melanated folks teaching African American history rubbed D and BJ the wrong way. But at any rate, DeJon did think about it, and he declined.

BJ and Tremon both decided to let their bodies heal before their football all-star games in the spring and to tighten up their relationships with Tracy and Cassie. Rory and Austin Macklin also were getting ready for the all-star football games by training and conditioning at track practice. Austin Macklin had the most recognition in track. He, Calvin, and Rory were all on the relay team with Reshaun Taylor the star sophomore. Cameron Mosby replaced Tyrell from last year in the high jump. Anthony "Tony" Phar would also be a standout track man. It was looking like someone was going to win some medals.

While the months started to fly towards graduation. BJ's knee continued to swell and dislocate. He starting to become more frustrated with his knee brace. Following physical therapy one day his father came up with a solution to keep his spirits up.

"They're hiring down at Providence." His father said to him.

"Providence, what's that?" BJ asked.

"Providence, the senior high rise." Pastor Timmons said. "They're hiring down there, and they are always looking for young men. I know the hiring supervisor."

Pastor Timmons also knew some of the church members who resided there.

"I'll go down there and put in an application." BJ said.

BJ had no problem with getting a job, the issue was this would be his first "real" job. He cut grass, helped with food share, baby sat from time to time, and did some side gigs for his parents. However, he never filled out an actual application. He didn't know what to expect.

"Will this interfere with my training?" He said to himself. *"Will I miss out on talking to colleges?" "This is my last few months here!"* All these thoughts were in his mind. He wanted to have fun.

Speaking of fun, it was the time of the year again. Prom, and BJ still hadn't asked Principal K about taking underclassmen. He eventually asked Principal K and Mr. Ericson the school VP. It was a no go.

"How am I going to tell this girl?" BJ said to himself.

It was going to be a leisurely conversation that night.

"Babe, I tried to ask them, and they said they could not do it."

Cassie was upset but she was very empathetic to BJ this time. Maybe it was because this was the last time.

"As long as you don't go with..."

"Come on, yo." BJ cut her off with humor in his voice. "I ain't crazy. Besides, Denise got a man."

Cassie wasn't buying it for one second. She was feigning like she had belief that Denise would back off.

"When doesn't she have a man BJ? More important, when did she stop liking you?" Cassie had a point. Cassie was more confident this time around.

"I don't know who I'm going to go with. I might go by myself." BJ said.

Weeks would go by, and BJ would start at his Providence job. They started him off as a dish washer. It was slow paced; however, BJ would eventually work on a method to keep it going like a cardio work out. It was hot and humid due to the steam and drying machine. Like BJ, his girlfriend also worked in the dish department at her job. Cassie worked weekends at Geneva College as a dishwasher and bus girl. She made decent tips and developed her own work ethic at such a young age. This is what attracted BJ to her in the first place. After BJ got use to the dishes, he started working on the tray line. The tray line worked like a human factory. The first person set up the menus for all the senior citizens in the high rise, the second person had to set up the drinks and desserts, the last person worked on the hot place and silver ware. Someone ran up the trays to the patients.

BJ would befriend two girls: one girl named Janelle who was close with Cassie, and an older girl from the 2002 class named Shaina. She went to Hampton University and came home for the summer to work. Both girls were funny and made life easy for BJ at work.

"Who you going to the prom with?" Shaina asked one day, while everyone was on break.

"I don't know, Cassie's too young." BJ said.

Janelle observed the conversation and chimed in later. "Maybe you should go with Shaina." She said.

"Nah, come on now, she's with Justin." BJ replied.

Later, Shaina inserted herself into the Prom date contestant slot.

"Me and Justin didn't even have a good time last year." She said quickly putting away the dishes that night at work. BJ asked her the following week when the dietary staff at work went on break.

Avalon was tapped out. Cassie wasn't trusting no other girls anyway.

"I'm excited!" Shaina said.

On the track, Beaver Falls was extremely competitive, and the senior boys continued to impress the surrounding towns. Rory Bibby Santiago was faster than a lot of folks knew.

Calvin was still recovering from the toe and was still faster than most of the competition. Macklin was *Macklin* and placed in most of the track meets.

"Next week, we got Quip." Rory said.

Like the basketball game from months before, this was Rory's last time of competing against the top dogs of the county. Many people were looking forward to watching this group of Tigers and Quips one last time.

The track was packed that afternoon at Geneva College. BJ's father was present, Cassie, DeJon, Tremon Barksdale, Kevin Barksdale was also present and everyone from Aliquippa it seemed like was there. BJ Timmons was at work.

"Keep me in the loop." He told his girl Cassie before he punched into work.

He called her from the work phone. Calvin, Reshaun, Cameron and Rory were getting ready to run. Austin Mosby and Tyler Marx were also getting ready for their events. Tyler was kicking butt on the track, and Austin was a stud at throwing the shotput. Dejon, Tremon and Pastor Timmons were all watching from the fence near the track.

Pastor would inform both Tre and D. "Y'all see all them dudes up there?" He said as he observed the bleachers full of Quips.

Pastor was not trying to instigate but trying to warn the young men. Pastor was aware that the tension would not ease up. The numbers grew of Aliquippa young men. The track was in Beaver Falls, but the Quips outnumbered the Beaver

Falls student body. They took over the bleachers. Later, Pastor Timmons would compare the number of men like crows on a power line.

"Aye DeJon…" Someone yelled.

"D… DeJon…D…!!!" Another person yelled.

"Aye what's up Nigga!" Someone else yelled.

Tremon started to get irritated from the nagging and sarcastic greetings from the Aliquippa natives.

"They talking to you like that, D?" Tremon said. "I know they talking to you, because they wouldn't be talking to me like that." Tre continued.

Pastor advised the young men to leave or keep their head on a swivel. They started to threaten DeJon. He knew that his loyalty to his friends would cost him, but not like this. DeJon wasn't the problem. Tremon wasn't the problem. The problem was that the Aliquippa young men didn't get the memo that they were guests. They had worn out their welcome. The taunting and intimidation factor had run its course. Now it was time to knuckle up once again. Even though it seemed senseless at the time, there was a point that needed to be made.

DeJon squared up with a young man and DeJon swung. *Boom!*" DeJon dropped 'em. Tremon chased three men who obviously were aware of his punching power. Tremon's cousin got involved and swung on some Quips. Rory tried to hop the fence and defend his boys. Holton held him up.

"You got too much to lose baby." Coach Holton said.

"O.G." Bobby James a young sophomore hopped the fence and dove on someone. Tyler Marx hopped the fence like he was running hurdles to run over and throw some haymakers (long punches). He didn't mind fighting if he had to. Mind you Tyler was the son of an alpha male, who loved to pump iron. Tyler wasn't nobody's punk. The melee lasted for about 7 minutes. Some young men were bleeding, and a few got hospitalized. Cassie called BJ from her cell phone.

"They up here fighting!" She yelled through the phone. "They hit my cousin with a stick! He's bleeding!"

BJ was confused, furious and worried all at the same time. "Wait, who?" He yelled back. "Calm down, where is Tre and DeJon?"

Cassie's voice started to crack, and she became more emotionally charged.

"I'm pissed! I'll call you back." She yelled and hung up.

Then she hung up. Cassie never hung up on BJ before. This caused BJ to become more uneasy at work. Janelle and Shaina came to his aide and offered advice. They both insisted that BJ stay calm and try to contact Dejon or Tre on break.

When BJ came home, his father told him in the living room- "I told them dudes. I knew something was going to happen. I just got off the phones with a couple parents. I had to check on a couple guys."

Pastor Timmons wanted BJ to stay put first before he did anything irrational.

"They blaming DeJon for this." He said to his son. "I can't

say it was DeJon's fault, but they were screaming his name before I left."

"Can I use the van?" BJ asked.

"Don't take my van to no fights." Pastor Timmons said.

When BJ got to Cassie's, it was a repeat from the basketball game. Grown adults were blaming one young man for 25 males fighting in the street. It was unfair and unsettling for BJ.

"Why did you hang up on me?" BJ asked Cassie.

"I had to. I panicked!" She yelled with conviction. "That's my cousin, I had to!"

"Nah, you could have told me where you were going." BJ interrupted. "You had me worried."

"I could have lost my mother... freaking..." Cassie interrupted back- "Don't snap at me! You understand that's my family. And your boy DeJon..."

"What about him?" BJ said.

The two would yell back and forth until Ms. Lisa intervened. She smoothed things out by letting both sides take turns expressing their concerns about the fight.

"What's DeJon going to do now?" Ms. Lisa asked.

1.If DeJon would have been on the track, would he have been safe? 2."Should Pastor Timmons took DeJon home when he left? 3.Would DeJon have listened? What about Tre? 4.If DeJon would have been on the "right" track running, would Tre had been ambushed? 5.What if BJ Timmons would have been there, would he have been injured or worse? Rory and Austin could have been hospitalized or incarcerated following the fight. Rory, Austin and Calvin were on the right track. DeJon, as it always seems, was on the wrong track.

D's Parking Lot (Spring 2003)

Power in a lot of ways is a game of appearances. DeJon had gained a lot of unwanted attention since the track meet incident and before that, the so-called betrayal on his friends from the Aliquippa community. Every weekend he had to be on a look out. He wasn't running or hiding, but he couldn't be caught slipping. Do you understand the difference? In the late John Singleton's movie "Boyz N da Hood," the character Ricky had been caught slipping after he got into a verbal confrontation with some neighborhood Bloods. DeJon had built up a profile for immediate confrontation from some of the boys from that neighborhood. Visitation to the mall became limited, and dances and parties always had a heaviness around it. There was always a feeling something could jump off. If this were a faster paced city, Dejon would have been in more danger. By the grace of God alone, he was able to adapt to all the surroundings. He also had courage to admit when his friends from BF were wrong. Plenty times, he informed his cousins and his friends to seize the bull crap. Speaking of grace, what ever happened to the Damon Grace, DeJon, and Tremon beef?

It wasn't over.

It was a typical spring Saturday night. The 2003 class as mentioned before were set in their routines. Ladies, working or working out.

"You going to the Elks tonight?" BJ asked DeJon.

"Yeah, I'm going, you?" DeJon asked back.

BJ began to warn DeJon – "Man they are saying that Damon going be there tonight on that bull…"

"I'm trying to chill, but it's like they won't let it go. I ain't thinking about that Nigga." DeJon said. I ain't trying to start nothing, everything going to be cool Rev. You gotta stop thinking like that."

The crazy thing was Dejon may have been feeling apprehensive, but he didn't want to put that on display. He sacrificed his true feelings of worrying to live out these last few months as a high school senior in peace.

"If he steps, I'm going to bust his ass," he said with a focused stare.

"Who keeps telling them to come down here?" BJ asked.

"All of them chicks want to see me get rocked." DeJon said. "My sister going stop a lot of that."

DeJon's sister also became a target due to the Beaver Falls girls putting a target on she, her cousin Tremon and Kevin, and DeJon's back. They were a close family and all they wanted was respect. Tremon hadn't committed to going to the Elks just yet.

"I don't think Tre going tonight, I just got off the computer with him." BJ said. "Tracey got something going on. Bibby working and Macklin will be there later."

It was a shame that 4 to 5 dudes had to get a head count in their own neighborhood. BJ, DeJon and the 2003 boys had become numb to school but vague to the fact they were men. All the noise surrounding them was self-inflicted at times. Even guys who weren't necessarily fighters like Calvin or Regis. Had to practice assertive methods with their neighboring brethren. A lot of hate had been put on these men from a stupid rivalry. Or this beef that had been cooking since these Tigers were freshman had been reeking with animosity, disrespect, and old school testosterone.

BJ had just finished his weekend shift at Providence. He went home, showered, and discussed the colors he was wearing with Shaina.

"I think this turquoise going to be sharp!" Mrs. Timmons said. "Y'all going to be looking good boy."

"I wish Cassie could go." BJ said to his mother as she chopped up some green peppers for the home fries.

She looked up at him and said, "One day she will have her day."

BJ started to shake his head. "I dread that day." He said back to his mother. "Nah, in all seriousness, I don't want to think about no man with my lady."

Mrs. Timmons gazed at her son and smiled. "Wonder what she's thinking?" She said.

BJ Timmons fixed himself something to drink and asked, "Can I use your jeep tonight?"

"Don't be doing nothing stupid tonight." Ms. Timmons said. BJ kissed his mother on the cheek and flew out the house.

As soon as he arrived, the dance floor was already jumping. BJ looked for DeJon. He ran into Carlos Clemons and Bullet. Macklin would arrive later. BJ spotted Cassie. He also spotted Damon. Damon was cordial with a lot of the Beaver Falls boys. He was related to Dre Lee. He was willing to bury the hatchet with Beaver Falls. But there was one guy that he couldn't let slide. DeJon Alford and whoever he rolled with. BJ spotted him on the dance floor and even approached him.

"Let's squash the beef man."

Damon stared at BJ, gave him a side look with suspicion and said, "My beef ain't with you, big man."

DeJon's sister noticed BJ talking to Damon. Cassie did too.

"BJ let it go." Cassie said. "I'm not down here for that."

BJ yelled over the loud music. "I'm trying to have some fun."

When DeJon came in, all eyes were on him like 2pac Shakur. BJ knew it wasn't over, DeJon made sure his presence was felt by strong greetings. He never made eye contact with Damon. Damon's loudmouth and hand gestures indicated that there would be no love for D. There were rumors going around that Damon had a gun and was willing to pop DeJon that night. D and BJ left early to avoid the blame gang. DeJon would have gotten blamed for anything that night.

When the two boys got to McDonald's to eat, someone must have informed Damon that DeJon was in the restaurant. Within 20 minutes the whole parking lot was packed with teenagers. Where was the police? DeJon and BJ thought the same thing. DeJon's sister begged DeJon to leave and even tried to threaten some of the people egging on Damon to fight her brother.

"Ain't no time for games, D!" Damon yelled when he entered the restaurant.

DeJon started to laugh. He was laughing to ensure that Damon knew that if he tried him that night, it wouldn't be a good idea.

Damon repeated it again. "Ain't no time for games, D!"

DeJon waived Damon off.

Damon rushed DeJon and threw a wild punch. The two immediately started rumbling like two studio wrestlers behind the scenes. DeJon unloaded a couple fast combos. Damon tried his best to throw DeJon around, DeJon was naturally stronger than Damon and Damon was crazier. He had nothing to lose. People started to get in the way of BJ. A few mutual friends of Damon and DeJon grabbed BJ one was a big man named Kevin Kirkland.

Carlos Clemons pushed a couple people back. He was home visiting from school. "Ain't nobody jumping in!" He said as he pushed a couple young men back.

Big Brian Pitts arrived grabbed BJ and yelled, "Nah Rev chill! Let them fight!"

Blood was everywhere! Damon's whole mouth was full of blood. DeJon had a scratch or two. He was yelling at Damon that he wanted more. Damon appeared hurt but he had one more trick up his sleeve. BJ broke loose and ran towards the car.

"I got something for you DeJon!" Damon said as his driver pulled up in the parking lot.

DeJon surprisingly sprinted towards the car. "What you got for me nigga?" He was screaming full of rage. Punching and kicking the car door. "Get out the car!"

Damon smiled- "I got something for you DeJon."

Damon tried to roll up the window and DeJon punched into the car. The driver said pop the trunk. Macklin grabbed Damon's hand and forcefully got him to not get out the car. DeJon was irate.

"Who want it?" That was DeJon's invitation to whoever wanted to fight him.

He was sick of Damon and the naysayers. The whole event took about 8 minutes. That's a long fight. Again, where was the police? Someone said the police ended up coming shortly after everyone left. The next day Tremon was furious with everyone. Why did Carlos not let anyone jump in? He asked BJ.

"Tre, D didn't want no one jumping in." BJ said.

Tremon started to hit his hand. "I wish I was there; I would have to do Carlos. I ain't letting my cousin fight no one while I'm there."

Tre was so serious.

"Tre you should have seen it." BJ said. "D rumbled and truth be told, Damon stole on him first."

The rumors started to fly that DeJon lost the fight-- a complete lie. In the end, it was all about respect. Damon wanted DeJon's respect. He got it, but he paid a price. DeJon didn't hate Damon, Damon was a classical wannabe tough guy. He was a street guy who didn't mind getting into sticky situations. DeJon never bragged about his own struggles that he was experiencing at home. He started to lash out more and more towards the end of the school year. He had pressure on him, and Damon had to be the recipient of that pressure. Damon liked to press buttons.

Would Damon have really shot DeJon? No one really knew. Truthfully, if it weren't for Macklin, Damon would have at least shot in DeJon's direction to scare him. DeJon was so mad though, that he may have forced Damon or the mysterious driver to shoot him. All the spectators that night in the parking lot witnessed a street fight that they would never forget. These two men had a long history of tension. Both neighborhoods continued to keep the "beef" going by using two motivators: drugs and women.

Drugs, you ask. Yes, Damon started to mingle more with Beaver Falls dough boys (dealers). He wanted to stretch his allies. Also, some of the Beaver Falls guys were his cousins. Women was an easy motivator. A lot of the BF gals continued to invite Damon to functions knowing he couldn't stand DeJon. Damon would have tried to even entice DeJon's cousins and sister. When you talk trash to a man's female cousins, that normally sparks violence. The other girls as stated before

250

wanted to see one of these boys laying in their own blood. Why would girls who grew up with these young men want to see that? If we had all the answers, there would be no need to share these stories. DeJon's smile before he took that shot by Damon symbolized something that BJ always said: *"Let your smile welcome the heartbroken and warn the heartless."*

DeJon had a way of making people laugh and knew how to lighten up the mood. He also smiled when trouble seem to be knocking at his door. That night he could have charged everyone five dollars for the fight and charged McDonald's a fee for facilitating the brawl. That night, it was DeJon's parking lot.

YOU GET 5

Towards the end of the 2003 school year, BJ started to press for making a solid commitment for college.

"You get five visits, might as well use them all." Austin Macklin said at the YMCA one evening.

"I think I'm going to walk on at Youngstown State and earn me a scholarship. "How's the knee?" Macklin asked.

BJ stared off into la-la land and sighed.

"I'm hurting, I'm pissed, and this knee brace is whack." BJ started to vent, and

Macklin cut him off. "Look man, you got five visits." He said biting into a homemade sandwich his mother made him. "Go on two more visits, take these S.A.T.'s and live out your last few months of high school stress free."

With Macklin, it was that easy. He had issues just like any teenager, but he didn't let them settle. He too was aching in pain. His shoulder continued to aggravate him. He just didn't have time to complain.

"Me and Bibby going to go to YSU and make names for ourselves." Macklin said to BJ on the way to the car.

"I'm supposed to go to New York to some junior college and then Massachusetts later on this month." BJ said.

BJ and Reverend Timmons ended up going to New York to visit with Hudson Valley Community College first. There he was escorted by the two-star defensive ends. They were the size of Refrigerators. When they came into the computer lab, Rev Timmons started to laugh out loud.

"How old is he?" Rev Timmons said to the coach.

Both Defensive ends were on their way to a big four-year college. They showed BJ the computer labs, the weight rooms, communication departments and the cafeteria.

"How far away are we from the Big Apple?"

The defensive end looked around to see if any coaches were near.

"It depends on whose asking." He said with a smile on his face.

"I can get you to upper New Jersey, Brooklyn New York in about an hour." The other defensive end said, "We go out all the time."

BJ liked the campus, and the coach was very honest.

"Bernard… Listen, since your grades are good, you might only want to do one year." He said as he looked through BJ's transcript. "If you work hard, I'm sure you'll have some offers. He delivered his message with confirming, sincere words.

On the plane BJ and Rev went over the pros and cons of Hudson Valley.

The following week BJ visited a small division two school in Boston, MA. This school was very patient, hospitable and BJ wanted to see what they were offering since they were persistent. When he arrived, they had his jersey hanging in the rafters. It was hilarious to BJ. What was even funnier was they happened to have his favorite meal in the cafeteria and a bible was on the head coach's desk.

"Let me pray with you Reverend." The head coach said to Pastor Timmons.

BJ looked at his dad with a discerning look. After the coach said his rehearsed, scripted prayer, he thanked BJ and drove he and his father to the airport. BJ made up in his mind, that Robert Morris would be the best choice or Pitt to stay close to Cassie. But with the injury of his knee, his uncertainty of what position to play and his undecided major. Junior college would be the best fit. At first, BJ wanted to take up pre-law with a criminal justice minor. Then he wanted to do something with radio and television. Then he just wanted to go division one. These childish thoughts all raced through his thick head. You know what BJ wasn't thinking? How was he going to tell Cassie? In his head he thought, *"I'm not telling her right away."* Was that fair?

Speaking of collegiate destinations, what about Calvin Hollywood Jackson? Since the bomb threat, his phone wasn't ringing as much. Did someone sabotage his chances to getting into a decent school? Sure, he caused some what a disruption to his progress, but this guy was still one of the best players in the state of Pennsylvania. Calvin had visited a junior college in Columbus Ohio and had been in contact with Robert Morris University. Calvin and BJ hypothetically could have been roommates. Their friendship would have soured though. Two Alpha males couped up in one room? Nah! They didn't even entertain the conversation but for about two minutes.

In another sense, why not? That is one of the biggest down falls for man of color. Men sometimes are very apprehensive to show their true feelings. There is a lack of confidence of hashing out their differences. Rejection seems to be put away at a young age and never visited again. Calvin and BJ should have gone over the pros and cons of their potential housing dilemma. If they would have gone to the same college/university, this would mean they would see each other all day, every day. College Football typically starts in the summer and ends right before the so-called holiday season. College basketball on the other hand, starts in November and can stretch all the way to March... if you're fortunate that is. These two if they could have done it again, would have at least visited the idea. Both men knew their tempers and there spacing issues. There big egos might not have fit into a freshman dorm room. Another scenario, DeJon, Blaire Ameen and BJ all could have gone to Junior college together in Kansas, New York or anywhere in the country. Their mutual friend Ascheley Brown was going towards the middle of the state to a technical college. Thaddeus Stevens was interested in DeJon and Blaire. Both Blaire and DeJon were smart enough and tough enough and both were figuring out life before their childhood ended. While BJ was visiting schools, these young men were being pushed out to the "real world."

Towards the senior prom, BJ and Shaina had more discussions about prom night including colors, transportation, and significant others.

"I know Cassie. I used to play softball with her in little league." Shaina said as the two were washing dishes in the dish room.

"Yeah, we been together almost two years now." He said while he was stacking the bowls.

Shaina started to take some plates back.

She slowed down to say - "She is so young!"

She began to stack some trays from dinner.

"Did you decide on a school yet?" Shaina asked.

It became clearer that BJ was holding something in.

"Nah, I haven't." He said, lying to himself and Shaina.

This white lie started to weigh him down. He knew he wanted to go to New York, but if he would have told another woman before his girl, strike one. Strike two: Shaina went to Hampton University and her relationship was on the rocks. If she thought she had an in, she may have sparked a potential fling. Not that men and woman can't be friends, but they were just starting to become close because of work. Strike 3: BJ wasn't sure what Cassie's response was going to be when he told her about New York.

BJ knew eventually he would have to sign some sort of letter of intent. He had met with some of the other high school football players who were playing in the local all-star game.

When the players were putting down the information, they wanted to have presented in the program they had to put down undecided or the college they had picked. BJ wasn't undecided he just didn't want to have that conversation with Cassie. Why not? Long distance relationships worked right? People did it all the time, right? BJ had already heard all the doubters through his girlfriend's conversations. There were a few times where the arguments were as if there was somebody in her ears.

There was.

Church members, family members and some of her peers all cautioned her. They all threw some pinches of hate and poured fountains of jealousy into their relationship. Why couldn't they let Bernard BJ Timmons and Cassandra S. Washington organically call it the quits? If the odds were so against these two, why couldn't they just let it happen? Sure, BJ couldn't prove it, but he felt it. BJ also had family members, teachers, church members throwing "salt" in the game. Throwing salt in the game means putting their two cents into what they thought BJ needed to hear. With prom approaching and then graduation, BJ wanted to have an easy exit out of High School.

Towards the end of April BJ turned 18. He had wanted to go out with Cassie the night of his birthday. He had it all planned out. Wake up in the morning, look at the cards from his parents and grandparents. Go to school, physical therapy for his knee and Cassie's. Simple, straight to the point, right? No way, no how. Denise had a great memory and wanted BJ's introduction to manhood to be rather tempting. The two had homeroom together as mentioned before. They had theater together also. They had been at a good place in their friendship. Denise seemed to be civil with Cassie, she had forgiven Cassie for her interference of giving BJ his senior player treats. That afternoon, BJ went to his locker because he needed to grab a literature book. When he opened the locker, he found a surprise. There was a cake! Not a piece, not a mini cake, a full-size cake sitting perfectly where he would typically put his coat or jacket. There was a gold necklace hanging on one of the hooks and a card. BJ didn't even read the card. He was shocked and a little scared.

When he found Denise in the hallway he asked to speak to her privately.

"What the hell are you doing?" He asked her.

She gave him a look as if he was the one crazy. "What?" Denise said. "We're friends, right?"

Denise was right, the thought was kind, the gift was all wrong!

"Timing Hun!" BJ said. "The timing is all wrong!"

Denise was able to get the locker combination from either a custodian or the homeroom teacher. She had to have had the cake delivered. She was rather clever!

BJ yelled - "I got a girlfrrrrr…"

"Je t'aime" - Denise interrupted BJ with an index finger to her lips.

Was this the end of the theatrics? BJ couldn't take much more. The funny thing was Cassie was on her way up to the third floor.

"What the hell did that chick want?" She asked after she

gave her man a peck on the lips for his birthday.

BJ was sweating like a coke dealer in court.

"She didn't want nothing." He said with an uncomfortable tone of voice. "She just told me happy birthday."

"Yeah whatever." She said.

Denise had a boyfriend, who was in the same homeroom as BJ. He was a nice guy who seem to be truly in love. If he only knew.

When a man turns 18, the world is supposed to open a little more. Chronologically, it means that a boy can go to certain strip clubs, after hour spots and go to a couple restricted places. BJ had another way to celebrate, DeJon and Tre wanted to celebrate with their boy. Their night got cut short due to a lack of daring ways. Tremon was a no-nonsense guy who never wanted to put his friends in jeopardy. These young men had sense. BJ wanted to be with his friends or his girl. He was boring, dull, and wanted to be safe. He was content going out for Chinese and catching a late-night movie. In his mind he still had the mindset that these people would be around forever. Was he right? Only time would tell.

Senior Prom
(May 2003)

It was the class of 2003's prom night and there were rumblings of some outside sources coming to crash the prom.

"They better not!" DeJon said the night before prom.

There was a young man named "Raul" who was coming to the prom that had been involved with the brawl at the track meet. He wasn't a participant, but he was a boisterous supporter of the Aliquippa population that day. He was a little older and some of his family members were talking about avenging their family member if Tre and the boys got out of line. It just so happens that BJ also got into a verbal altercation with his friend Brittany's boyfriend. He also stated he was thinking about crashing.

"I'll be yelling, 'not tonight'!" BJ Timmons said on the phone with DeJon.

Some of the girls from BF begged Tremon, DeJon and BJ not to get involved with any foolishness. If it weren't for God, Raul had no chance.

"I ain't thinking about him man." DeJon said. "If they get stupid then we gotta get nasty." He went on. "This is our last prom and I'm trying to chill."

BJ was ignoring the fact that he was upset that he couldn't take Cassie to the prom and the weeks were going by quick. Shaina was overly excited, and she ensured that she and BJ to have a good time. Cassie also ensured BJ's consciousness would be protected because she trusted him. This was the last time she would have to be on the receiving end of the trust game. She must have had some good instruction from Mrs. Lisa. Or let's give her the benefit of the doubt. She was maturing. She may have not known it at the time, but it was evident. She even assisted BJ with his flower choices. It wasn't easy for her, but she was aware of the circumstances. If BJ and she would have got into an argument before Prom or even the night before, this would look bad on her end. She believed BJ did every possible to see if Mr. K would allow her to attend. They just couldn't bend the rules. Not even for Mr. K's favorite class.

The night had come, and everyone was looking rather sharp! Blaire Ameen was on the prom court with Ascheley Brown's sister. The two looked great together. Most folks weren't used to seeing Blaire dressed up. He was normally a jean, t-shirt, and Air Jordan's guy. Tremon and Tracey as usual were the template of a young power couple. Ascheley (A B) Brown, DeJon, Rory, Regis, Macklin, Calvin, Daron Shakespeare, DeWarren, Nate, Fife, PJ.... Everyone looked great! It was time for everyone to line up with their dates.

This was it, the last time they would all be together before graduation day.

Did these men process this defining moment?

BJ and his date Shaina were lined up right in front of Calvin Hollywood Jackson and his date Eleanor Brooks. She was the daughter of Jet magazine model and she had been friends with the boys since grade school. BJ drifted away in his head. He took it all in. In his mind, this was the night of the Grammy's, Oscars, or Heisman Trophy ceremony. All in one. He was happy to see all the gentlemen and their dates but more important he was happy to experience this moment knowing that he wasn't stressed any more. He had an idea he was going to New York or Dayton, Ohio. He knew that Cassie was going to be waiting for him in the morning when the prom was over, and he also knew that these guys were going to have the most fun they could ever have in high school. He started to tear up the closer the couple got to the stage. He kept playing old moments in his head: DeJon running wild in J.V. football games, DeJon fighting Damon almost to the death, and then DeJon was called with his date.

One of Tracey's friends. A.B. was called and his date Sharon from the junior class. BJ thought about how he had saw his friend battle all the jokes of him having alopecia. He took it, he accepted it, and he let the stares and jokes mold him into an awesome human being. Rory Santiago and Sharice Winters was called. BJ thought about when Rory arrived; the quiet assassin who came from the West Side of Pittsburgh. All of them miles on the bike, now he was riding in the "Bat Mobile." DeWarren and his girl Shayla were called. BJ thought about how much he wished he would have gotten closer to DeWarren a.k.a. Pong following the basic foods class. Pong had a lot to offer. All these names were called by the masters of ceremony.

After the names were called, the parents, friends and loved ones would take pictures. After BJ watched Regis, his date and Tremon and Tracey, it was his time to be called. When BJ walked out to the auditorium with Shaina, everything seemed to go in slow motion. He looked for Cassie and Mrs. Lisa. He looked for his parents. He was blinded by camera flashes.

After all the couples were called, the Prom Queen was announced, and the teens were asked to get on the bus to head to the hotel. Cassie and BJ kissed. BJ promised Cassie he would be back later. Shaina was much more polite than BJ's junior prom date. BJ took a picture with Shaina's boyfriend Justin also. He spent some time on the Northside of Pittsburgh the same time BJ was there.

"Take care of my girl man." He said shaking BJ's hand.

In theory BJ was a good guy. You never tell a man to take care of your lady.

On the bus, Shaina and BJ discussed life in an HBCU.

"Hampton is beautiful, you would love it." Shaina said.

"I think that's where little Nate (Lewis) is going."

"Yeah, he'll like it." She said.

She started to ponder on her next question. "Where are you going next year?"

BJ started to sweat and play with the buttons on his vest. He knew it was coming. Shaina blinked her eyes rapidly and started to smile ear to ear.

"You're going far away, aren't you?" She said confidently.

BJ nodded his head.

"And how does Ms. Cassandra feel about that?" She asked.

"I really don't know; I think she's scared." BJ said. "She has been very supportive, and I love her."

Shaina played the role of a beautiful therapist for the first 20 minutes. Shortly after the direction of the conversation shifted. The two young adults started to compare their proms from this year and last year. The strange thing was for BJ he assumed she had a successful relationship up to this point. He was a little off in his assumptions. It wasn't that she trashed Justin by any means, they just had adversity like all couples: long distance, Justin's past relationships, lingering girlfriends, the rumors. She sounded like she wondered if it was time to cut ties. So, then BJ displayed active listening.

He did until the comment was made.

"How come you never said nothing to this girl, or that girl?" She asked.

It was as if she was fishing to see if BJ had a type or he was pursuing the next girlfriend. BJ didn't want to seem naïve, but he didn't want to open the door for a potential awkward moment. Maybe it was too late! Shaina admitted she thought BJ and a few guys were handsome, but they were always off the market. Again, no one was saying that Justin was a bad guy, but he had some questionable qualities. Truth was that BJ had a lot of respect for him and his family. The tension between Big Rob and BJ from his sophomore year was simmered because of Justin and his family. Justin's people came to BJ's house to smooth things out. BJ and Justin went to the same elementary school in Pittsburgh before they both moved to Beaver Falls. He had respect for him, however his lady sounded like there was about to be change a coming.

The night went smooth as expected. BJ and Shaina danced a few times and the boys grooved until the wee hours of 3:30 am. 50 Cent, Ja Rule, Jagged Edge and Eminem's top hits played on repeat it seemed. The high light of the night was Nate being hypnotized. None of the boys were sure if he was acting or truly hypnotized. Nate had a habit of falling asleep easily. It was late though, so who really knew? BJ, Dre Lee and A.B. danced the night away. Regis who the classes best dancer also seized to capture the moment. BJ wondered what was going through everyone's head. Tracey and Tre looked like they were ready to take the next step in their relationship. They reminded everyone of a married couple because they clicked on all cylinders. Four years they had been dating, BJ wondered if they were thinking about their next batch of obstacles. Like Shaina said earlier, there are a lot of distractions when you date someone that is far away. Tre was going to Howard University and Tracey was going to school close to home.

BJ and Shaina went to breakfast with some of the couples from the prom. Macklin and his date, Rory Bibby Santiago and his date Sharice, and some other couples. Everyone was tired and ready to eat. BJ was text messaging Cassie towards the end of his breakfast. By this time in 2003, text messaging wasn't free, but it was free on the weekends. Does this make sense? Certain phone companies had different plans like they do today. If you went above 50 text messages on Rev. Timmons's phone, then it would cost him... not on the weekend though.

Macklin and Rory were ringing up their bills and Macklin

mentioned something about being cool with one guy that Rory didn't particularly care for.

"That's your problem man, you're cool with everybody!" Rory yelled pounding the table. "Even Jesus had enemies." His anger was glaring all over his face.

Macklin tried to calm him down because to him, it wasn't that serious. Even though these two were on their way to college together, they were vastly different. Rory had a reserved fiery spirit about certain things. Austin Macklin was speaking on his friendships with guys surrounding the county. Austin Macklin was like the Mayor of Beaver County. It's not that Rory had an issue with befriending people. But he wasn't too trusting. Maybe it was because of his upbringing. Maybe it was because of all the scraps he had been in. He wanted to set the record straight how he wanted to start his college experience with being cool with everybody.

Sharice asked Rory a few times to calm down. It was getting late, and Rory was probably just getting cranky. BJ observed the two friends arguing with conviction of taking too long to get back to his sweetheart. BJ started to look down at his phone then look at Shaina.

He said to her, "You ready to go?"

She said "Yes, I got to work tomorrow."

"I got to work Sunday night." BJ said back.

On the way home, BJ had to let somethings off his chest.

"When I pulled up to get you, your stepdad was talking really crazy." BJ Timmons said looking straight forward with one hand on the staring wheel.

"Yeah, he always talks like that." Shaina said.

"He asked me do I know where I'm at, this is 2nd Avenue and …." BJ kept going. "I only respected him because I know your family and I have respect for you. No disrespect, 2nd Avenue don't mean shit to me. If I didn't want to ruin our friendship, I would knock on the door and settle my issue."

Shaina looked confused but not surprised. "He's a simpleton." She said as she put her hand gently on his shoulder. "BJ let me ask you something, is that what's on your mind?" She asked looking him in his eyes.

Truly that wasn't on BJ's mind at all. Maybe on the back end, but no. He didn't know how to close this night. He worked with Shaina, he knew her relationship was on the rocks, and she looked like she wanted closure on how he felt about her.

"No Shaina, I could care less about him, I just want you to know…" He said.

Shaina cut him off, "That you ain't no punk? Everybody knows, BJ ain't no punk.BJ is a fine young man." She said with a huge smile.

BJ walked her to her door and thanked her for coming to the prom. "The pleasure is all mine."

"Good night, hun." Shaina shut the door slowly.

In some instances, most men can see the excitement of wanting to go to the next level with a college girl. She was his co-worker who just came home for the summer trying to pay for tuition. But hypothetically speaking, what could happen with that fling? She goes back to Hampton, BJ's going to New York or Dayton. How would the mood be at work? Would folks catch on? What about Cassie, Justin…? These are all the components young men should keep in mind when they are flirting with the idea of having a side woman, fling, girlfriend… etc. In BJ's mind he thought, *"Nah I'll keep sharpening my husband skills with building a stronger relationship with Cassie."* It was attractive to the ladies; Shaina touched briefly on that when the two talked. Most folks love to break up a good thing… most simple-minded folks that is.

The next day following Prom was the traditional picnic. All the teens from surrounding areas go to Kennywood, which is a Greater Pittsburgh landmark. Cassie and BJ had a blast. Rollercoasters, Ferris wheel, haunted houses and all the games you could imagine. There was a lingering thought though in both teen's heads. What is going to happen to us in the next couple months? Cassie asked on the ride back home. The ride from Kennywood which is located in West Mifflin, PA to Beaver Falls was about one hour or so. The question opened a discussion that would take about that long, until Cassie's younger cousin Gino threw a stuffed animal and hit BJ in the back of the head. BJ as usual took things overboard. He wanted to spank the young lad for interrupting his conversation with his gal. However, he was saved by the bell. Directing his anger towards the goofy twelve-year-old made it easy to reject Cassie's questions about the near future. It's not that BJ wasn't worried equally as she was.; it was just he wasn't trying to talk about it after such a great time.

They had taken pictures, held hands, and were kissing and

hugging. BJ had won so many prizes. Then the song "*How you gonna act like that*," by Tyrese came on

"Exactly…" BJ said under his breath. "You trust me?" He asked her with his hand caressing her shoulder blade.

She nodded her head, then looked down.

"I just don't want to think about it." She said with sadness in her voice. "Time is flying. You haven't made a choice."

BJ gripped the staring wheel tighter and said "Mm Hmm." BJ hesitated. "I think…I think I'm going to go to the junior college in New York. If Dayton doesn't offer me this full package."

She sighed, "Robert Morris is out the question for you and Hollywood (Calvin)."

BJ shook his head and said, "I don't want to be that close."

She put up her index finger, "Hold up!"

BJ cut her off immediately before she could speak. "Nah, before I got hurt you was cool with me looking at Tennessee State, Michigan, Syracuse, Purdue."

"Is that what you think?" She said back. "Are you an idiot? What the hell is wrong with this guy?"

The two would go back and forth about 30 minutes until both looked like two empty headed cartoon characters in a car. Her eyes were red and baggy from crying. BJ's jaw line was about to explode.

"Listen, I love you." BJ said hitting the staring wheel.

"Period, yo!"

When the two pulled up to Cassie's house one of her older cousins swore, he saw BJ being aggressive with her.

He asked her "Everything ok up there?"

BJ became defensive due to Cassie's face looking like she had just been torn up emotionally.

"She's cool man." BJ said to the cousin.

"I'm not talking to you!" He said to BJ walking closer to him.

"Well now, I'm talking to you!" BJ yelled back. The cousin hit two bottles together as if he was a Roman soldier.

From what BJ could remember the guy had a little rep, but BJ would have destroyed him due to the guy being blitzed (high) out of his mind. Ms. Lisa came outside, and BJ's father Pastor Timmons was called to de-escalate the problem.

When BJ came home, he was sure that it was over. The relationship was crushed, he was thinking... *"Why not just end it now?"* It would have been smooth, sensible and no one would have judged him. The famous song by Ralph Tresvant came to mind. *"Do what I Gotta Do."* That night he thought about the argument that occurred and that was simmering to boil over later. *"What was going to happen next? If I stay in this relationship, will I be stunting her growth emotionally and mentally? Will I be a selfish jerk if I don't feel as safe with her going to Christmas dances, proms and other functions?"* All these thoughts were on his mind. And for the first time that night, he thought about how bad he was slowly hurting this girl.

"Iron sharpens iron" a wise man once said. Both these teenagers were Iron. Cassie, whether she knew it or not, was a lot like iron. She was hard to break, and she continued to challenge him-- not intellectually, but subliminally. He pondered on what God was thinking. *"One day, I may have a little girl. Do I want her dating a senior? Was I technically violating some laws?"* In his mind, he loved her and wanted to be with her for eternity.

"How could I just end it like that?" That's what BJ Timmons said to himself before going to bed.

Meanwhile Calvin Hollywood Jackson and Rory Bibby Santiago were patching up all the loose ends before leaving high school. Calvin had heard some chatter about a school in Virginia.

"What about us?" His girl Bianca said. "I mean are you just living here?" She hollered at him one night. "I mean, I cook, I clean…"

Calvin held up his hand. "Wait a minute! "Ain't that what you're supposed to do as a mother? If I wasn't here, what would you be doing?" He asked. "I don't bitch and moan about reading to your kids. Helping them with their homework."

Bianca started to tear up.

"Don't cry now!" Calvin said. "Aye, last I checked; you're married! You got some big nigga hounding me like some maniac."

She couldn't take the fact that Calvin was 18 and he was the man in her life. But was it official? She had a legitimate beef with her young man. He hadn't committed to a school or her. Or maybe she knew the deal. She knew what she signed up for. Bibby was also facing some heat. Sharice started to ask more about the summer plans. Sharice had plans for summer trips while Rory needed to get ready for his all- star game and later college football camp. This was primary, he believed the two were already solid in their relationship.

All three of these men had no idea what the future would hold with their lady folk. No doubt about it that the three had their minds headed in a collegiate direction. Rory, Calvin, and BJ all were living different lives and dating women in different age brackets. All three women could be seriously hurt emotionally. Sure, Bianca was a mother of three and had a crazy husband. She still had feelings for Calvin and the truth was, it was he who didn't want to let it go. Sharice was a brainiac who could go anywhere when her time came. She was only a junior though and she was unaware how to keep a loose cannon like Rory at times. Cassie, she was so young and without the assistance of her mother, she didn't have a chance… not because she wasn't the best thing in BJ's life. It's because she was up against life and all the challenges that came with it. No man has ever beat father time or his older cousin, life. She was up against all of it. The girls would become women. The distance would be further. The schedules would become complicated. All in all, both Cassie and BJ were up for the challenge. Shaina his prom date would continue to inform him weeks to come how college life can be hard on relationships from a realist perspective. You need that… sometimes.

Nothing Else to Prove

The time had come when all the 2003 class would get ready for the final run. The prom was over, and now it was time for senior projects, senior trip and the final lap was approaching for these young men. Nate Lewis and Bibby were finishing their senior project with class and charisma. Austin Macklin had put together a great scrap book for his coaching debut with the Little Tiger's program. Regis put all the academic gifts to work while volunteering at the local library. Tremon put up the signs for the High School every morning. Calvin re did his neighborhood playground and basketball court. Ascheley Brown also did a collaboration project with the Tiger Pause basketball tournament. He and Calvin really put their hearts into that because this is where it all started for them: "Chains" and 2nd Avenue."

Darren Shakespeare, being the undercover musician he was, made a compact disc full of beats. But BJ was procrastinating on his finishing touches with his senior project. With the help of his mother Sabrina, he was able to put together a collage of his work with the Sunday School department. All the volunteering and fellowshipping with the children was fun and it opened a vision of wanting to help others. There will always be another brother or sister who could use your help. You didn't have to dunk a basketball or hit a baseball out the park. Just be yourself.

"B.., I think this is good." Ms. Timmons said while she was assisting him put on his tie.

"I don't feel like doing this man." BJ said.

His ma smiled at him and said... "But just think, this is it."

She was right, this was it. BJ had already been boiling all week because his African American History teacher gave him a high C instead of B minus. This would cause him not to graduate with honors. He was livid and just ready to bounce.

"Ma, I don't want to go to graduation."

BJ's mother had a puzzled look on her face. Then she made a sarcastic remark. "You are joking right? Come on Bernard."

She called him that when she was about to go off.

"You realize how selfish that would be? Your grandparents are coming. Your nieces and nephew, Lisa and San (Cassie)."

"I'm just ready for it to be over." BJ said staring off into the ceiling.

"Don't worry it will be soon enough." She said. "You can never get it back." She said to him as he walked out the door.

She was right. No matter what the past is permanent.

The staff had to judge your senior project on your exit interview. It was a requirement for some of the seniors. BJ killed his exit interview. The boys had to walk around and wait for some of their classmates to finish.

"This is it man!" BJ said walking around in the hallways and through the lounge area.

Mixed emotions were running through BJ's body. He was ignoring some of the obvious realities of maturing. Letting go. No more lunch arguing. No more running through the hallways hitting the signs. Certain teachers were ready for you to go, and certain teachers were not. Tears were shed and hugs were given. Mr. K the principal was incredibly happy and sad at the time. He loved the 2003 class. In a way it was like seeing some of his kids grow and leave. As BJ walked down by his locker one last time, he closed it and said in the words of the savior, "It is finished."

WHAT WOULD THEY SAY?

One of the reasons BJ Timmons didn't want to go to graduation, was because there was a mixture of emotion was going through his body daily up until that point. He struggled with endings in movies so internally he was starting to fear change. In a man's life, change is inevitable. One thing is always for sure, there will always be change. So, why didn't BJ have closure? Believe it or not, he was starting to feel weird about Dougie Benson and DeJon Alford not being a part of this thing called graduation. It just didn't seem right.

He knew it was a wacky ceremony for mostly family members and loved ones to snap pictures, but these men fought with him. They pushed him and put their lives on the line at times. What would they say? First let's establish who they are: all the naysayers, cynics, and critics. They would rejoice that Dougie never finished. DeJon would eventually finish and go to job corps like he said. BJ knew Dougie and DeJon had futures. It sucked, it stung, therefore BJ was struggling with closure. Really, closure is hard for some people.

Blaire Ameen was right there. He, too, would choose to go

to job corps near the Philadelphia area. He was already under the realization that he was no longer a ball player. Central Elementary, to backyard football, playing in the projects, Friday nights to....? That's just it, there was still left on the table. Pastor Timmons really believed it. He would tell his son to suck it up and understand that they were men now. not boys and it was time to start their new path, a new chapter. No closure though. What would people say about Blaire Ameen? A.B. (Ascheley Brown) tried to get him to come to Lancaster with him. He knew Blaire needed the right push and those two had been close since first grade. It was time to let go.

The news had got out that Allen Fife and Calvin would not walk for graduation. Once again BJ was thinking about Calvin's mother and grandmother getting that fulfilment of watching their son and grandson complete the mission. Calvin wasn't mad, so why was BJ? It was the principal. What did this man need to do to walk? It was very awkward looking at folks happy during commencement rehearsal. He was pissed and everyone knew it. He showed up 20 minutes late for rehearsal.

"This is butt." He spent the rehearsal deflecting his true feelings which was he was going to miss these fools.

It was all about to change in hours for Nate Lewis, Darren Shakespeare, Pong, Paul Joseph (PJ), Macklin, the girls, and the young guys. What was going through their heads? What would people say when the next classes were asked about the 2003 class?

"What was Darren Shakespeare like?"

"Could he really hoop?"

"A.B. ...Dougie Benson...DeJon.... who were those guys?"

"Tremon Barksdale, Calvin Hollywood Jackson, Regis Bolden..." I heard those dudes beat the varsity in the 9th grade."

Would the next few classes continue the legacy? Lance Jamison, Cameron Mosby, Brandon McDowell, Kevin Barksdale... would these guys continue to press the issue of wanting to dominate? Dominate on the hardwood, field, track, parties, classroom, parking lots, churches. It was like Alpha training 101. Not necessarily outwardly like a boisterous lion. It could be humble and meek. It could be intellectual and nonchalant confidence. These guys all had these gifts. Now one may say, why did BJ care? He didn't care about what they thought or said. How would they tell their stories to their kids? What would they say? Would their memories fade away? Was some of this fairytale of a long run of runner up sporting events in vain? Did they only talk because they had the same color jersey on? Or they were members of the same church, or their parents thought they would be good fits for one another? What would they say when it's all over?

The day of graduation, BJ and Cassie laid up and watched television before it was time for him to get ready.

"This is it." He said to her. "Why you crying?" BJ said with his arms open trying to give her a hug.

"Come on BJ!" She said walking closer to him. "It's going to be over."

She put her head in his chest. "I know one day it had to come, but damn man."

She was full of tears and could barely get her words out. He held her for about 10 minutes and told her.

"I'll be back." He said it like Arnold Schwarzenegger in Terminator 2.

The night had come, and it was time for the graduation. Regis, like Regis does, was full of strong words to push his brethren through to the next stage of life. The chorus sung and the awards were given. To see Rory, Darren and Nate get their honor awards made BJ forget all about coming up short. Regis took many awards that night. Tremon and BJ sat a few seats away from one another. Their names were called up like any graduation one by one. Then it came and went. *"BJ Timmons..."* just like a blink of an eye. 7th grade to graduation night. Just that fast. When the caps were thrown into the air, BJ left early to hold his emotions together. He played the song *"Oh Father"* by Pastor Troy and drove through Tiger Alley. That's how he envisioned it. He couldn't handle closure.

When he pulled up back to the house, everyone was already outside ready to take pictures. BJ's two sisters and their husbands, Cassie and Mrs. Lisa, BJ's niece and nephew and his grandparents. He took the pictures and told Cassie he would be up.

"How you feel kid?" Pastor Timmons asked BJ.

BJ hugged his mother and said, "It's over man. I got to get out of here."

BJ ended up just laying with Cassie until the early morning. She cried, they watched movies, she cried again. He waited till he got in his car and then... he cried too.

"It's over man." He said to himself. Not the relationship. The time... it was over.

God has some mysterious ways of sitting you down. We asked so many questions, wanting closure. Like a spoiled child we forget all the gifts and good times. It's a part of growing up. Dealing with pain, losses, and closure. It's what they would say about these 2003 Tigers. *"They lost, they had growing pains, they got over it. They are now doing these great things...."*

Tremon Barksdale, Rory Santiago and Austin Macklin would all play in the East vs West Football game and contribute to the outcome of the game. It was awesome for BJ to watch the guys play on tv. They would all go division 1 to play football and start a new legacy at their respected Universities. Youngstown State and Howard. There may never be a dynamic wide receiver duo like Rory Santiago and Tremon Barksdale. Darren Shakespeare would go to Edinboro in Erie PA to pursue an educational career. It was in his nature to lead by example. He would always be the "standard" the model to "Christlike" behavior. He wasn't perfect, but damn close.

Ascheley Brown, DeJon Alford and Blaire Ameen would all choose Tech schools or Job core. These three would eventually venture out to find life after sports. DeWarren Pong Ford also pursued his passion with culinary arts. *"God is good and so was his cooking."*

Nate Lewis, PJ and Regis would all head to Virginia to three different schools. PJ went to Virginia Tech, Regis attended University of Virginia, and Little Nate Lewis was heading to Hampton.

After Graduation, Calvin would get his diploma and head to

play at a school called Ferrum College. It was also in Virginia. So, who knows, maybe he could get up with some of the fellas. He needed to get out of Beaver Falls and change his look on life. He dominated from kindergarten to college ball.

BJ made the tough decision of choosing Hudson Valley Community College in Troy, New York. Dayton was holding on to his scholarship, but he didn't get the score to get in. Some folks don't test well. He ended up playing in the Pennsylvania vs Ohio all-star game. Cassie recorded it and took pictures with him when it was over. BJ forgot about his knee injury and worrying for one last night. He even forgot to wear his knee brace! The closure was a struggle because he knew if Rory, Tremon and Macklin were healthy along with his knee, they could have made another run to the state in both football and basketball. He would later earn a full scholarship to Delaware State University. Crazy how things turn out, ain't it?

God makes no mistakes. It was meant for these young men to fall short but not to quit. It was meant for these guys to taste a little success and a little humility. Some guys even harshly ended their careers premature. But in the end, these guys wouldn't be forgotten because there was too much evidence running through that community. Though they would leave, the impression they left with their fans and their supporters would never leave. Those Tigers went through wars and for that. They earned their stripes.

And that's what they would say.

The End

###

Special Thank you

To those individuals who took the time to push me to get through the days of writing, thinking, thinking, and writing again. My deepest regards thank you. Alonna Carter, Shawn F. Coleman, Reggie Rockymore, Lewis Colyar and all the creative writers on God's green earth. Thank you so much. All the Beaver Falls Families who assisted me with putting my story out there. It was a collective effort and I love you all.

This is my creed.

I believe first in God, the same God in which my ancestors Abraham, Isaac and Jacob believed in. I believe in Jesus Christ and that he is my Savior until the day I leave this planet called earth. I believe in the family unit, brotherhood based on biblical terms. That being salvation and acknowledging the Elohim.

Bernard Tench III

Feb.1st, 2021

9 781956 876208